OUT-OF-COUNTRY

WOUNDED WARRIORS
OUT-OF-COUNTRY

The Untold Story of the Vietnam War

Ron Aigotti

ISBN: Softcover   978-1-5144-1019-6
             eBook   978-1-5144-1018-9

Print information available on the last page

Rev. date: 10/08/2015

To order additional copies of this book, contact:
Xlibris
1-888-795-4274
www.Xlibris.com
Orders@Xlibris.com
723871

CONTENTS

PROLOGUE

FEW AMERICAN CITIZENS would disagree with the observation that the Vietnam War was probably the most tragic event to befall the American people since the the Imperial Japanese surprise attack on Pearl Harbor in December 1941.

The Vietnam War's devastation was not limited to the loss of thousands of lives; the maiming of bodies and minds or the terrible waste of the worlds resources. A major, irrevocable injury was inflicted on the American psyche. We were all personally, politically, spiritually and psychologically effected.

The conduct and the outcome of the war irreparably altered the way Americans now view the waging of war in general; the influence our politicians exert over the conduct of wars; the motives and the effectiveness of our military-industrial complex and the competency of our military leaders.

Many excellent volumes—both fiction and non-fiction—have been written about the terrible residual effects of the war on its survivors, their families and those Americans killed while stationed 'In-Country; that is, in Vietnam.

The story which follows is an attempt to portray the profound effects which the Vietnam War had on those American military personnel who remained stationed 'Out-of-Country'; that is, not in Vietnam, and thus suffered no physical war injuries or casualties. Yet these men and women also carry permanent, deep scars of this dreadful conflict.

CHAPTER ONE

The Black Wall

A BRIGHT, EARLY-MORNING, autumn sun glistened off the highly polished surface of the black marble wall. The October air of the nation's capitol was crisp and unusually clear considering the amount of atmospheric pollution in the huge city. Two middle aged couples silently approached the Vietnam War Memorial. The second couple, which was in line behind the first, husband on the left and wife on the right, seemed a little hesitant in their approach. The woman was dragged back by her husband's halting steps.

"Michael, what is your problem? You haven't been yourself since we talked last night about coming here with Joe and Judy. Are you all right?" asked his wife Kathy.

Michael stopped at the flagpole, with the stars and stripes at half-mast, about fifty yards from the wall. The first couple, Joe and Judy O'Mara continued on to the wall.

"Yes, I'm fine. I just don't want to be here. That's all. I told you that last night. You go ahead I'll wait here," said Michael.

"But Michael?"

"Just go ahead, will you," said Michael in a rare display of impatience towards his wife of twenty-three years.

Her eyes turned moist and red as she briskly walked on to the wall.

"Where's Michael?" asked Judy.

"Oh, he's sitting back there under the flag."

"Why? What's wrong? Is he sick or something?" asked Joe O'Mara.

"No, at least I don't think he is. He just doesn't want to be here."

"Why not? I didn't know that he felt that way about it. He should have said something at dinner last night," said Joe.

"He's really acting strange. It's not like him," said Kathy.

"I'll go talk to him. Why don't you gals go on to the monument. We'll meet you there in a few minutes unless he won't come, then we'll meet you back at the car."

Joe walked back to the bench where Michael sat slumped forward, elbows on his knees, face buried in his hands and his back to the Black Wall.

"Hey, Mike. Are you okay? What's the matter?"

"I'm fine," said Michael suddenly sitting upright. "I just don't want to go near that goddamned black wall. That's all, it's as simple as that."

"Huh?" said Joe startled at Michael's atypical, blunt response. "Why not? Did you have some close relative who was killed in-country? You've never mentioned anyone."

"No, I didn't. But it's a farce, a fiasco, an attempt at appeasing the unknowing masses by the politicians and the military brass," said Michael trying to suppress anger.

"Hey, better keep it down, Mike. There are a lot of people here that feel different about this place."

"I don't give a damn what other people think or if they hear me."

"Okay, okay Mike," said Joe putting his arm on Michael's shoulder and patting it gently. "Let's go back to the car and talk about it."

The two men walked back in silence several dozen yards toward the parking lot until their wives had caught up to them. Kathy walked alongside Michael and Judy was next to Joe.

"So, what's with the wall, Mike?" said Joe.

"Yes, Michael. What is it?" said Judy keeping her voice soft.

"It's a travesty, that's what it is," he answered.

"But why? In what way? I've never knew you felt this way about it. I mean, I knew you hated the Army and our time in the Army during Vietnam. But it's been twenty years now since we got out and you've never said a word about it since," said his wife.

"In what way?" Michael answered. "I'll tell you in what way. Because there should be at least five more names on the damn Black-Wall-thing, maybe even more."

"How do you know they're not on it? You didn't even get close enough to look," said Judy.

"I don't have to. The people I'm talking about didn't die in combat that's how I know. As if there weren't many other people who suffered. As a matter of fact, some of these people didn't even die, not in the physical sense that is," said Michael.

The two women looked at each other in puzzlement. But Joe understood. He just nodded his head in affirmation.

"You're talking about Bobby Joe aren't you? The Bobby Joe Parrish who died from that weird overdose at Fort Riley, that's it, isn't it?

Michael just nodded his head.

"But Bobby Joe was hooked on drugs long before the Army and Vietnam," said Joe. "He would have probably O.D'd anyway," he added.

"We don't know that. Maybe if he had gotten some real psychotherapy and support instead of that crap the Army put out he might have had a chance. People have kicked the habit, you know?" Michael said.

"Yeah, one in a thousand kick the habit, maybe. Be realistic will you?" said Joe with a facial expression of frustration. "Okay, okay I suppose it is possible. I'll give him that much," Joe added after a moment of contemplation.

"Thanks, but that won't give Parrish back his life, will it?" said Michael staring at his hands.

"But that's just one name. Who are these other people who died, or didn't really die? as you put it," said Joe.

"All right, first there was Colonel Anderson, remember him? The half-assed career medical officer who ran the hospital like a clearing house for 'Nam, remember him?"

"Yeah, of course I remember him. But he died of natural causes long after he got out," said Joe.

"Yes but his death was still caused by the stress of that whole stupid war and maybe. . . maybe by the pressure from me, too," said Michael painfully.

"Oh, don't be ridiculous. There you go again with one of your guilt trips just like a good Roman Catholic," said Joe throwing up his arms.

"And what about Pvt. Guiterrez?" asked Michael pacing anxiously.

"Now wait a minute we don't know how he got that virus. It could have happened to anybody," said Joe.

"True enough," said Michael. "But we do know where he contracted it. In Vietnam, right? And if he had stayed out-of-country he wouldn't have contracted it. Right?"

"Maybe, maybe not," said Joe.

"But that's a big maybe. And *maybe*, just *maybe* C. D. Highsmith wouldn't be spending the remainder of his wretched life in a mental hospital. Perhaps he'd be a practicing attorney, or a doctor, or a nurse, or something. But he wouldn't be a psychiatric basket case like he has been for the past twenty years."

Joe didn't, or couldn't disagree. He just sat silently listening as Michael raged on. "I guess so," he said shrugging his shoulders.

"And leave us not forget the man who lost his soul in that goddamned war," said Michael.

"Wait, now you lost me. Who was that?" asked Joe.

Michael continued more calmly now, "I ran into a friend of mine here at the AMA meetings. He's a surgeon, a thoracic surgeon. He used to practice with my friend from medical school, Tom Adams, before Vietnam."

"Oh yeah. The one who got. . . got that virus from Pvt. Guiterrez. What's he doing now?" asked Joe cautiously.

"What's he doing? He's a drunk living on the streets and in flophouses. Ended up getting divorced, lost his family and never did go back into practice after Vietnam. Lives on handouts and at soup kitchens. He's in and out of the VA hospitals all over the west coast trying to dry out. But he never quite makes it."

"Oh, sorry. I didn't know," said Joe.

"Do you think you'll find his name on that . . . that goddamned wall?" asked Michael.

"You know that we won't," said Joe.

"Do you think you'll find the names of any of the thousands of the broken bodies, minds and souls that should be there?" asked Michael mockingly.

"No, I'm sure I won't. And I won't find your name on it, either, Mike," said Joe.

"What? what do you mean?" asked Michael.

"It's clear to me now that a large piece of your heart and soul was killed at Ft. O'Malley, too," said Joe. "I didn't realize that the scars it left on you were so deep," he added.

Michael shrugged his shoulders, wiped the moisture out of his eyes and got back into the car. Joe and the women got back into the vehicle. Not another, single word was exchanged in the thirty minute drive back to the hotel. And the topic of the Black Wall, Vietnam or the U. S. Army never came up again in the remaining days of the medical convention in Washington, D. C.

CHAPTER TWO

Uncle Sammy Wants You

"THIS DISTRICT COURT in and for the county of Los Angeles California, for November 22, 1967 is now in session. The honorable Judge Thomas O. W. H. McCullough presiding. All please rise," the bailiff resounded in a booming baritones voice while striking his gavel thrice. The few spectators, the attorneys and the accused stood ceremoniously as the judge strode into the courtroom. Judge McCullough, appearing as authoritarian as possible, walked up the steps to the bench and stood for a moment surveying the courtroom. His full head of silver-gray hair, his thin, black pencil mustache, dark rimmed glasses and granite-like chin atop his full six-foot, two inch, portly frame added to his already majestic ambience.

"All may be seated. The first case bailiff, please."

"First case, your honor. The county of Los Angeles versus Mr. Jesus Lopez. The charge is assault and battery, creating a public nuisance and a domestic disturbance. The victim is the defendant's wife, Mrs. Rosa Lopez."

"Is the defendant represented by council?"

"Yes, your honor. Mr. Charles Townsend is defense attorney and Ms. Charlotte Cutner is the prosecuting attorney."

"How does the defendant plead?"

"My client pleads guilty, your honor with a plea for clemency."

"Clemency? On what grounds, counselor? The record shows that this is your client's fifth offense on these very same charges," said the judge.

"Excuse me please, your honor. May I speak?" asked a clergyman dressed in a tattered, shiny black suit and a white collar that was closer to yellow-gray from wear.

"And who might you be, sir?" asked the judge.

"My name is Father Hector Gonzalez. I am the pastor of St. Teresa's, the parish of the Lopez family. I have dealt with this family for many years."

"I object your honor," interjected the prosecuting attorney.

"Objection over ruled, Miss Cutner. Sit down."

"Ah, a good catholic man of the cloth should be given his due respect. You may speak father."

"Jesus Lopez is a good father and husband. He always works hard and brings home the pay envelope. Once in a while he drinks too much and forgets himself. But he comes to church every Sunday and gives generously in the collection. I beg his honor not to lock him up in jail, for his children's sake. Who will provide for them?"

"I see your point. Thank you father. I'll see what we can do. Be seated, please."

"Thank you, your honor."

"I object judge on the grounds of relevancy. What has the defendant's church attendance got to do with his guilt or innocence of the charges?"

"Objection over ruled," shouted the angry judge. "I told you to sit down, Miss Cutner. I'll decide what is and what is not relevant in my court."

"Is Mrs. Lopez in the courtroom? Please come forward if you are," said the judge.

Very slowly and meekly a thin, frail woman wearing a faded, threadbare, house dress stood up and came forward.

"Are you the defendant's wife?"

"Yes, your majesty, I am."

Several snickers and giggles arose from the spectators. The judge slammed his hand on the bench and bolted from his chair. "Order in the court. We'll have no more of that."

"It's 'your honor' not 'your majesty', dear lady. But you may simply address me as judge."

"Thank you, judge. You excuse me, please. I ain't too smart."

"That's all right. What do *you* think I should do with your husband for beating you?"

She lowered her head and eyes to consider the question. The right side of her lower lip was still swollen and split. She closed one eye to concentrate because her left eye was black and blue and already swollen shut from the recent beating. Then she glanced over at her husband to see if he was watching her. The judge deliberately avoided shifting his glance toward the defendant. Mr. Lopez glanced back at his wife with a stern expression and clenched both his fists so she could see them.

Finally she responded, "I would like to have my husband back home with me and his children, judge . . . please."

"So be it," said the judge after no deliberation and slamming his gavel down once.

The prosecuting attorney stood up curtly and attempted to speak. The judge stared at her fiercely and coiled himself like a rattlesnake ready to strike. She sat down in frustration and said, "what's the use, anyway."

"Now, Mr. Lopez I know you didn't mean to hurt your wife and that you were influenced by the effect of the alcohol on your mind and soul."

The judge instinctively put his hand on his hip pocket to check for the presence of his own hip flask without the slightest bit of embarrassment.

"You will be required to attend mass each and every Sunday. You will spend one hour afterward being counseled by Father Gonzalez on the evils of drink. Mind you, if I ever find you in my court again I'll lock you up and throw away the keys. Do you understand that?"

"Si, si. Yes, your honor. Thank you so much," said Jesus bowing profusely as he left the court room.

"Next case."

"The next case, your honor, is that of the city and county of Los Angeles versus Robert Joseph Parrish."

"What are the charges?"

"Let's see, your honor. Possession of controlled substances-marajuana, PCP and heroin, twenty-two ounces of heroin. Attempted illicit sale of said controlled substances; resisting arrest, and assaulting an office of the law with a broken beer bottle."

"How does the defendant plead?"

"My client pleads guilty to the lesser charge of possession, your honor," said Ralph Spencer, Parrish's attorney.

"Oh really," said the judge. "I see by your record, young man, that you have six previous arrests on similar charges Have you been in my court before?"

"No, your honor. I just moved here from my home state of Georgia."

"And why did you leave your home state so suddenly?"

The defendant hesitated.

"Well, Mr. Parrish?" the judge pressed.

"Bobby Joe, your honor. Everybody calls me Bobby Joe."

"Never mind that just answer the question."

"Well, I just wanted a fresh start on some new turf and . . ."

"Don't lie to me Mr. Parrish. I have reliable information that you were ordered by the court to leave the state of Georgia because of your repeated disregard for the law. Is that not correct?"

"That ain't true. That judge and all them high-brows in Atlanta just don't like white trash like me," he answered in anger.

"That will be enough of that kind of talk," said the judge slamming down his gavel. "Another outburst like that and I'll find you in contempt and add more time to your sentence. Understood?"

"Yeah, I mean, yes, your honor."

"Your honor I apologize for my client's disrespectful behavior. He's been under some unusual stress, lately."

"Oh, really. What kind of stress besides the obvious current type?"

"Well, you see, he just heard yesterday that his older brother had been killed in the fighting in Vietnam."

The entire court room fell silent and held its collective breath for just a split second in total sympathy with Bobby Joe.

"I see. In that case your apology is accepted, counselor. Our boys in uniform deserve every ounce of respect we can give them."

Bobby Joe's face turned crimson, the jugular veins bulged in his neck as he lost complete control.

"I want to kill every goddamned gook in this goddamned world for killing Virgil," he yelled waiving his arms above his head. Then he slumped back into his chair and sobbed.

"I'd like to request a recess, your honor," said his attorney.

"Of course, counselor, of course. This court will recess for two hours and reconvene after lunch. I'd like to speak to you and your client in my chambers in one hour Mr. Spencer."

"Yes, your honor."

Every one left the court room silently, solemnly.

Later in the judge's chambers Parrish and his attorney sat alone waiting for the judge.

"What do you think he wants?" asked Bobby Joe

"I don't know. But I do know this. You'd better pull yourself together and show more respect to the court or he'll throw the book at you. He'll put you away for a hundred years if you don't."

"Yeah, I guess you're right. But I don't take too well to kissing ass even to save my own skin. All my life people have been trying to get me to kiss up. They say it's for my own good. But I ain't gonna do it. Ain't nobody better than me and ain't nobody gonna push me around and treat me like dirt."

"That's it. That's the attitude that'll get you hung someday."

The judge finally entered the room. The warmth of the two ounces of scotch whiskey still caressed his insides, calming his frayed nerve endings.

"So you want to kill every gook in the world, do you? I'll assume that means Vietcong and not judges. Well, this desire of yours just might present a solution to your obvious guilt and intransigence."

"What does that mean, judge?" asked Bobby Joe.

"I think the judge is trying to work out a plea bargain instead of sending you to prison for a hundred years," answered his attorney.

"It means, Mr. Parrish, that what you need to learn is discipline and respect for authority which I don't think you'll get in any prison. Truthfully, I don't think you'll ever get it but I'm willing to give you another chance at it," said the judge.

"I don't follow you, judge," said Bobby Joe.

"Just listen, Bobby Joe," said his attorney.

"What I propose is that in lieu of a long prison term that you volunteer for military service for three years. Army, Navy, Marine Corps or Air Force, that's up to you. But I would suggest the Marine Corps. They'll teach you some real discipline and they won't molly-coddle you either. It just might make a man of you. And you just might get to kill some of those 'gooks', as you call them, and avenge your brother's death in the process. That is, if you can cut it."

"Oh, I can cut it all right. Don't you worry none about that your honor. Yeah, I like that idea. Kill me some gooks. Sounds okay to me."

"Now just a minute Bobby Joe. You'd better think about this for a little while. There's a war going on over there. You just might get killed yourself," warned his attorney.

"Yeah, I know that. But at least I'll have a weapon to fight back with. Not like being in the state pen. A bunch of guys can jump on you, beat you up, rape you or whatever they want. You ain't got a chance unless you got a weapon. Then you're the king."

"Well, you discuss it with your client and then let the court know your decision. Your case will be held over for two weeks. After that time you will present documented evidence of your client's enlistment, and acceptance, into military service for three years. If not, I'll pass sentence and he'll go to jail for a long, long time. Understood?"

"Yes, your honor," answered Bobby and his lawyer.

"In the meantime he's released into your custody. And I intend to hold you completely responsible for his behavior and reappearance in this court."

"Don't worry, your honor. We'll go down to the U.S. Army enlistment center right now," said the attorney as he left the chamber.

"You mean today?" said Bobby Joe.

"Yes, today. The sooner you're off my back the safer I'll feel. And if you try to skip town I'll personally make sure the bail bonding company takes every cent your mother has left. Mark my words," said the attorney.

"Okay, okay. Cool it man, cool it. Today it is. Why not?"

*   *   *

Several hundred miles away in Atlanta, Georgia, C.D. Highsmith was discussing his draft notice with Sgt. Major Kincade.

"Look, Sergeant, I just. . ."

"It's 'Sergeant-Major', if you don't mind."

"Okay, Sgt. Major. But I just graduated from law school and I have a ton of education loans to pay off and I can't do that on a U.S. Army lieutenant's salary for four years."

"I can't help that, boy."

The black attorney felt the hair on the back of his neck bristle at the racial-put-down but he restrained his anger.

"All I know is that your college deferment is up and 'Uncle Sammy Wants You'," he chuckled.

"But four years, that's a long time. I can't believe this is happening to me."

"There is another choice for you, though."

"You mean a way out."

"No, not a way out. You'll still have to serve but you can soften your hitch."

"Really, how?"

"It's simple. If you accept a commission as an officer and play at being a lawyer you'll serve four years. But if you enlist in the infantry as a buck private you'll only have to serve two years."

"But then I'm more likely to go to Vietnam and see combat, right?"

"I don't think so. The Army's not stupid, you know. They know you're an educated man. And probably one of the few Negro lawyers around. They won't risk losing such a valuable man in combat," said the sergeant who was obviously a good liar.

Highsmith thought for a moment. "Can I think about it and call you in a day or two?"

"I'm afraid not. You'll have to decide now."

Highsmith hated to make snap decisions but he had no other choice.

"Okay. Okay, then, I'll do it. Two years in the rank and file has got to be better than four years even with a commission."

"Good. It's settled then. I have the papers right here. Just sign on that line or make your mark." Another dig from the good Sgt. Major. "Now, you report back here tomorrow morning at 0600 hours for your induction physical."

"Okay, sergeant, and thanks for your help."

The sergeant grabbed him by the elbow as he turned to leave, pulled him vigorously against his body and shouted in his face, chin to chin, "that's, yes Sgt. Major. And don't you forget it, boy. You gotta start learning respect for superior rank and you'd better start learning right now. You got that, boy?"

"Yes, Sgt. Mayor."

"Dismissed," he shouted.

Another recruiting officer who had over heard the entire exchange nudged the Sgt. Major aside after Highsmith had left.

"Yes, what is it Sgt. McCoy?"

"You didn't tell that recruit the straight scoop. As a commissioned officer and an attorney his hitch would only be three years not four."

"Well, now ain't that a shame. I guess I got a little mixed up there. But it's too late anyway he already signed up."

"But that's a violation of army regulations, ain't it? You could get court martialled if anybody found out.

He grabbed Sgt. McCoy by his shirt front, pulled him against his chest, chin to chin, and said, "Now, I don't know anybody who'd risk his neck and career to tell the brass, Do you?"

"No, no, Sgt. Major. I guess not."

Kincade relaxed his grip and mockingly straightened McCoy's shirt.

"Besides, I think it's better all around for the Army to have as few niggers and spicks as possible giving orders to our white boys. Don't you?"

"Yeah, I mean, yes Sgt. Major, if you say so."

"Good. Now get back to your duties. And remember, 'loose lips sink ships, and careers, too.'"

Clarence Darrow Highsmith was totally unaware, as was everyone else until after the war, that the vast majority of enlisted men and women who would see combat in Vietnam came from the ethnic minorities, especially the blacks and Hispanics.

*   *   *

Three thousand miles from Los Angeles in New York City's Whitehall Street Army recruiting station Dr. Michael Angelo Rizzuto was being sworn in as a Captain in the medical corps of the U. S. Army along with hundreds of other physicians. He looked around the crowded room and noted that many of the doctors carried their personal medical records and x-rays with them as they waited. Most had not even yet had their induction physical examination, including Michael. He leaned over to the man sitting next to him who also had his medical records with him.

"Excuse me, my name is Michael Rizzuto, internal medicine, Brooklyn."

"Hi. Joe O'Mara, radiologist, Massapequa, Long Island."

"Hi. What's with all the medical records a lot of you guys are carrying?"

"Well, many of us feel, including me, that we have medical conditions that disqualifies us from military service in spite of our previous college deferments. We brought our medical records and statements from our personal physicians to plead our cases."

"Oh, I see," said Michael.

'What a bunch of hypocrites,' thought Michael. 'Don't they know there's a war on and the communists are trying to expand their sphere of influence all over the free world? Who else in the world can stop them but us? I guess they have no sense of patriotism and are only worried about their own hides. They're just like those creeps demonstrating on the college campuses. They make me sick.'

His thoughts were broken by the thumping of combat boots up on the wooden stage platform in the front of the room. Marching in before them was the medical officer in charge of the recruiting station. Five foot four inches tall, at least twenty-five pounds overweight and dressed in combat fatigues he was what was known as 'Gong-Ho Army'.

"My name is Lt. Colonel Cannon," he said as he rested his right hand on the pearl handled revolver in his right hip holster. There was a matching set on his left hip.

"Now, gentlemen, I notice that many of you have medical records, x-rays or what-have-you tucked under your unpatriotic, bleeding-heart-liberal little arms. Well, you can just forget it doctors. As far as the U.S. Army and me is concerned if you can practice medicine as a civilian you can damn well practice it in the Army."

An obese, sweating, nervous man stood up in the audience and shouted, "but I've already had two heart attacks. Any undue physical or emotional stress could kill me."

"That's tough, doc, but you're in. Even if you're a quadriplegic and we have to wheel you in on a stretcher, prop up your head to read x-rays, you're in the army now. Period! Now sit down and shut up."

Everyone in the audience was stunned by his bluntness.

"Now remember, men. Every one of our boys you patch up 'Out-of-country'—that means in the States—gets to go back 'in-country'—that means in 'Nam—to kill more of the Vietcong, otherwise known as V.C."

He started to march off the stage, his right hand still resting on his revolver amidst groans, boos and cat calls from the crowd. Some even threw their medical records and x-rays at him, frisbee style. It was a perfect example of the contempt and disrespect many of them would show toward the army during their two years of service.

One of the few silent exceptions was Michael Rizzuto, at least for now, who said to himself, 'Would you look at these animals. Regardless of their political views of the war you'd never know they were a group of physicians. What disgustingly unprofessional behavior. I am ashamed to call them colleagues.'

"I don't see what the big deal is," Michael said to his new acquaintance Joe O'Mara. "We'll still all be practicing our profession while we're in the army. Two years isn't a lifetime."

"What about those of us who are unlucky enough to go to Vietnam, I mean, 'in-country,' and get shot at. We could get killed, you know."

"Yeah, but I hear that is very unlikely, that we'll go over seas I mean. I also understand they really protect their medical officers very well over there. Anyway, it's mostly surgical-types and general practitioners who go to Vietnam."

"Yeah, that's what I've heard, too," said O'Mara obviously still dismayed.

"So what are you worried about? You're a radiologist. You're safe just like all the non-surgical specialists in this room."

"My brother's a general practitioner in Colorado. He's being sworn in today like we are. He's got a wife and four girls."

"Oh, I see. I'm sorry, Joe. I didn't know. But I hear that the casualty rate among Army doctors is less than one percent including wounded, missing in action, prisoners and fatalities."

"Yeah, but that's not very comforting. If you're one of the one percent that's a hundred percent for you and your family."

Michael fell silent.

"God, he loves his wife and those kids and that horse ranch of his," said Joe.

"What's your brother's name? Maybe I've run into him at medical conventions or somewhere," said Michael for want of anything else to say.

"George, George O'Mara III, named after our father and our grandfather, and our great grandfather before him just like the first-born-male has been named in our family for generations," he answered with and exaggerated, jovial, Irish brogue.

CHAPTER THREE

Medical Boot Camp

FORT SAM HOUSTON in San Antonio, Texas was the basic training post for all medical officers and medical service corps personnel. Therefore, all doctors, nurses, pharmacists, corpsman and hospital administrative-types were assigned to Fort Sam for seven weeks of basic training. It was also the location of one of the major consulting and referral hospitals for complicated military medical cases.

Michael Rizzuto and his family arrived in San Antonio late one February evening for the seven week stay at Fort Sam. That night the overnight temperature had dropped to an unusual ten degrees above zero. Joe O'Mara and his family had an apartment in the same complex off the military post.

"Well, here we are at last, honey," Michael said to his wife Catherine. "Why don't you arouse the kids while I go get the key to the apartment from the superintendent."

"All right, Michael. San Antonio looks like a nice community. I think we're going to enjoy our stay here," she said.

"Yes, I think so, too. And with the O'Maras next door we'll have some new friends and some support."

"And with an Army captain's pay of nine thousand a year we'll finally have some money to have a little fun after all those lean years as an intern and resident", she said.

Just as Michael was about to ring the doorbell to the superintendant's apartment a man came rushing out of the door almost knocking Michael down the steps.

"Oh, sorry, mister. I didn't see you at the door," said the man.

"It's okay. I'm Dr. Rizzuto. I came to get my key to my apartment. We just got into town and we're exhausted."

"What's your apartment number?" the super asked.

"Let's see. It's 14A," said Michael reading it off his apartment lease.

"Oh, that's too bad. That's one of them that was damaged with the freeze," he said.

"What do you mean, one of them?" asked Michael.

"Well, I was just running over there now to turn off the water. Seems this crazy cold-weather-snap froze the pipes in that apartment, and a lot of others, and busted them. Water all over the place."

"Oh, no. Are there any other vacant apartments we can use?"

"I'm afraid there's not. Ain't there nobody you can spend the night with?"

"No. I don't know anybody in San Antonio and I have no relatives here."

"What about that other doctor that came in earlier. What's there name? O'Hara, I think it was."

"You mean, O'Mara. But I hardly know him. We only just met. I couldn't impose on him and his family."

"Not much other choice, Doc. I doubt you could even find a motel in town tonight, what with all the other military fellas arriving, unless you want to spend the night in your car."

"Hey, Mike, Mike Rizzuto, is that you?" called a vaguely familiar voice from across the court. Then Michael recognized it as that of Joe O'Mara.

"Oh, thank God," muttered Michael. "Yes, it's me, Joe."

"What's up? You got a problem?"

"Yeah, sort of," answered Michael.

"Come on into my place. We'll see if we can work it out."

Michael walked across the court briskly as he saw lightning and heard thunder overhead.

"What's this? Thunder and lightening in the middle of 10 degrees temperature?" he said to the superintendent who walked across with him.

"Yep. Anything's possible in Texas. Weatherman's calling for severe thunderstorms, large hail and flash flooding. Something about two fronts colliding or some such nonsense," said the super.

As they approached Joe O'Mara's apartment door Joe said, "where's your family?"

"Oh, they're waiting in the car."

"Well, get them on in here, too, man," Joe insisted. "They're liable to catch their death out there."

Michael ran back to his car to get his wife and his four year old daughter.

"It seems our apartment has no water, honey. We're going into Joe O'Mara's place until we can figure something out."

"I won't hear another word about it," said Joe's wife, Judy. "You and your family will stay with us until your place is ready to live in and that is that. Joe, you and Michael go over to their place and bring the mattresses from their beds over here. Go on now, hurry up."

After arranging the two mattresses on the cramped living room floor the Rizzuto's argued that they could not let the O'Mara's sleep on the floor, too.

"After all, you guys were good enough to share your place with us. We couldn't take your beds away from you. Besides, you've already got three kids of your own in the bedroom. The five of you could not fit comfortably out here, Judy, but for the three of us it will be just fine," said Cathy Rizzuto.

"Whatever you say, Cathy," said Judy. And they both knew instantly that they would be friends forever.

"We'd better get some Zs. Roll call is at five in the morning," said Michael.

"Roll call? Five a.m.?" said Joe. "What are these Army guys, crazy? Surely that's just for the dog soldiers and recruits. They don't really expect doctors to be there at that time?"

"Yes, that's what is says in our orders. All newly assigned military personnel, officers and all, are to report to the parade grounds at five a.m.," said Michael.

"Orders? What orders?" said Joe.

"You know, Joe, that huge stack of papers you threw next to the spare tire in the trunk," said Judy.

"Oh, those orders. Is that what they were? You didn't actually read all those pages did you Mike?"

"Yes, I did. But it was only two typed, double spaced pages of orders."

"Go on. There had to be at least a hundred pages in that package," said Joe.

"That's right, there were. Two original pages and forty-nine copies. That's the U. S. Army way of doing things. Forty-nine to lose and one to use," said Michael.

"It's no wonder our taxes keep going up and our national debt continues to grow. What a waste," said Joe.

"I think it's a throwback from the old days when so many levels of the bureaucracy needed a copy to approve uniforms, livings quarters, weapons and so on," said Michael.

"Ah, come on now. Don't go defending a rotten system. I'm sure some General's brother-in-law or bosom buddy owns a paper and ink factory near the place where these are printed. At a hundred copies a man I'll bet he's bringing in millions and contributing to the General's retirement fund," said Joe, with no show of humor.

"Come now, Joe, really. Surely, you don't actually believe that?" asked Cathy.

"I most certainly do. These regular career Army guys are just like the politicians. They perpetuate the system by over-doing everything and their business buddies make a fortune. Then when you retire they give you a nice, plush vice-presidency with a big, fat salary. They put you in charge of golf outings and skiing weekends for the new Army guys coming up to get them into the system, too."

"Oh, cut it out, Joe. Now you're beginning to sound just like your father," said Judy.

"Yes, I am because he's right. He saw it happen in World War II, too. That's what this Vietnam thing is all about, you know. Big bucks. The economy needs a boost so you turn up the heat in some war somewhere, generate military spending and jobs. It's just the way FDR did in 1939 to get out of the great depression," said Joe, who was beginning to get hot.

Michael sat quietly listening until Joe mentioned his hero, Franklin D. Roosevelt.

"Now just a minute, Joe," he said, trying to remain calm. He liked his new-found friends a great deal and didn't want to offend them.

But he continued, "several others have made that same accusation against FDR but no documented proof of any kind has ever been turned up. It's all pure supposition," he said.

Joe backed off not because he was convinced but because he like the Rizzuto's, too. Michael was one of the few fellow doctors and colleagues he did like. And now that he saw that Michael, although soft spoken, had the courage to stand by his convictions he knew he had found a kindred spirit. He knew Michael was not a go-alonger like so many physicians he had known.

"Yeah, I guess you're right, Mike. I never have seen any proof, at that. But you have to admit that this Vietnam War stinks of corruption and incompetence," he said.

"I agree that the running of this war has been questionable so far, very questionable. However, I think the principle is right and the intentions are good. At least Hitler and the Japanese made their goals clear and proceeded openly even if it was after clandestine preparations. But these commies are something else again. First Castro pretends to fight for democracy and against dictatorship, then when he wins the guerrilla war with our help he says, "April-fools-day, everybody. I'm really a communist dictator myself". Then the North Koreans and the North Vietnamese start harassing their southern neighbors and before you know it the whole free world is threatened by a cold, subversive war in order to make world communism dominant."

Joe, Judy and even Cathy were impressed with Michael's sincerity and conviction.

He went on, "Oh no, Joe, I don't believe in war, and killing, and aggression but I'll die before I see my kids live under the yoke of an atheistic, dictatorial system like communism or anything that smells like it. No, never, not at any costs, under no circumstances."

The entire room, even the children, was completely silent and taken with Michael's passionate, soft spoken but sincere anti-communist dissertation.

"Yeah, yeah, Mike, I see your point," said Joe.

Cathy and Judy were moved, also, but pensive. They each had slight tears in their eyes. Their only thoughts were for the safety of their husbands, the fathers of their children.

"We'd better get some sleep. Four am is not too many hours away from now," said Judy.

"Four am? We've got to get up at four. These Army guys are not just crazy they're hysterically insane," said Joe turning out the lights.

"Just absolutely insane, daffed they are," he said as everyone chuckled. Then they closed their eyes for a few hours of well deserved, albeit fitful, sleep.

Sleep, however, came with difficulty for them and was frequently interrupted by loud claps of thunder and eye-twitching lightning. The children were awakened several times and were crying intermittently throughout the night.

"Oh, it's no use trying to sleep," said Joe. The adults agreed and spent the rest of the night talking, drinking coffee and catnapping on the living room floor after putting all the children together in the one bedroom.

Finally at 3 am the women started making breakfast since they were wide awake, anyway.

"We might as well get ready now and be at the post a little early," said Michael.

They showered, shaved and dressed in rotation, and as quietly as possible to avoid waking the children.

"Boy, oh boy. Just listen to that rain pouring down. It sounds like a deluge," said Joe.

"I wonder if we'll run into any flooded streets?" said Michael.

"I doubt it. Didn't you notice all the spill-ways and viaducts in this town. Looks to me like these people are prepared for the worst," answered Joe.

"Yes, I did notice them now that you mention it. But I still think we should leave a little early, just in case," said Michael.

After a hardy, but leisurely, breakfast Michael and Joe started up Michael's 1967 Plymouth Barracuda and exited the parking lot. They turned left out of the driveway toward the post. The street was a moderately steep uphill grade.

"I can't see a thing, Joe. The rain is coming down in torrents. I can hardly see the headlights striking the pavement."

"Yeah, it's like swimming under water with your eyes open in the filthy East River in Brooklyn. . ."

The car suddenly mushed to a slow halt. It was not like hitting a brick wall or anything. It was more like bogging down in the mud. The engine was still running but the vehicle just couldn't move no matter how far down Michael pushed the accelerator. Finally the engine stalled and the headlights started to dim.

"What the hell was that?" said Joe.

"I don't know. Hey, look the headlights are going out, too. The rain is so heavy I can't see anything . . ." Michael said squinting to try to see ahead.

"Look, look," said Joe. "Is that water rippling against the headlights? Yeah, it is. It is water. We're in a river or something. Holy shit."

The Plymouth Barracuda slowly began floating down the hill. Both men jumped out and were shocked to find themselves standing waist high in a torrent of water.

"Close the door," yelled Michael over the roar of the rain, the flowing water and the thunder, "before the car fills up," and he made a gesture with a wave of his hand to Joe.

Both men sloshed their way to the rear of the car to halt it's progress down the hill but the current from the flooding street was too strong for them.

"Get on this side, Joe. Let's try to push it and guide it back into the parking lot," shouted Michael.

The drive way had a slight uphill incline and the lot was about four feet above street level which put it even with the surface of the flowing water. The air trapped under the wheel wells and in the passenger compartment buoyed up the vehicle but the current was still strong. However, pushing together they were able to turn the car and guide it into the lot. They pushed it another twenty feet to the center of the lot and safety. They were both thoroughly drenched as the pouring rain flowed over their faces like a shower head on a Saturday night.

"Come on, let's get back to the apartment and check out the families," shouted Michael.

"Yeah. Holy crap, it's pouring so hard I can hardly see the lights in the windows" said Joe when Michael stopped him.

"Wait," said Michael.

"Wait for what?"

"Quiet. Listen. Do you hear something?" asked Michael

"Yeah, sure," answered Joe, "like I'm standing under Niagara Falls."

"No, no, I mean a voice calling for help."

They strained to hear and cupped one ear each toward the street.

"Help! Please somebody help," they heard a faint, muffled cry over the din of the rain. They ran back to the parking-lot driveway and stopped to listen again. The voice became slightly louder.

"It's coming from that way down the street." They started in that direction.

"Wait, I have a flashlight in my glove box. I'll go get it," said Michael.

He was back with the flashlight in seconds and flicked it on. Nothing. He took out the batteries, wiped them on his T shirt under the armpits which were still miraculously dry. It worked, the light went on. He aimed the beam in the direction from which the voice had come. At first they saw nothing. Then Michael raised the light a few feet up a utility pole.

"Hey, there he is," said Joe.

"Where?" asked Michael squinting through the pouring rain.

"Raise the light up the pole a bit. I thought I saw a bare foot. Yeah, there. Hey it's a lady," said Joe.

Sure enough, five feet up the pole and only a few inches above the surface of the water, a middle aged woman clutched a Bus Stop sign while her legs were wrapped around the pole. Michael and Joe waded the two hundred yards to where the lady was trapped. She was crying hysterically.

"It's all right, ma'am. You're safe now. We'll get you out of here to a safe place," said Michael.

The rain had begun to subside and the sky brightened almost imperceptibly. The woman continued to sob.

"You're gonna be okay, lady. You can calm down, now," said Joe.

She struggled to speak.

"My son, my son, save my son," she finally choked out.

"Your son? Where? Where is he?" they asked. They looked up and down the torrent of water still flowing by.

"Over there. In that viaduct. The water washed him away from the bus stop. I tried to hold on to him. He's only eight years old. Please, please find him. He can't swim."

Both men looked, momentarily, at each other in stunned disbelief, .

"Mike, do you want to go?" said Joe as he pulled off his shirt, then leaned against the post and raised his feet above the water surface to remove his shoes.

Michael hesitated almost frozen and dumb founded. He didn't want Joe to discover his terrible fear of drowning.

"No, no, you go, Joe. I'll help the woman down and into the apartment," said Michael.

Joe waded a few feet into the viaduct. Every few yards he plunged deeply down into the viaduct, and then came up for air after a few minutes . . . without the boy. After several more tries he finally came up with the boy and towed his limp body toward the parking lot. By this time Michael had gotten the woman to safety in the parking lot. The boy's lips and fingertips were ashen grey, his limbs flopped around like a rag doll.

Joe placed the boy on the pavement face down and compressed his chest wall to express the water out, even though he was exhausted after the difficult swim.

"Here, not that way," said Michael, "let me do it. I saw a new method called CPR in a medical journal."

He rolled the boy on his back, gave him a few puffs of breath into his mouth while pinching the boy's nostrils closed. After three or four puffs he placed both hands on his breast bone and pressed down hard four or five times in quick succession. This action vigorously compressed the boys heart between his back bone and his breast bone, as the boy's mother watched in silence.

Water spurted gently out of the boy's mouth but he made no spontaneous respiratory effort. The woman continued to sob, shiver and wait for some response from her son. Joe kept checking his wristwatch.

After twelve minutes Joe said, "Mike it's no use, he's gone. You can stop now. It's been twelve minutes."

"No, no. I can still bring him back."

"No, you can't, Mike. Remember, brain death after six minutes of no oxygen to the head," said Joe, gently.

"Never mind the physiology lecture. I can do it, I know I can."

Now Michael was crying while trying to muster more strength and to catch his own gasping breath. Joe put his hand on Michael's shoulder.

"Let me alone. Get your hands off me. I can do it, I can do it."

Michael finally slumped to the wet pavement exhausted. The mother now kneeled silently next to her son's lifeless body too stunned and emotionally spent to cry any longer. She gazed forlornly into the pavement. Joe took off his soaking wet jacket and stretched it out over the boy's body.

"Come on, ma'am, let's go inside. Come one, Mike get up. We've got to call the authorities and get this lady out of those wet clothes before she catches her . . . before she catches pneumonia."

"Yeah, you're right, Joe. We are doctors, aren't we? We've got to go through all the motions now, don't we?" mumbled Michael.

"Let's stand up, Mrs. . . Miss, What is your name ma'am?" The mother couldn't answer or move.

Michael and Joe gripped her under the arms and began to walk her slowly back to the apartment. Her legs were flaccid as she dragged one foot in front of the other scrapping her bare toes along the rough pavement with a soft, grating sound. The rain had stopped and the sun was peaking over the horizon.

"Just take it slow. We'll help you. There's no hurry," comforted Michael. "You're going to be okay. We'll take care of everything. Don't you worry about anything."

Although they were only a hundred feet from the apartment door they traveled what seemed like a hundred agonizing miles. Michael just wanted to let her go and run as fast as he could, as far away from Texas, the U. S. Army and Fort Sam Houston as possible.

They finally reached the apartment. Joe kicked against the door while holding the woman up to get the attention of the wives quickly. Judy and Cathy opened the door quickly but were startled at what confronted them.

"Joe, Michael. What are you doing here? It's almost 7:30 a.m.," said Cathy. Then they noticed the woman literally hanging suspended between them.

"Who's that? Oh, never mind that now. Just bring her into the bedroom," said Judy. "I'll get those wet clothes off her."

"You're all soaking wet right through to the skin," said Cathy.

"Honey, you'd better call the police and an ambulance," said Michael.

"Why? What's happened?"

"First, call them, I'll tell you the whole story while we change our clothes," Michael faltered on the words.

"There's . . . there's a body of a dead boy out there in the parking lot."

"A boy? Who's boy? What boy?" asked Cathy.

"He was only eight years old. That's his mother in the bedroom with Judy. I don't know his name or her's either. See if you can get her to speak. I think she's still in a state of emotional shock. Me too," he said, "me too."

They waited for the ambulance, the police and the coroner which took several hours because of the flooded streets and roads. After all the forms and technicalities were taken care of the mother began to speak. She told them where her husband worked so he could be notified. Michael and Joe insisted on being the ones to break the news to the father, face-to-face, rather than over the telephone. The father collapsed upon hearing the shocking news just as his wife had done. They spent the rest of the afternoon and early evening trying to console the parents as best they could.

Finally, at 8:40 p.m. they staggered, exhausted, back to the apartment.

"Where have the both of you been? We were so worried," said Judy.

"We stayed with those poor folks for a while. They needed somebody, right now. They're from California and they have no family here," said Joe

"It seems the boy was their only child," said Michael.

"Well, they can always have more. They're still young and they'll eventually get over it. Life must go on," said Judy.

"No, I'm afraid not," said Michael. "Have anymore children, I mean. Apparently Mrs. Nichols, that's the mother, had a hysterectomy shortly after Sean was born. She'll never be able to have children again," he added.

"Well, they can always adopt. I understand that adopted children are among the most lovable of children," said Joe.

Judy and Cathy agreed but, as mothers themselves, they wondered, in their hearts, if it would be exactly the same.

"I'm sure it's too late to report to the post now," said Joe.

"Of course you can't report now. You are both totally exhausted. I'm sure when you explain the circumstances they'll understand, they'll have to," said Cathy.

"Oh, I'm not so sure about that," said Judy.

"Why do you say that?" asked Cathy.

"Because I know the Army."

"Oh, really. And how do you know so much about the Army?" asked Cathy immediately regretting her curtness after she had said it.

"Because my father was a career Army man. He wasn't an officer but a Sgt. Major. I grew up on Army posts all across the country and in Europe for awhile, too," said Judy. "Then when he retired and we had all grown up he deserted us and my mother who had stood by him all those years. He took up with some geisha girl in Tokyo. We haven't heard from him in years. Oh well, that's another story. Anyway, he was 'regular Army'. Everything had to be done by the book, cold steel discipline all the way. Didn't have an understanding, forgiving bone in his whole body. For him, and for us, there was only one way—-the U.S. Army way—-no ifs, ands, buts or I understands about it. That's why he stayed in the Army so long. Thirty years of Army regulations. There was no other way he could have made it that long, otherwise," she added.

"Well, we'll just have to take our chances," said Michael. "We'll report to the commander of the post first thing in the morning and explain. What's the worst thing they could do to us? send us to Vietnam to kill 'gooks'," he said smiling in a failed attempt to be humorous. No one laughed.

"Michael! Don't say things like that. That is not funny," said Cathy throwing her arms around his neck and burying her face in his shoulder to hide her moist, red eyes.

"Sorry, honey. I was only kidding."

"Yeah, I don't think we have to worry about that happening," said Joe. "I hear they only send surgeons and general practitioners over 'In-country'. At least that's been the history of this war, so far."

Judy smiled and nodded her head in agreement but in her heart she knew that the only predictable thing about the Army was it's unpredictability.

"Let's check the schedule and see what time we have to report tomorrow," said Michael as he searched through his papers.

"Ah, yes, here it is. Let's see. It says we are to report to roll call at 6:45 am and then start classes at 7:00."

"Oh joy," said Joe. "Tomorrow we actually get to sleep in for a whole hour. It'll seem like only a half day of work."

Everyone chuckled and they vowed to turn in early after a late supper.

CHAPTER FOUR

A. W. O. L.

THE FOLLOWING MORNING Kathy was at the kitchen sink trying to scrape the burnt edges off the toast while the bacon and eggs were frying. She looked out through the window when she heard a vehicle drive up and park across the parking lot. There were two M.P.s inside the vehicle. They turned off their headlights but keep the engine running. It was 5:20 am by the kitchen clock. She shrugged and thought nothing more about it.

"Come on everybody," she said softly not to awaken the children. "Breakfast is on. Get it while it's hot."

Michael, Judy and Joe tiptoed out in their stocking feet and sat at the table. The clock read 5:31 am precisely.

"Pass the butter please, Judy," said Michael.

Suddenly there was a loud pounding at the front door which startled everyone and awakened the children who immediately began crying.

"MIlitary police. Open the door immediately and everyone will stand in the center of the room," shouted two deep, husky voices.

"What the hell is going on here," Joe yelled back as he angrily stomped toward the door and threw it open. He was shocked and amazed to see two large MP's confronting him with their 45 automatic pistols drawn, cocked and raised ready to be lowered to the firing position.

"Hey, are you guys crazy or something? We've got women and kids in here. Put those guns away," growled Joe. They ignored him and held their position.

"Captain Michael Rizzuto?" asked one of them.

"No, I'm Cpt. O'Mara. That's Cpt. Rizzuto over there. What the hell gives? We're doctors not gangsters or spies."

"Sorry sirs but you're both under arrest," said the younger, more aggressive policeman.

"Under arrest? What for?" said Michael as he lay his hand on Joe's shoulder trying to calm him down. He gently maneuvered himself between Joe and the M.P.'s who were standing nose to nose, toes to toes with Joe.

"AWOL, sirs," answereed the more mature, reserved MP, Sgt. James. "You're both absent without leave, and twenty four hours and"... he paused to look at his wristwatch... "thirteen minutes, 36 seconds late for roll call."

"Holy shit," said Joe stamping his feet and waving his arms. "Twenty-four goddamned hours late and they're ready to thrown us in San Quentin for life."

"Easy, Joe, easy," said Michael. "Listen. . . ah officers, policemen whatever you guys are called," he added.

"Just by our rank, sir. Sgt. James and Corporal Peters."

"Okay, Sgt. we can explain all this. You know about the flood but then there was this woman and her son. The flood washed the kid away and. . ."

"Save it for the court-martial, sirs," said Corp. Peters with as little respect for their rank as Sgt. James would allow.

"Court martial? Why you dumb assholes. You're not taking me anywhere without a fight," said Joe ripping off his shirt and tie revealing an impressive physique from his college football days.

"Hold on, Joe," said Michael, bear hugging him around the waist trying to subdue him. He was not doing very well being at least 50 pounds and lighter and 5 inches shorter than Joe. "They're only doing their jobs, follwing orders," he added. But Joe would not be denied. He now had Corp. Peters' shirt front in one hand and his other hand cocked to throw the first blow. Both Peters and James had their night sticks raised.

"Joseph, Joseph. You stop that rowdyness this instant," yelled Judy with an authoritative tone which reminded Joe of his mother's tone. He didn't like it but he always withdrew.

"You are scaring the kids and me to death. All of you. Now start acting your ages and behaving like educated gentlemen, immediately."

Joe and Michael backed off as did Peters and James. Judy continued to get everyone calmed down and the situation stabilized while Joe and Michael got dressed to go with the M.P.'s to the post. They returned from the bedroom to find Peters holding two pairs of handcuffs and two pairs of leg shackles.

"Now hold on just a goddamned minute," said Michael, "this is where even I draw the line. You're not putting those things on me like some common criminal for the whole world to see."

"Sorry, sir. It's orders," said Peters.

"Back off Peters," said Sgt. James. "They're not dangerous or likely to try an escape," he added.

"But our orders are that all prisoners—bar none—are to be shackled when they are brought in."

"Well, technically you're right but we can stretch the rules a bit, that is, I can. We'll just put on the handcuffs once we get them into the jeep," said James.

"I won't be a party to disobeying orders, Sgt. . ."

"I'll take full responsibility. Now move out Peters," said James firmly.

Michael and Joe got in the back seat of the jeep. They put the handcuffs on them and then Peters tried to put the leg shackles on.

"Oh no you don't," said Joe as he kicked Peters hands.

"Ouch, you're gonna be sorry you done that, sir," said Peters.

"Goddamn it Peters. Cut it out," said James.

"Oh, are we really?" said Joe. "Well just remember, ball buster, we're doctors. And we're going to be on this post for seven weeks. We'll probably get to know all the doctors on the post. So if you get sick, I mean real sick, you'd better drag your sorry ass off the post and find a civilian doctor because we just might let you're steel plated hide die."

Peters paled and then flushed with the real but improbable threat.

"Joe? What the hell's wrong with you? We took an oath, you know. We couldn't do that," said Michael.

"Speak for yourself, Michael. I didn't take any oath. Even if I did I wouldn't have to save anybody I didn't want to. You remember we made that exception when we joined the AMA," he said winking and smiling so Peters could not see him. Michael winked back.

The jeep pulled up in front of Ft. Sam Houston Headquarters. The M/P.'s took Joe and Michael into the waiting room outside the commanding General's office. The General came out shaking hands with another General when he spied the two medical officers in handcuffs. The waiting room was crowded with people which did not discourage the General from speaking his mind, loudly.

"Well, well, well," said the general in his most authoritative intonation. "What do we have here? Two more spoiled rotten doctors who think they're too high and mighty for the U. S. Army?"

Michael paled and Joe smiled, threw back his shoulders sticking out his chest.

"Now get this, you two prima donnas. You'll either fall into line or I'll personally see to it that your privileged asses are shipped to Vietnam on the next flight out."

"But, sir, you don't even know the charges or the circumstances yet. How can you. . ." muttered Michael.

"Don't ever speak to a superior officer until you are given permission to speak," said Sgt. James.

"I don't need to know the details *doctor* because I know how you pill pushers and charlatans think. You're all alike. You all think your ass rides twenty feet above the sidewalk because you have an M.D. after your name. If I had my way I'd replace all of you with a good career Army corpman. Probably save more lives in the process."

Joe lowered his head, cocked it toward Michael and whispered, "I hope this bastard gets sick while we're here, real sick."

"What was that, Captain?" said the General.

"Oh nothing, General, sir, your highness, sir."

"Get these smart asses out of my sight. Take them to Col. Foster. Let him deal with them. He's a regular Army doc. Let him handle it."

The M.P.'s yanked on the handcuffs turning Joe and Michael around toward the hospital commander's office.

"And you tell the Colonel I said to throw the book at them. I want them to act more like soldiers and break them in the process, the good-for-nothing-sons-of-bitches," muttered the General storming back into his office slamming the door behind him.

On the long walk across the compound to the hospital Michael expressed disbelief over the mild slap on the wrist despite the harsh talk they had received.

"I don't get it. Why didn't he throw us in the stockade or give us something more severe than a tongue lashing. He could have ordered us to Vietnam right now."

"Are you kidding, Mike" said Joe. "They can't do without us. We can't patch up their mangled bodies and broken minds locked up in a cell somewhere. There are no substitutes for doctors. You can always make another tank commander, supply officer in ninety days of training but it takes years to make a surgeon. They know that, we know that, and they know we know it. That's why they get so pissed off at us. We are indispensable and they hate us for it. Nice feeling, isn't it?"

"Maybe so but they can still send us to 'Nam," said Michael.

"No, not us non-surgical types like you and me. We can't operate on anybody. We're not trained for that. We'd only get in the way 'In-country'. They know that, too," said Joe.

The tension in Michael's neck muscles began to relax as he understood the rationale of Joe's wisdom.

"How do you have so much insight into the Army ways?" asked Michael.

"My wife. Did you forget? She's an Army brat. She knows them inside out thanks to her Dad.

"No talking while under arrest," said Corp. Peters.

"Stuff it, Peters," said Joe as they entered the waiting area outside the office of the hospital commander, Lt. Col. Richard Forest. Forest is a career Army medical officer; eighteen years of service and two years away from retirement on a full pension at 50% of his pay for life. He was not about to rock the pork-barrel boat and jeopordize his promotion to full Colonel.

Michael and Joe went in and sat down in front of the Colonel's desk as he was ostensibly finishing up some paper work, trying to look as official and military as possible.

"Oh, I didn't hear you come in. What do we have here? Sgt. James."

"Captains Rizzuto and *O'Hara*, sir. AWOL for 24 hours."

"That's O'Mara, bird brain. You know M like in mother if you had one," said Joe.

"Now, now doctor. Let's remember our educational background and our manners. After all physicians are supposed to be gentlemen and scholars."

The Colonel stood up at his desk. Joe had all he could do to keep from laughing out loud. The Colonel's five foot, one inch height, 128 lbs of grissle and bone did nothing to add to his image of *commander*. His graying red hair cut in a close military style crewcut didn't add any improvement. Nor did his small beady eyes which appeared even smaller behind the thick eyeglasses he wore. When he removed the glasses his left eye turned grossly inward.

"So, gentlemen tell me the whole story and don't leave out any of the details. I'm sure we can work this all out, amicably. Sgt. James remove the handcuffs, please," said the Col.

"But they're prisoners, sir" protested Corp. Peters.

"It's all right, Peters. I'll take full responsibility," said the Col.

"Up yours," said Joe and chuckled. Michael elbowed Joe in the ribs, "cut it out Joe, will you? Enough's enough."

Joe shrugged his shoulders and smiled.

They then told the complete details of the previous day and night including the frozen water pipes in the apartment, the flashflood, the woman on the utility pole, the dead boy and the hours spent trying to console the parents. When the finished Col. Forest seemed unmoved. Then a gentle knock came at the door.

"Come in," said the Col., Corp Peters stepped inside, saluted and said, "another fact you might note, Col. They are out of uniform. The uniform of the day was supposed to be dress greens, not fatigues, sir."

"Our other uniforms were all wrinkled and muddy from the water in the viaduct, you ninnie," said Joe.

"Thank you, that'll be all Peters. It will be noted in the record. You're dismissed," said Forest. Peters left muttering to himself angrily.

"Now, gentlemen," the Col continued, "your actions and courage were indeed outstanding as physicians. However, your primary status here is that of a soldier, first and foremost. Your role as physicians is secondary."

"Oh, for Christ sake. Are you shitting us or what?" said Joe.

Forest ignored the comment, paced back and forth in front of the desk with clasped hands behind his back strutting as militarily as possible.

"Now as far as your conduct as soldiers and officers over the past," he paused to glance at his wristwatch, "twenty-four hours, forty-two minutes, and eighteen seconds has been appalling."

"Talk about your Hippocratic oath. This guy's taken his oath to Zeus, the god of war, the flaming asshole," said Joe.

The Col. stopped his marching, raised his eyebrows, considered a rebuttal but decided against it and continued. "Now, as to your punishment. . ."

"Excuse me, sir," interrupted Michael. "Did you ever practice medicine? as a civilian, I mean," he added.

"Well not in the usual sense. You see I went to a military primary school and high school. I was Army ROTC all through college and medical school. Upon graduation I took all my post-graduate medical training in the Army and at military hospitals. I'm military all the way. I went into the medical corps, and medical school for that matter, because it seemed a sure-fire way to have a successful military career," he concluded proudly.

"So, what are you going to do to us? Colonel, flunk us out of medical field service school?" said Joe.

"Oh, no I couldn't do that. If I did you could never go to Vietnam in the service of your country. No, no, it's already been decided as standard policy for all doctors. All medical officers *shall* successfully complete medical field service school. Some will get A's and B's, most will get C's with an occasional D or two for the record," said the Col looking straight at them while transfering his gaze from one to the other rythmically as if counting. One, two. One, two. Left, right. Left, right.

"No, I will do nothing to stifle your ability to function as physicians. In fact you'll get to do more doctoring than you bargained for while at Ft. Sam. In addition to attending your regular classes and training you will both be required to make rounds on all the critical ill patients at the hospital—that's sixty beds—before or after classes, which start at 7:00 am, seven days a week. And there'd better not be any deaths on your ward, either."

"What?" said Joe who had jumped out of his chair and thrusted his body against the Colonel's whose nose struck Joe's shirt at the first button above his beltbuckle, "that is physically impossible."

"Begging you pardon, sir. But it will not be possible to give competent care to those patients under those circumstances," said Michael. "And Joe is a trained radiologist. He hasn't given direct patient care since he was an intern several years ago. I'll have to do it all myself" he added.

"Well, I guess you'll have to adjust to the situation, then. He can review all the x-rays for you and you can teach him how to be a real doctor again. Might come in handy at his final duty station or in Vietnam," said the Col. smiling.

"It's not all bad, Joe. At least we'll be practicing medicine and seeing really sick patients who'll need our help. I guess we can find consolation and strenght in that," said Michael.

The Colonel giggled in a slow, soft, sardonic chuckle, then he added, "in addition, you will conduct the dispensary and sick call at the stockade three times a week."

"Stockade Dispensary? What's that?" said Michael.

"That's sick call at the post's jail. That's where all the incorrigables are kept. You know, guys going AWOL—like us—guys faking sickness to get a medical discharge, the worst of the worst," said Joe.

Now the reason for the Colonel's sadistic giggle had become obvious.

"That'll be all gentlemen. You're dismissed. Remember, roll call is 0645 and classes start at 0700. What you do with all your *free time*"—again the giggle—"is your business."

Joe and Michael got up to leave, turned and walked toward the door.

"Excuse me, captains. Didn't you forget something?"

Michael, when he suddenly realized what the Colonel was referring to snapped to attention and give an acceptable salute which he returned. Joe just watched in disgust. Then without coming to attention and still slouching he raised his left hand to his face and placed his left thumb on the tip of his nose in a mocking salute. They both turned and departed.

CHAPTER FIVE

The Stockade

SGT. MAJOR SAL 'Rocky' LaRocca was slowly pacing in front of the open faced cells in the stockade at Ft. O'Malley, Kansas. He wore the usual facial expression which told the inmates, that which it had signaled for several weeks, "go ahead, you punks. Just say something to piss me off, I dare you. Just look at me crooked and I'll crucify you."

He continued his deliberate, taunting pace. His combat boot heels were clicking toward his favorite spot, the cell of Bobby Joe Parrish. "I can get a rise out of this scum bag nine times out of ten," he thought.

"So, red-neck, are are you making it without your weeds and your heroin to fry your make-believe brain? "Rocky taunted.

The man in the next cell chuckled.

"Quiet you, or do want to clean every latrine on this post with a toothbrush?" he scowled.

There was no response, which of course was the best response, unless one was demanded. Then you answered," no sir, or yes sir, or yes Sgt. or no Sgt. having no idea which was expected and hoping for the best.

"Well, Pvt. Parrish. I asked you a question and I expect an answer."

Bobby Joe hesitated knowing full well that he was condemned no matter what he said. Still he said nothing.

"Stand at attention when a superior addresses you," the Sgt. said.

Bobby Joe stood up slowly from his steel springed bunk from which the mattress and blanket had been stripped as punishment for some minor infraction. He ambled over to the center of the cell and stood at attention, more or less.

"Yeah, I makin' it, sir," he mumbled.

"No, no you goddamned ignorant douche bag. Sgt. Major, it's Sgt. Major. You only address officers as 'sir', not non-com's. I can't stand the sight of you no more, Parrish. You're gettin' just like these coons and chiquita-bananas you've been caged up with here. You're a disgrace to the white trash that born you. Corporal Miller take this piece of garbage and throw him into solitary confinement for ten days."

"On what charge? Sgt. Major," asked Miller. LaRocco flushed and gritted his teeth.

"I'm sorry but you know the regulations, Rocky. I gotta put something on the books for the brass," said Miller.

LaRocco's tension relaxed momentarily. "Yeah, of course, you do," he smiled. "Ah. . . put down insubordination and disrespect to a non-commissioned officer. That's vague enough to cover the REG'S, ain't it?"

"Yes, I guess so Rocky. That's cool," said Miller.

Bobby Joe's temper in the meantime was reaching the boiling point but he waited until he was outside of his cell and closer to LaRocco. As Miller was putting the shackles on his ankles Rocky strode past Parrish just close enough to tempt him. Bobby Joe worked up a large collection of saliva and mucus into his mouth. He spat it smack into the middle of LaRocco's back. BJ laughed as he watched the spit slide down the smooth, starched, fressly pressed surface of the Sgt.'s fatigue uniform.

LaRocco stopped momentarily and then with cat-like quickness he spun around and kicked Parrish hard between his legs and deep into his genitals. Parrish fell to the floor, curled into a writhing, groaning ball of burning pain.

"Make that thirty days in solitary, Miller. And add assaulting a superior officer for you damned regulations," said Rocky. He leaned over, ripped the shirt off the back of Parrish's still quivering body. He gave it to Miller to wipe the spit off his back. "And make sure he puts that shirt back on and keeps it on until he gets out of solitary."

"See you later, Parrish. And you know you're going to see me again. In fact, I'm gonna come visit you every day that you're in here. You'll be my own personal, special case for military rehabilitation. I'll give you all my expert attention," he said laughing sadistically.

Just like clock work La Rocco visited Parrish at 6:30 am every day to lay on some new indignity to spice up his thirty days in solitary confinement.

First he was stripped down to just his khaki boxer shorts on the pretext the he might try to hang hmiself with his other clothes. He stayed that way for 24 hours a day in the cold, damp confines of his cell for the full 30 days. His mail was withheld from him, as scant as it was. But he missed his regular issues of 'Hustler' and 'Playboy' magazines. His rations were reduced and very frequently excessively salted through some *accident* in the kitchen.

On day number 15 Sgt. LaRocco visited him as usual and dragged him out of his cell for some *rehabilitation and special counseling.*

"Now let see, Private Parrish. I've been examining your records. According to this you've been in the Army sixty days now—an anniversary kind of, isn't it— and you've served forty-five days of it in the stockade. That comes to one day of good time for every three days of bad time. And since bad time don't count toward your three year enlistment it ought to take you about nine years to serve out your hitch in this man's Army. It's too bad I'll be retiring in six more years. Unless I decide to go for 30, that is. I'd kind of like to be around to see you complete your successful military career. I'd like to sort of . . . make sure your rehab program doesn't get bogged down, if you get my drift."

"Don't worry about it, though. You'll be getting out of the stockade in 15 more days and you'll be assigned to C company. And guess what? I'm getting transfered out of the stockade duty to . . . you guessed it, C company. So we ain't gonna be separated after all. Ain't that a nice coincidence?"

"C company?" muttered Parrish being barely able to speak after 15 days in solitary and total silence. He had almost forgotten the sound of his own voice. "Ain't that the company guys go to when they're getting ready to go to 'Nam?"

"Well, ain't you the smart one. Maybe you've got a brain after all. Yeah, you got it right. We're getting ready to go to Vietnam," said Rocky.

"That's okay with me. That's why I joined the freeking army, to kill the 'Cong." said Parrish.

"But you're so close to retirement why would you risk getting your head shot off in-country?" asked the guard.

"Because that's the only way to quick promotions in the U.S. Army and that means more pay on retirement. And maybe I could wangle a Purple Heart for some little injury. That ups the booty even more," he added.

"Yeah, me too. I gotta get me some VC scalps before it's all over," said Parrish still standing at quasi-attention.

LaRocco suddenly lashed out with his night stick, which he always covered with foam rubber to prevent bruising when he went into the stockade. The blow sunk the end of the stick into the pit of Parrish's stomach.

"Who said you could talk? punk," said Rocky. He grabbed Parrish's hair and threw his doubled over body against the wall. Parrish's head whiplashed against the concrete with a crack.

"Speak only when you're spoken to. Throw this creep back into his cell, corporal."

"What about his remaining time in the solitary? Rocky," asked the Corporal as they walked back toward the stockade gate.

"What about it?" asked LaRocco.

"Don't you see? If he stays in there until he goes back to the unit at C company he'll look like he just got out of Auschwitz, which he knid of did," said the corporal.

"Oh, yeah. I see your point. Okay, let him out a week early into the regular stockade area. And see to it that he gets three square meals a day with two helpings of everything. If he can't eat it all force it down his gullet throw a stomach tube. I want him fat and sassy for his pre-deployment training."

Parrish was moved out of solitary but was given maximum security and extra guards around the clock. He was served six meals a day and was forced to eat every scrap sometimes to the point of almost vomiting back the excess food. But the corporal had stolen some anti-vomiting medication from the dispenary and gave Parrish an injection of it before each meal to subdue any vomiting. Parrish gained 14 pounds in the week of forced feeding. When he transfered to his unit he looked fairly normal, in weight at least, but his animosity toward Sgt. LaRocco had deepened and intensified.

"Hey, man. Where are you from?" asked the man in the bunk next to Bobby Joe Parrish's. "My names Tucker. Willie Tucker from Toledo, Ohio."

"Georgia's my home but I lived in LA before I joined up," said Bobby Joe.

"You joined up? What are you out of your goddamned head?"

"I had no other choice. It was either three years in the Army or five years of busting rocks in San Quentin," said Bobby Joe.

"San Quentin? What for?"

"For dealing and shootin' up," he answered.

"They were going to give you five years just for that?"

"Well, it wasn't the first time. . . and there was some other problems between me and the judge."

"You still shooting up?" asked Tucker.

"Nah, I've been clean for a month, now."

"How'd you manage that? It ain't that easy to quit. I know that for a fact," said Tucker.

"I've been in the stockade for awhile."

"So what? You can always get the stuff even in the stockade if you got some bread and know the right guards."

"Yeah, I was getting it for awhile. But then they put me into solitary. When you're in that hell hole you can't get it for any price," said Parrish.

"Oh, I didn't know that. I've been in the stockade but I ain't never been in solitary," said Tucker.

"Yeah, well it's a bitch, believe me. I ain't never going back in there. I gotta get to 'Nam to blow away the VC."

"You need some stuff for shooting up? I can get it for you anytime," said Tucker.

"Nah, I'm clean, now. I'm gonna try to stay that way so I can get my training done and go to 'Nam, a. s. a. p., baby."

"Ten-hut," came an unexpected shout from Sgt. LaRocco as he and Cpt. Williams, the company commander, marched into the barracks.

"Everybody open up your foot lockers and put all your personal effects out for inspection," said LaRocco.

Unannounced, spot inspections were a tradition in the military for decades but with the current prevalence of illicit drugs they were even more frequent. In the past the Sgt. of the unit would drop some hints so his man could be prepared since the adequacy of inspection reflected his ability to manage his unit. But not this time.

Williams and LaRocco proceeded down the row of bunks and foot lockers with only an occasional, cursory derrogatory comment. When they reached Parrish's bunk LaRocco cleared his throat and nodded to the captain.

"Oh, oh," thought Tucker, "Parrish is in for it."

"Open that foot locker, soldier and pull everything out of it," said the captain.

"Yes, sir," said Parrish as he neatly removed all the contents and layed then on his bunk.

"Come on, Parrish, come on. Hurry it up, the captain ain't got all day," said LaRocco who then began pulling out all the contents and throwing them on the floor.

"Unroll all those socks," said the Sgt.

It was obvious that they were searching for illicit drugs and not for signs of uncleanliness.

"Open that jar of deodorant," said the captain.

The captain put one finger into the creamy substance, searching it carefully. Then he wiped his messy finger on Parrish's blanket and pillow.

LaRocco was busy squeezing the contents out of the toothpaste tube and the tubes of shaving cream. He deliberately did this over the bunk making the creamy goo spill all over the blanket and pillow. Bobby Joe winced but didn't say a word but stood at attention as the bogus search continued.

All the packets of his clothes were turned inside out, the in-soles of his shoes and boots were removed, every compartment of his wallet was opened and all his family pictures were removed and thrown on the floor. Nothing was found.

"He's clean, sir," said LaRocco.

"Not quite, Sgt." said the captain as he picked up a pair of Parrish's combat boots, "not quite."

He turned the boot over with the heel and sole facing upward. A small chunk of mud was lodged in the angle where the sole and heel met. He flicked it out with his finernail onto Parrish's uniform.

"You don't keep yourself and your space very neat, Parrish. "Thirty days of latrine duty for this man, Sgt." he said.

"Yes, sir, Captain."

The barracks came to attention with a snappy salute as the Captain and the Sgt. left without even bothering to inspect the remaining bunks. It was clear they had finished the task for which they had come.

Bobby Joe turned to Tucker and said, "when can you get me some of the *grass* and 'H' you talked about?"

"As soon as you want, and all you want," said Tucker.

"Well, I want, and right soon."

The next day at dawn began the long, tedious training and indoctrination process for the the troopers having the potential for combat in Vietnam.

Parrish, Tucker and the rest of their platoon staggered into their barracks around dusk.

"Man, I am really bushed," said Parrish throwing himself face down on his bunk. "After I get me some chow I'm going right into the sack," he added.

"No you ain't, soldier," said Rocky LaRocco who had quietly walked into the barracks.

"Shit, I ain't," said Parrish who apparently had not immediately recognized LaRocco's voice. He rolled over and sat quickly upright when he finally realized it was LaRocco.

"That's right, Parrish. It's me, LaRocco, remember your personal rehab counselor. Did you forget about your latrine detail the Captain gave you yesterday. Now snap to it. Go get some chow in the mess hall, because you're gonna need it. Report back here to me in twenty minutes. No, you better make that fifteen minutes, and not a second longer."

"But that ain't hardly enough time to digest never mind eat any food," said Bobby Joe.

"So what? Then eat fast or bring it with you," shot back the Sgt.

"What? Eat in the latrine? That ain't very sanitary," said Parrish.

"Yeah, why not? You ain't worried about germs are you? Well don't because you got bigger things to worry about," said LaRocco as he left the barracks.

Bobby Joe changed his clothes quickly and started to head for the mess hall. Tucker stopped him outside the barracks.

"Hey, man. Wait up," said Tucker

"I can't wait. I anin't got much time."

"You want this stuff you asked me to get, don't you?" said Tucker as handed Parrish a small packet .

"Yeah, yeah. Sure I do. I need it bad, now," said Parrish. "What did you get me?"

"There's four joints in there and three bags of 'snow'," he answered.

"Heh, heh. That's great man. Thanks."

"It's okay, Jack. But don't thank me now. Just remember me on payday when the eagle shits."

"Sure, sure brother. I'll remember. See you later, man," said Parrish.

Bobby Joe ate a double helping of everything he could bolt down in the short time he had and stuffed the extra bread and cookies into his pockets. He ran back to LaRocco's quarters still munching on a pork chop. Rocky was standing outside waiting for him.

"You're forty-five seconds late, soldier. That means tomorrow you only get twelve minutes to eat."

Bobby Joe didn't react or respond. He knew better and just stood at attention.

"Good," said Rocky. "Now you're getting the idea." They marched double time to the latrine area and went into one of the buildings. It contained a dozen stools, a dozen urinals and dozen small sinks.

"Now, Parrish. This is your own personal, little rehab center. You will clean every square inch of every stool, sink, urinal, wall, floor, mirror and hardware and make them sparkle. I want to be able to see my handsome face in those faucets by the time lights-out comes. That's twenty-two hundred hours or ten o'clock in civy time. And you'll do it everyday. Have you got that?"

"Yes, sir. I mean yes Sgt. But what if somebaody comes in to use one of the stools or urinals before I'm done?"

"Then you'll wait until he's finished and then you'll clean it again."

"Oh, yeah. Okay. I mean, yes Sgt."

"I'll be back at 2200 sharpf. Now hop to it, soldier," he said and marched off into the darkness.

"Well, I'll be damned," said Parrish. "I ain't cleaning up after no dog faces like me." He thought for a moment and surveyed the latrine building then pulled over a trash can, turned it upside down and stood on it. Using his handkerchief to prevent burning his fingers he unscrewed the single light bulb illuminating the latrine door and sign. Once inside he used two trash receptacles to barricade the door from the inside.

"Now, any body got to go will just have to go in the bushes. I ain't cleaning this place but once a day and only once."

When securely locked inside he spooned and heated one of the bags of heroin and mainlined it into a vein. Then while flying high he lit up a marijuana and sailed through the cleaning job a good ten minutes before 2200 hours.

"Yes sir. When you gotta get something done fast there ain't nothing like using rocket fuel," he laughed.

Bobb Joe went along in this fashion every night for eleven nights without a hitch.

- -

"Well, Sgt." said Cpt. Williams. "It looks like you were wrong about Parrish. He's been a good soldier and he's kept his nose clean. He actually seems to delight in every dirty detail we give him."

"Yes, sir, I noticed that. I'd have bet my stripes on that punk screwing up but he ain't done it. . . yet," said LaRocco flushing with embarrassment.

"There's got to be something funny going on here," he thought. "And I'm gonna find out what it is. That red neck, piece-of-garbage can't be that good. I know my white trash garbage real good." At that point he decided to pay Bobby Joe a little surprise visit in the middle of latrine duty the following night after mess.

Sgt. LaRocco modified his original plan after thinking it over and proceeded to the latrine ten minutes before Bobby Joe was due to arrive. He hid himself inside a locked electricians utility closet and waited with the door opened just a crack.

Bobby Joe arrived and went through his usual preparation of unscrewing the light bulb, barricading the door and juicing himself up with Heroin and grass. Leaning against a sink he tied a tourniquet

around his arm and began his injection. Sgt. LaRocco had eased the
door of the closet open just a bit wider and watched until Bobby Joe
finished his injection. Suddenly surging forward he flung the door
open with a start, Bobby Joe jumped and dropped the syringe on the
floor.

"Well, well, well. Looky what we got here, will you," said the Sgt.

After dropping the syringe Bobby Joe tried to flush his remaining
heroin bags and joints down the stool.

"No, no don't waste that good stuff. You're gonna need it for
later. So this is how you been able to handle all the crap we've been
throwing at you, heh? Get yourself all juiced up with *horse* and *grass*.
Why I'll bet you could clean every latrine on Ft. O'Malley and never
blink an eye while you're on this juice."

"This is the first time Sgt. I swear it," said Bobby Joe.

"Oh, yeah," said LaRocco. He grabbed Bobby Joe's arms and pulled
up his sleeves. "Then what's all those railroad tracks on your arms?"

"Thems old ones from years ago," Bobby Joe lied.

"No they ain't. I know fresh track marks when I sees them," said
LaRocco who then swiftly brought his knee up into Parrish's groin.
Bobby Joe feel to his knees moaning softly.

"Don't lie to me. Those are fresh tracks. I've been around scum like
you too long not to know all your tricks. Don't try to fool old Rocky
he's too smart for the likes of you."

"So, what happens now, sarge. I guess it'll mean the stockade and
more solitary confinement for me," said Bobby Joe with a tinge of
defiance.

"Now that's where you're wrong, Bobby Joe. Your uncle Rocky
is trying to help you to get to Vietnam. I ain't got nothing against
hopheads, really. Matter of fact that makes them the best combat
soldiers and the best VC killers. No, there'll be no court martial or
stockade for you. Why, you can even stay on that stuff as long as you
don't get sick or O. D. or nothing like that."

"What? You're jerking me around, ain't you?"

"No, I mean every word of it. In fact I'll get you a clean supply of
needles each week and show you how to shoot up the right way, the
clean way. That's the only way you get sick from this dope stuff is using
dirty needles, poor technique and adulterated fluff."

"How do you know so much about it?"

"I got a lot of friends in the medical corps who owe me some favors. They taught me a lot. I'm gonna have them test your dope to make sure it ain't got no talcum powder, quinine or other bad adulterants in it. Yeah, Uncle Rocky's gonna keep you well enough to kill some 'gooks' in 'Nam."

Rocky remained true to his vow by keeping Bobby Joe supplied with sterile needles, alcohol swabs and unadulterated dope. And Parrish remained on heroin and pot becoming more deeply dependent and addicted as the weeks of combat training passed.

CHAPTER SIX

Yellow Escape From 'Nam

JOE AND MICHAEL rushed across the quadrangle of the parade grounds to get to the hospital to make their rounds.

"This really pisses me off," said Joe.

"You might as well calm down and make the best of it, We only have a few weeks of this duty until we're assigned to our permanent Post," said Michael. "Where do you think we'll get sent to?" he added.

"Fort Riley, Kansas. The armpit of the universe," said Joe.

"Kansas? What makes you think of Kansas right out of the blue?"

"I don't think, I know," said Joe.

"You know? And how do you know?"

"Oh, I know this Spec 4 in the C.O.'s office. He told me."

"You mean he just decided to give you this information."

"Well, not exactly. He needed light duty assignment for a few days and I just thought I'd negotiate a little trade," said Joe.

"You are unreal," said Michael.

"At least now we don't have to wonder about 'Nam. The wives will be relieved," said Joe.

They broke into a slow jog across the parade grounds to get to the hospital since an unexpected Texas thunder shower had started.

Fortunately they had very few patients in the critical ward the Colonel had assigned them and they felt them could still give them good medical care.

"Luckily for us there are few really critical cases today so I think we can finish up quickly and get to our other duties," said Michael as he went down the list of patients.

"Hey, I think I know this guy," said Michael. "It says, Major Thomas Adams. I had a Tom Adams in my fraternity who was two years ahead of me in med school," he added.

"May not be the same guy. Tom Adams is a pretty common name, you know," said Joe.

"Yes, I know. But this guy's a chest surgeon, he's from California, he's a couple of years older than me, just like the Tom Adams I once knew. That's too many coincidences. Let's see where he went to med school. Yes, he graduated from Creighton U. two years before me. That's got to be him," said Michael.

"What's his diagnosis? Nothing serious or fatal, I hope," said Joe.

"I don't know. Let's check his chart," said Michael. "Let's see . . . it says here infectious viral hepatitis. He should easily recover from that. As you know that kind of hepatitis is rarely serious, let alone fatal. Let's go talk to him. He's in the contagion ward in bed number six."

They walked the line of beds and came to number six which contained a very yellow, deeply jaundiced, quite ill white man. He looked very emaciated and weak.

"Hey, Tom? Tom Adams, is that you? It's me Michael Rizzuto. You remember me from Creighton U. don't you?"

The man struggled to turn his head and open his eyes which were deeply sunken into their sockets and ringed by dark brown-yellow circles.

"What? Who?" said Major Adams. "Oh, you? Yeah I remember you, Mike Rizzuto," he mumbled with difficulty as he tried to swallow over his thick, dry tongue.

"Yes, that's right Mike. Take it easy, Tom. Don't try to talk or move. Save your strength," said Michael who instinctively assumed the role of physician when he realized how sick the Major actually was. He quickly felt the thick texture of the hot, dry, yellow skin; checked his weak, thready pulse; examined his feebly beating heart; and they felt his enlarged, very tender liver.

"Something's wrong here, Joe. He's not supposed to be this sick with infectious hepatitis. I'm going to move him over to the intensive care unit right away."

As they moved away from the Major's bed Michael noticed all the other jaundiced patients who also had hepatitis and were jaundiced.

But they were all sitting on the edge of their beds talking, reading or playing cards. All except for one Hispanic man in the bed next to Adams' who appeared as sick as the Major. Michael quickly examined him as he had the Major.

"Private Guiterrez? Can you hear me?" he said. No response. "He's from the same outfit and station in Vietnam as Tom, Joe. We've got to move him to ICU, too."

The nurse and corpsman who were in charge of the ward reported to Michael and Joe.

"Nurse, please move these two men to ICU, immediately. Place them on the critical list." He then rattled off a long series of medical tests to be performed, prescribed oxygen and highly nutritious intravenous feedings. "Oh, also notify their families about their critical status so they can be prepared for the worst," he said in closing.

"Yes, Captain," the nurse answered.

"Not Captain. Doctor, it's Doctor," said Joe sarcastically, "we are doctors."

"Not now, Joe. There's no time for any of your hate-the-army attitude. We've got work to do," chastised Michael. "Something doesn't fit here and we've got to find out what it is."

Michael and Joe worked extra hours for the next three weeks trying to bring Tom Adams and Guiterrez back to good health. They visited them three, and sometimes four, times a day. Major Adams slowly but steadily improved while Guiterrez slowly deteriorated.

On the twenty-seventh day the Major became more alert and strong enough to converse coherently.

"How are you feeling today? Tom," asked Joe.

"Good, I'm feeling much better thanks to you and Michael. How's Guiterrez doing?"

"Not so good," said Michael. "He slipped into coma last night from liver failure. I don't think he's going to make it."

Tom Adams didn't say anything but he broke out in a cold sweat and his hands trembled slightly. When he realized Michael had noticed he pulled himself together.

"I knew it," said Michael. "I knew it. You're sacred shitless, Tom, because you know, as I know, that this isn't a case of benign infectious hepatitis.

"What do you mean?" said Joe.

"I remembered it the other night about a week ago. The whole fraternity house, thirty-seven medical students, including Tom Adams and myself had infectious hepatitis at the same time. I recall it exactly now because we were quarantined for six weeks. They brought in tutors who were hepatitis resistant to give us classes so we wouldn't all flunk out."

"So, what does that prove," said Joe.

Tom Adams interdicted, "so no one can have Infectious viral Hepatitis twice. Once you've had it you are immune to it for the rest of your life."

"But you can still get the other type of viral hepatitis called Serum Hepatitis or Hepatitis B," interrupted Michael.

"Oh, yeah. I remember that now," said Joe. "You forget those little facts as a radiologist. So what's the difference? Tom's recovering and he'll be eligible for medical discharge when he's fully recovered."

"The difference is that there's only two ways to get Hepatitis B and that's from a blood transfusion, which Tom has never had, or by main lining drugs with unclean needles. Now that's how Guiterrez got his. You can still see all the needle tracks running up and down his arms. But not Tom. He's got no needle tracks or marks. . . except for one. Right, Tom?"

Tom didn't answer but simply cast his eyes away in shame.

"Oh, yeah. Where?" asked Joe.

Michael hesitated but he knew he could trust Joe to keep Tom's secret.

"Shall I tell him Tom or do you want to?" said Michael.

"No, Michael, you go ahead," answered Tom.

"On the dorsal vein of the penis," said Michael.

"What? Where?" said Joe in astonishment. "You have got to be kidding," he added.

"No, I'm not. It's an old drug addict's trick. When all the veins in their arms and legs are completely scarred shut from hundreds of needle sticks they go there to find one of the few remaining patent veins to main line their drugs. Of course, that vein eventually scars over too . . . and then they die in acute drug withdrawal," said Michael.

"Good grief, that's awful," said Joe. "But why would Tom do that, and only once? He's not a druggie. You're not are you?" he added.

"Do you want to answer that one Tom or shall I answer this one, too?" said Michael.

Tom didn't respond so Michael continued. "No, Tom's not a druggie. But he injected himself deliberately with one of Guiterrez's dirty needles so he would contract Hepatitis B. What I don't know is why he did it. Only Tom knows the answer to that one."

"You must have been out of your freeking head," said Joe. "You could have been dying just like Guiterrez. Whatever possessed you to do such a crazy thing like that?"

"Desperation. Hate. Hate for this whole goddamned, stinking war and this stupid Army. And don't forget temporary insanity which will be my official plea. After ten months of trying to patch up the broken and shattered bodies in the jungle with second rate medical facilities and supplies. I was going out of my 'freeking mind'. But what really tied it was the civilians. Women, kids, old people, babies scalded beyond recognition by the goddamned napalm. Bodies torn to shreds by shrapnel from anti-personnel minds. Pregnant girls with their bellies ripped open by the mortars with the fetus half hanging out and still half alive. That's what possessed me, you horse's ass," he shouted.

Joe and Michael were frozen in time unable to speak. Their minds fighting not to visualize the horror Tom was describing and trying not to see themselves in the midst of these same horrific scenes.

Tom Adams was sobbing softly as Guiterrez in the next bed loudly sucked in his last gasping breath, then gave out with the familiar death rattle, and expired. Adams raised his head and looked at Guiterrez when he heard him take his last strained inspiration.

"Yes, I hated it so much I even risked what's happened to him. Even if I get cirrhosis and die of liver failure in ten or twenty years it's better than living and going back to see all that crap *In-country* again."

"But what if you had been caught? said Michael. "It would have meant a dishonorable discharge, a court martial and public disgrace. They might even have revoked your medical license. What then? What if you couldn't practice medicine and surgery in the states? Surgery has been your whole life. I remember how dedicated to it you were in med school. You would have blown all that?"

"Yes, I would have even blow all that to get out of Vietnam and out of this stupid Army. I'm not sure I could ever put a scalpel to living human flesh again, anyway," said Tom.

Joe sat on the edge of the bed next to Adams where he was sobbing again and said, "sure you can, Tom. Sure you can. You just need some time and peace of mind away from all this. You'll be back doing surgery again someday. And you'll be the best damned thoracic surgeon in, where is it you are from Southern California? Yeah, the best in all of Southern California, just give yourself some time. You'll see, and don't worry your secret is safe with us. This will never appear in your record. Right, Michael?"

Michael hesitated for just a split second torn between his ideals of truth, and loyalty to a friend. Finally he answered, "Right, Joe. Tom, no one will ever know except we three."

Tom slumped over into Joe's lap. Joe wrapped his arms around him cradling him like a crying child. Michael walked over and stood at his side placing one hand gently on Tom's shoulder and lightly rubbed his back with the other.

*   *   *

The following days at Ft. Sam Houston seemed more serene and pensive for Michael and Joe now as they professionally went about their medical duties. They tried to put Tom Adams's secret out of their minds but they could only bury it in a shallow grave in their hearts. Their vow of secrecy was kept but with great difficulty since they would only discuss it between them. Even their wives were not made privy to the episode, as much as they would have liked to share it with them.

Tom Adams fully recovered in body and mind, at least, if not in spirit, and received an honorable medical discharge. He decided to backpack around Europe for a year or two before considering returning to his practice in California. Joe and Michael never heard from him again. Private Guiterrez was given a military hero's funeral and was placed to rest in Arlington National Cemetery under the proud faces of his family. They never learned the real cause of his death. The death certificate listed the causes of death as liver failure due to viral hepatitis.

*   *   *

"Well, well, how are my two favorite Army doctors doing today?" said Colonel Robert Forest the Ft. Sam hospital commander. "Are we keeping you men busy enough? Do you have enough to do, yet?"

Michael said nothing ignoring the Colonel completely and continued to examine the patients on rounds.

"At least we're still functioning as real doctors, Colonel," said Joe.

Michael breathed a deep sigh of frustration over Joe's unbridled mouth.

"Is that so? As it says in the Hippocratic oath, which I'm sure both of you have taken, a physician is also supposed to be a teacher. But you men don't seem to be doing any teaching. I feel obliged to remedy that hiatus in your duties. Therefore, I've just made some additional arrangements for you both. After all I wouldn't want to suppress any of your professional zeal."

"Oh, really, Colonel. How considerate of you. You shouldn't have done this just for us. How will we ever repay your kindness?" said Joe.

"Starting next week, Monday you will both be assigned to teach classes at corpsmen's school. Report to my office after you've finished today for the class assignments. Don't thank me, gentlemen and think nothing of it. No repayment is necessary, either. Just tell your grandchildren about me when you tell them your Vietnam War stories," said the Colonel as he walked away chuckling.

Michael and Joe plunged ahead into their teaching assignments and put all animosity aside after their usual griping about it.

"Why should we go out of our way to do anything for this stinking Army?" said Joe.

"Because it's better then going to 'Nam and getting shot at or whatever. Did you forget already what Tom Adams went through?" said Michael.

"Sometimes I wonder if it is better," said Joe.

"As much as I hate that regular Army S.O.B., Colonel Forest, what we teach those corpsmen just might save some lives during this idiotic war," said Michael.

"Yeah, of course you're right, Mike," said Joe.

That evening Michael and Joe obtained the records on all the student corpsmen to become familiar with their educational and personal backgrounds.

"Looks like all these guys are conscientious objectors," said Joe.

"There's nothing wrong with that. I kind of admire a man who refuses to kill and then volunteers to help the wounded instead," said Michael.

"Yeah, me too. Especially when you consider that they'll be out in the field getting shot at themselves but they won't be able to shoot back. They're not allowed to carry weapons, you know."

"No, I didn't know that. Wow, that takes real guts," said Michael leafing through the files.

"Hey, here's a peculiar record. It seems this guy is a law school graduate. What's he doing in the ranks, and as a corpsman yet?" said Michael.

"Here, let me see that file. It's got to be a mistake. What a waste of an educated legal mind," said Joe.

"Highsmith, Clarence Darrow, that's his full name. Hey, he's in your class, Mike.

"Yeah, I saw that. I'd like to talk to him about this sometime," said Michael.

Michael taught his first corpsman training class the following Monday. In his typical idealistic fashion he inspired his students and infected them with his enthusiasm for the medical sciences and medical practice.

"You will hold in your hands the knowledge and ability which could determine whether a wounded soldier lives or dies. You must study continuously to maintain your competency, practice frequently to improve you clinical skills and be ever diligent for every single clue involved in the care of the patient," he said closing his first class to resounding applause.

"Class dismissed. You have your reading assignments. Be prepared for unannounced quizzes at all times."

The class started to depart.

"Specialist (Spec) 4 Highsmith," he called out.

"Yes, sir. Here, sir," Highsmith answered.

"I'd like to speak to you privately, please," said Michael.

"Yes, sir," he said uneasily as he began to worry if he was in for more racial harassment, or for being a conscientious objector or a displaced attorney.

He stood at attention before Michael's desk waiting for the tirade to begin.

"At ease," said Michael waiting until the classroom was cleared. "Sit down, Highsmith. Sit down and relax. There's no problem, Clarence. May I call you Clarence?"

"C.D. is okay, that's what everyone calls me. Just C. D."

"Okay, C. D. I was just curious about your background," he said.

C. D. immediately thought he was going to be ridiculed for his race just as he was by the recruiting sergeant when he enlisted.

"Yes, sir. What about it?' he said defensively.

"Now don't get your hackles up. I didn't mean your racial background. I meant your educational background. What's an attorney—tops in his class no less—doing in the Army, without officer's rank and a corpsman, yet?"

"Well, that's a long story, Captain."

"I've got time. I'd like to hear it, if I'm not being to nosy. I don't mean to pry."

"No, that's all right Captain. I've got nothing to hide or to be ashamed of."

C. D. began to elucidate the story regarding his enlistment to shorten his military obligation; and how, after a few weeks of basic training and learning how to kill people, he decided not to fight. In order to avoid a court martial and possible imprisonment he volunteered to be a corpsman, just as many others had done.

"I've got to give you credit for having the courage to stand by your convictions, C. D. There's not enough of that kind of courage around these days."

"Thank you, Captain."

"You can call me Michael. I don't like being addressed by rank. Except perhaps for the title doctor, of which I am very proud of but I don't consider that a ranking. I consider it a privileged title."

"Somehow, I knew that sir but I couldn't call you by your first name. Suppose I just call you Doctor."

"That's fine, CD, whatever you're comfortable with. Okay, you can go now. I'll see you in class in the morning. If you need any help with anything you just call me or come over to my quarters. Here's my address and phone number." They shook hands and separated.

"Thank you, doctor," said C.D. as he walked toward the door.

"By the way C.D. I think you have all the makings of a fine corpsman. In fact you could be an excellent physician," said Michael.

"I've never given that possibility any thought. But thanks for the complement."

"Just calling them like I see them, C.D. Maybe you ought to give it some thought. . . about going to med school when you get out of this Army, I mean."

"Yes, sir. I *will* think about it."

*   *   *

A week later the corpsmen and physicians were jointly scheduled for a practical class in wound debridement. This is a surgical procedure of trimming away the raged, unclean edges of a combat wound in order to allow for better healing of the edges and with a lower risk for infection.

Joe had acquired a jeep from a cooperative motor pool sergeant. It actually was another one of Joe's skillful trade-of-favors maneuvers. It did shorten the travel time between their multiple duties so Michael reluctantly agreed to Joe's pragmatism.

Michael looked over the schedule while Joe drove the jeep across the Post. Dawn was just beginning to break on the horizon. Another cool night in San Antonio was giving way to the usual warmer, humid daylight hours.

"Wound debridement, heh? I wonder how they plan to find real wounds or will it be just films and diagrams?" said Michael.

"I don't know," said Joe. Then he suddenly jammed on the brakes as they heard what were clearly loud cracks of rifle fire. The cracks were soon followed by the sound of crying and wailing.

"What the hell was that?" said Joe.

Both men were standing up in the jeep trying to ascertain the origin of the shots and cries.

"Are we under sniper fire or what?" said Michael.

Several more shots resounded followed again by the almost human sounding cries. They almost sounded like the cries of little children in pain but they had more of an animal quality. Both men looked toward the building where their debridement class was scheduled.

"I think it's coming from the building we're going to," said Joe.

"Yes, you're right, it is. But it's kind of a muffled noise like it was in an enclosure. You know, like a garage or a basement," said Michael.

"Yeah, that's it. It's coming from the basement."

Joe spun the jeep out quickly and spirited it away in the direction of the sounds, ignoring both speed limits and stop signs.

"Wow, take it easy will you. They'll be debriding our wounds if you're not careful. What's gotten into you, anyway? Those shots weren't fired at us," said Michael.

"I know that. But I just remembered where I'd heard those cries before. Those are the cries of wounded animals like I heard when I used to hunt deer with my dad. Once you hear that blood curdling, mournful cry you never forget it. I've never hunted deer again since I fatally wounded a doe years ago that cried like that for hours until we found her and my dad shot her through the head," said Joe.

"You mean you think they're shooting deer in the basement of that building to give us real wounds to debride. Why that's crazy, Joe."

"Maybe those are not deer cries but they are definitely the cries of wounded animals," said Joe.

They jumped out of the jeep, the motor still running, hurried through the front doors and down two flights of stairs to the sub-basement. Two M. P.'s were standing guard at the barred doors to a secured room. Joe tried to push past the guards but the M.P.'s crossed rifles to block the entrance.

"Sorry, sirs. You can't go in there. Only authorized personnel allowed."

"Get your ass out of my way," growled Joe.

"We're doctors and Captains and that's an order soldier," said Michael hoping their rank would have some influence.

"Yes, sir. I can see that you are, sir. But you're still not authorized to enter," the guard persisted.

A Master Sergeant had heard the ruckus and came to the door. Leaving the door partial open he looked out to investigate.

"What's all the fuss? What's going on out here, men?"

Then he noticed the two captains and snapped off a salute which Michael returned but Joe didn't.

"Begging your pardons, sirs. I'm Sergeant Makowski. What can I do for you?"

Joe pushed his way through the door catching everyone off guard. The two M.P.'s were thrown aside like two bowling pins. He thrust himself inside the large basement room.

"Holy shit," he said. "Would you look at this," he called over his shoulder to Michael. The guard tried to stop Michael from entering the room.

"It's okay," said the Sergeant They've already seen enough to know what's going on anyway. Go back to your Posts and close the door behind you. I'll handle this."

Michael and Joe glanced around the room in disbelief, their eyes bulging and mouths opened. Ten or twelve small animals—goats, sheep, and calves— lay on the concrete floor. Fresh blood was pouring from rifle wounds and poured down hill toward the iron drain in the middle of the room. All the animals were still alive but more or less unconscious. However, several of them were semi-conscious and were letting out an occasional cry while thrashing about.

"Hey, give those moving ones some more pentathal and morphine. Get them back to sleep," said the Sergeant

"Are you authorized to perform this . . . this slaughter, Sergeant?" asked Michael barely able to speak with the anger lodged in his throat.

"Yes, sir. It's done for each and every class of doctors that comes through Ft. Sam for field service training school. Twelve to fourteen animals every eight weeks, depending on the class size. It's been done this way since World War II," said the Sergeant reluctantly.

"What the hell for?" said Joe.

"For authenticity, sir. Wound debridement can only be taught on real wounds."

"That's bull shit. Every doctor that graduates from med school has debrided a lot of real human wounds by the time he's finished his training. This goddamned butchery is not necessary," said Joe.

"I'm sure that's true for you doctors but it's not for corpsmen, sir. They need real experience before they go to 'Nam. They'll be doing most of the debridement in the field, not the doctors," said Sergeant Makowski.

"You could have at least put them down to a sufficient level of anesthesia with ether or chloroform," said Michael.

"We're not authorized to handle those general anesthetics, sir. There's too much risk of explosion." It sounded like the Sergeant had been thoroughly prepared to answer these criticisms.

"Don't hand us that crap. Those anesthetics are used all the time in hospitals with a few simple precautions even the Army could manage," said Joe.

"Sorry, sir. Orders is orders and that's what we've been ordered to do."

"Orders, orders. That's the Army's answers to everything whenever you don't have a plausible excuse for your actions you just say, 'it's orders'. That's what the Nazi's said when they were on trial for Auschwitz and Treblinka," said Michael. "Who signed those orders, Sergeant?"

"The medical corps commander, sir, Colonel Forest."

"I might've guessed it was that asshole," said Joe.

Michael and Joe stormed out of the building and into the jeep which still had it's motor running. They sped across the Post to Colonel Forest's headquarters even faster than they had when they first heard the shots being fired.

The Colonel's office had just opened. There was no one in the waiting room, not even a guard or secretary. They barged into the Colonel's private office. He was sitting behind his desk talking on the telephone.

"Yes, Sergeant Makowski. I see, yes. They just walked in without permission to enter, I might add. I'll take care of it. Get back to your preparation for the class," the Colonel was saying. He gently and calmly placed the phone on the receiver.

"So what is it this time, doctors? Can't you stand the sight of a little blood and pain?" he said mockingly.

"That's not the point, Colonel and you know it," said Michael.

"Oh, really. And what is the point, then?"

"There's no need to make those animals suffer that way," said Joe. "You just don't give a damn, do you?" he added.

"Watch your disrespectful mouth, Captain. I've had just about enough of your impudence and insubordination."

"Oh, stuff it, you creep," said Joe.

"Cool it, Joe. Cool it will you," said Michael. "Now look, Colonel, I can understand the corpsmen needing the experience but the doctors don't need it. Instead, the Army could send the corpsmen to one of dozens of big city emergency rooms to get some real human wound exposure. . ."

"That will be enough, Captain Rizzuto," the Colonel interrupted. "The Army has seen fit to use this procedure for over twenty-five years. And until they decide to change that procedure you will follow orders and follow the book as they wrote it, period."

"Oh, I get it. It is not yours to question why, it is yours to simply do or die. Is that it? Colonel," said Joe.

"Right," shot back the Colonel. "And you will both follow those orders to the letter or I'll see both of your butts shot to hell in Vietnam. Do you understand that, doctors?"

They didn't respond, they were paralyzed by the thought of being separated from their families. This threat was to be the constantly swinging axe over their heads for the next two years.

"Now, you *will* report to that lab, immediately, and get on with it. Sergeant Makowski will report to me at the end of the class as to your conduct in that class. Dismissed,"

They left the office abruptly and without the courtesy of the customary salute when leaving a superior office an oversight that would persist throughout their Army careers.

Their jeep now practically crawled back across the Post to the lab building.

"No sense in stalling, Joe. We don't seem to have any choice," said Michael.

"The hell we don't. We can just pretend we had an emergency at the hospital. We can go over there right now and fake it," said Joe.

"I doubt that would work. If I read the Colonel right I'm sure he has spies all over this Post. You saw what Makowski did," said Michael.

"I guess you're right but I hate to let that bastard win. Let's go real slow and maybe the animals will die before we get there."

But they weren't that lucky. They ambled into the lab to find everyone, all the doctors and corpsmen, waiting for them to start. Sergeant Makowski was awaiting them at the door.

"You Judas," said Joe to Makowski.

"Sorry, sirs, but I'm under direct orders from the Colonel," said Makowski.

Michael put on a rubber apron, rubber shoe covers, and rubber gloves. He walked over to a table, with a bleeding animal lying on it, where he found C.D. Highsmith and three other corpsmen waiting for him. They were ashen gray and perspiring just standing next to the suffering animal.

"Let's get on with it, men. But first, push some more pentathal into this animals vein. I don't want to see one of its muscle fibers twitch, even once," said Michael.

Highsmith reacted immediately and put the animal under as deeply as possible without killing it. Michael began the careful, meticulous steps of debridement explaining the procedure as he went along.

"Oh, my gosh," came the cry of Joe's voice from the next lab table, "my poor animal just died. I must've given it too much pentathal. What could you expect from a radiologist. Well, I guess we're done for today, then."

"Not at all, sir. You and your men can assist Captain Rizzuto with his animal. I'm sure he wouldn't mind." said Makowski.

"No, no that's all right Sergeant I think we've learned enough about debridement," said Joe.

"I'm afraid I must insist, sir. I think Colonel Forest would want it that way. Would you like me to call him and ask him, Captain?"

"No, that won't be necessary, Sergeant, I'll accept your judgment in that regard," said Joe. Then he walked over close to the Sergeant and whispered, "if you get a serious illness you'd better have the ambulance take you to a private hospital in town, you bastard."

Sergeant Makowski started to smile until he looked deeply into Joe's eyes and realized that he might be deadly serious. He broke into a cold sweat.

"I'll remember that, Doctor," he said.

"Come on, Joe, don't talk like that. Let's make the best of this fiasco," said Michael. "At least these guys might learn enough to save a life."

Joe took up his position opposite Michael at the table and assisted in the debridement.

"Hey, you're not a bad surgeon for a radiologist," said Michael.

"Yeah, my dad was a terrific surgeon. I started working with him in his office when I was ten years old. He was great. He was my inspiration. Even a thick-headed Irish kid like me couldn't help learning something under his tutelage." A tear welled up in Joe's eyes. "He'd turn over in his grave if he could see me now. I hate this freeking Army. I don't blame Tom Adams for doing everything he could to get out," he added.

"Shut up will you," said Michael. "Did you forget our vow of secrecy to him?"

Joe didn't answer but he chastised himself for shooting off his big mouth. The corpsmen at the table raised their eyebrows and rolled their eyes in astonishment but no one said a word.

Joe slowly and sneakily reached his hand under the surgical drapes, disconnected the syringe of pentathal from the IV set up and proceeded to pump large quantities of air into the goat's vein by opening a petcock on a sidearm. Within seconds the goat began to convulse, gasped for air and then ceased breathing.

"Oh, oh, I lost another one. I guess I'm just bad luck wherever I go," said Joe smiling a smile of innocence.

Michael shook his head knowing full well what Joe had done. Sergeant Makowski threw up his hands in frustration.

"I guess that's enough lab experience for now. Besides at this rate we'll run out animals soon. Everyone report to room 306 for a film and lecture by Captain Rizzuto on the treatment of wound infections," said the Sergeant

"Good grief, Joe. You're going to get us sent to 'Nam yet," said Michael.

"No way," said Joe. "Don't sweat it, will you Mike," said Joe.

CHAPTER SEVEN

The Armpit of the Universe

AFTER COMPLETING FIELD service school Rizzuto and O'Mara were sent to their permanent Post hospital, O'Hern Army Hospital, at Fort Riley, Kansas just as Joe's insider information had said. C.D. Highsmith was sent to Vietnam after graduating corpsmen school at the top of the class. He was determined to make good on his vow to Michael Rizzuto, "to bring life, not death out of the maniacal chaos of war".

Michael, Joe, and their families tried to settle into some semblance of normalcy surrounded by the alien activities of military life. It wasn't going to be easy and they sensed that immediately.

"I just don't understand these regular, career Army types, Mike. They act as if the war was created just to further their military careers," said Joe.

"Don't you think you might be exaggerating just a little bit?" said Michael.

"Maybe so, but just look around you. All the career people are Gong-Ho with their buzzing around all spit-and-polish. They train with such enthusiasm; they talk about going to 'Nam to see some action and speed up their promotions."

"So what? That's their job. They're professional soldiers. They're suppose to believe in their work," said Michael.

"Yeah, but look at those kids in the training trenches, they're are scared shitless. It's their lives that'll be on the line not the career guys. Everybody knows that throughout American history it's been the draftees that win the wars. The career guys just get promoted," said Joe.

"I don't have any evidence of that. Sure, they have tough exteriors but I think that's just to encourage the rest of us."

"You don't know them yet. How can you say that?" said Joe.

"And what makes you know them any better? We got here the same day, remember?" said Michael.

"Well, I can just feel it. And I know my father-in-law. I've heard him say it a million times about WW II and the Korean War and I quote, 'the top brass is always right. They know what's best for this country not a bunch of politicians in Washington'. Blind obedience, that's what they believe in."

"So, what's wrong with obedience? You teach it to your kids, don't you?" said Michael.

"Yeah, yeah, I do. But it's not unconditional and blinded from reason. Unquestioned obedience to superior rank is what the Nazi's used in their defense of their actions at the Nuremberg trials regarding Auschwitz and Treblinka, remember?"

Michael shook his head, "that was different. It's just not the same."

"Oh really, well, just keep your eyes open, my friend. We've got two more years here unless we go to Vietnam. We'll see who's right."

Evidently Joe and Michael's reputation had preceded them from Ft. Sam Houston. In very quick order they were ordered to report to the hospital commander's office at 6:00 am for a briefing on 'special duty'.

Michael was determined to make a fresh start for himself and Joe. He made sure they were at the commander's office early; their shoes had a mirror-like shine; their brass polished to a star-like sparkle; hair cropped close in military style; their uniforms impeccable. They waited for a full hour outside the office of the commander, Lt. Colonel Samuel Anderson, Medical Corporal Anderson was a general surgeon by training with twenty-seven years of military service. A sign on his office door said, Regular duty hours: 0700 to 1700 hrs.

"This is enough to piss off the Pope," said Joe angrily pacing up and down the corridor.

"Just cool off, Joe. I'm sure it was just a mistake, typographical error on the orders," said Michael.

"Don't count on it. You can be sure that ninny, Colonel Forest, talked to his regular Army buddies here to put the screws to us."

Michael decided not to argue the point. Eventually, a corporal arrived, opened the office and instructed them to wait.

"Lt. Colonel Anderson is at an important meeting he'll be here shortly," he said.

At 9:15 am Colonel Anderson walked down the corridor to his office, went in and closed the door to his private office, completely ignoring Joe and Michael. Another twenty minutes went by.

"If this guy is trying to get my dander up he's doing a good job of it," said Joe.

"Just relax, will you? He's a busy man. He must have some tremendous responsibilities," said Michael.

At last, the office intercom buzzed and the Colonel said, "you can bring in Captains O'Mara and Rizzuto, now."

"Now don't forget to salute, Joe and don't be disrespectful. Let's try to get started right. We've got to change our reputation if we want to survive these next two years," said Michael.

"All right, all right. I'll give them the benefit of the doubt, for now," said Joe.

They marched into the office, gave a crisp, proper salute . . . to an empty chair behind a vacant desk. Bewildered at first, they simply stared. Then the momentary silence was broken by a gentle, methodical, soft cracking sound behind them. They turned around to see the Colonel stroking a line of golf balls, one at time, into a cup on a green-carpeted putting area which mechanically returned each ball along a runway back to his feet. A half empty, glass, coffee pot was sitting on a table along with the scattered pages of the 'Stars & Stripes' military newspaper.

"No one told you men you could be at ease. Face front and remain at attention," said the Colonel.

Michael snapped to and turned back around. Joe did the same but more slowly and casually. He whispered, "what did I tell you, Mike?"

"No talking, please until you are asked to speak."

"So, my friend Colonel Forest tells me you are two doctors who refuse to behave like Army captains. Well, we'll just have to see about that. Just keep in mind that you're only one signature away from Vietnam . . . my signature on your orders. Those orders have already been cut. All I have to do is date and sign them and make a call to Fifth Army headquarters. Do you understand?"

"Yes, sir," said Michael. Joe said nothing. Michael elbowed him in the ribs.

"Yeah, Colonel, sure," said Joe.

"Good. Now we understand each other."

Michael was quite impressed with the Colonel. But Joe wasn't. He noted that even though the Colonel tried to appear tough his upper lid was sweating and his fingers trembled as he admonished them.

'He's more afraid them we are,' thought Joe. 'He's a wimp trying to look tough.'

"You're dismissed. Report to Corporal Haskins out front for your special assignments."

"Yes, sir," said Michael. They turned, left the office and stopped at Haskins' desk.

"So what's this special assignment jazz, Corporal?" said Joe.

"You'll both have your regular hospital duties, including night call rotation every fourth night, officer of the day—-that's emergency room duty in doctor lingo—-and then there's dispensary duty at the various camps each morning—that's morning sick call at 0600 hours. Here's a list of the dispensaries," said the corporal handing them each a sheet of paper.

They looked for their names on the list and ran their fingers across to the dispensary to which each of them was assigned. Michael's assignment was the stockade dispensary and Joe's was at Camp Bullock. They noticed that there was an asterisk next to the name of each dispensary they were given.

"What the hell does this asterisk mean?" said Joe.

They looked to the bottom of the page for a legend to explain the asterisk. There was a strange explanation. Joe read the legend aloud, "armed escort recommended."

"Well, you see, sirs, there are some pretty tough dudes at those two dispensaries. The title *stockade* speaks for itself and Camp Bullock is where we keep all the druggies we are trying to rehabilitate."

"Is that the large, barbed-wire-enclosed area we noticed on the outskirts of the Post?" said Michael.

"Yes, that's it. Heroin Heaven or HH we call it," said the corporal smiling. "It's a new facility. It was Colonel Anderson's idea to try to rehabilitate the drug addicts and return them to active duty stations instead of to Leavenworth. It's been open for two months now."

"Has it been successful?" asked Michael.

"Oh, yes, very successful."

"How many men have been rehabilitated so far?" asked Joe.

"Ah . . . none, none yet that is. But they ain't killed nobody yet and nobody's escaped yet even though dozens have tried," the corporal chuckled.

"You call that a success?" said Joe.

"No, I don't but the Colonel does and the commanding General agrees with him. I send some very glowing reports to Fifth Army headquarters each week. *'Stars and Stripes'* had a big feature article on it last month. It'll be a huge feather in the Colonel's and the General's caps when they retire in a couple of years."

"How serious are they about this armed escort business?" said Michael.

"Well, sir, whenever I go down there I don't go without the escort, I can tell you."

"It must be for real, then," said Joe.

"And the Colonel? What about when he goes down there?" asked Michael.

"He takes double the escort and he wears a side-arm himself, a 357 magnum. It's not official but it does kill better."

"I thought medical officers—doctors that is—weren't suppose to carry weapons?" said Joe.

"That's right, sir, they ain't. But I don't think anyone's going to report the Colonel, do you?"

"Do we get combat pay or *under-hostile-fire* pay when we go down there?" asked Joe trying to be sarcastic.

"No, no, sir, I don't think so. But if you were regular Army I'll bet it could be arranged," said the corporal just as sarcastically.

"What an Army," said Joe.

"You ain't seen nothin' yet, doc. You ain't seen nothin'," said the corporal.

*   *   *

The following day Michael and Joe were off to their respective sick call dispensaries bright and early expecting a moderately busy day.

"Good morning Captain Rizzuto," said the non-commissioned officer in charge of the stockade. "Name's Master Sergeant Schultz. Follow me, sir. The patients are waiting for you in the sick call room."

"How many patient's are there to be seen today?" asked Michael.

"Sixty, sir."

"Sixty?" said Michael astonished. "That's an awful lot of people to see in two hours. Is there an epidemic or something?"

"No, sir, It's just the usual number."

"How many prisoners are there in this facility?" asked Michael.

"Seventy-five, sir, counting the ten men in solitary confinement."

"There can't be that many really sick men in here," said Michael.

"Oh, they're not really sick, sir. But we can't deny any man when he asks to see the doctor. If we do, they just write to their congressman and claim they have leukemia, tuberculosis, or Lou Gehrig's disease or some such nonsense. Then they claim they are being denied medical care. That will bring on a so called *'congressional inquiry'* letter and then the amount of paper work becomes staggering."

"Don't they have to have some kind of proof of those diseases to make those claims? I mean, an abnormal x-ray, a blood test or something to substantiate their claim?"

"No, they don't captain. And they can demand to be examined everyday of the week or write to their congressman everyday if they like. And when a *congressional* comes through, you, the treating doctor, have to drop everything and the get the paper work to the Colonel within twenty-four hours."

"And just how many cases of leukemia or 'Lou Gehrig's' disease have been turned up this way?"

"Well, I've been an NCO for stockade dispensary for nine years and I ain't seen any yet."

"What a waste of time, man power and money," said Michael.

"Yes sir, but that's the way the politicians and the public wants it. And you know politicians run this man's Army just like they run this war, which is the reason we ain't gonna win it."

Michael entered the sick call area to find sixty men lying on the floor, or in the few chairs available, sleeping soundly. On each examining table there were also two men sleeping. He went to the first table and picked up the first medical record. It read, 'major complaint', sore feet.

He leafed back through the record and saw that the man had been to sick call everyday for the past thirty four days for the same complaint-sore feet. There were also several foot x-rays, all were reported as normal, consultations by orthopedic surgeons and podiatrists who had each reported, normal feet or no disease. There had also been three congressional inquiries initiated by the man, result— no disease found, fit for military duty.

"Pvt. Whitaker," said Michael shaking the man. Both men on the gurney awakened abruptly but one left quickly to lie on the floor with the others.

"Yes, sir, doc, right here, sir," said Whitaker.

"What is your problem? Whitaker," asked Michael.

"It's my feet, doc. They're hurtin' all the time."

"Where, exactly, do they hurt?"

"All over. They hurt all over, doc."

"You mean to tell me the pain is all over, both feet, from the ankles to the toes?" asked Michael.

"Yes, sir, that's right. You got it."

"Is the pain worse at any one particular time or another? I mean like when you're walking, standing, sitting or sleeping?"

"No, sir, they hurt all the time, day or night, sleepin' or awake. Of course, they do get a little worse whenever I march or do anything like that."

"I don't know, Whitaker, you seemed pretty comfortable sleeping there on the stretcher a few minutes ago," said Michael skeptically.

"Well, I just looked like I was sleepin' but I wasn't, not really. I was in real terrific pain, believe me, I was."

"You were snoring and putting the Zs away pretty good, it looked like to me."

Whitaker didn't answer.

Michael did a very thorough physical examination from head to foot. In his perusal he notice several needles tracks, fresh and old, on Whitaker's arms.

"Could it be you're feeling no pain because of those needle tracks from shooting up drugs?"

Again no response.

"These last two punctures are quite fresh, no more than three or four hours old. How do you get dope when you're locked up in the stockade?"

Whitaker didn't answer but he was beginning to visibly sweat. Then he shot a glance toward Sergeant Schultz.

"Excuse me, sir, but you've already spent twenty minutes with this man and you still have fifty-nine cases to see," said Schultz.

"I don't care about that, Schultz. I want blood and urine samples collected from this man to be tested for illicit drugs—cocaine, heroin, barbiturates, the works. Do you understand? And I want a thorough search made of this entire stockade—every cell, clothes, foot lockers, bunks, everything."

"Yes, sir, but I'll have to clear it first with Colonel Anderson and the General," said Schultz.

"Then do it," said Michael.

Michael sent Whitaker back to his cell and continued his same meticulous examination of each of the other fifty-nine men in sick call.

"Pardon me, captain, doctor, sir, but Colonel Anderson wants to speak to you on the phone," said Sergeant Schultz.

Michael was examining a black man named Paterson who had been complaining of headaches for the past seven months that he had been in the Army. Six of those seven months had been spent in the stockade.

"Just a minute, Sergeant, there's something peculiar about this case," said Michael.

"I don't think he's in a mood to be kept waiting, captain," said Schultz.

"Oh, all right, give me that phone. Paterson, you sit down in this chair and wait," said Michael.

"Hello, Captain Rizzuto, what is that nonsense about searching the stockade for drugs.?" said the Colonel.

"Yes, sir that was my order. I've found that several of the prisoners have been mainlining drugs while incarcerated. I thought I'd call . . . ."

"Never mind any of your save-the-world crusades, Captain . . ."

As the Colonel ranted and raved Michael continued to look at Paterson's face, then his eyes and then his hands. He noticed something unusual and he completely shut out the Colonel's tirade, mentally.

"That's it," he said. "That's it! I see it now. How could I not have noticed before?" he said absentmindedly into the phone.

"What? What's that? Captain," said the Colonel angrily.

Michael still fixing on Paterson hung the phone up abruptly.

"Look, Sergeant, his left pupil is larger than his right. And notice how his left hand trembles slightly when he's at rest. I think this kid is really sick," said Michael.

"What does that mean, Doc?" said Paterson.

"Never mind that now. Just sit up on the table, Paterson. Sergeant, close the curtains and turn off the lights," said Michael.

"What?" said the sergeant.

"You heard me, just do it. And get me an ophthalmoscope."

"A which?" asked the Sergeant

"You know, the battery powered light to look at the back of the eye," said Michael.

"Oh, yeah one of those. I'm not sure where it is. Nobody's asked for one of those in a long time," said Schultz.

"Well, go find one then," said Michael as he continued to examine Paterson. He gently struck Paterson's knees and ankles with his little rubber-tipped, reflex mallet which he carried in his pocket with his stethoscope. Using a safety pin he tested Paterson's senses of touch and pain perception. After several minutes Schultz returned with the ophthalmoscope.

"Now, close those curtains and hit the lights like I said before," said Michael.

With the room darkened Michael looked at the back of Paterson's eyes which is technically called *the optic fundus.*

"Sure enough. There it is, a little bulging of the disk in the middle of the fundus. Just as I thought, increased intracranial pressure," said Michael.

"Thought what, doc? Am I sick, bad?" asked Paterson quite frightened.

Michael placed both of his hands on the soldier's shoulders.

"Now just relax, Paterson. Don't go jumping to any conclusions."

Michael lowered his voice a few decibels and said gently, "I think you have a growth there, a brain tumor."

"Oh, God, no. I tried to tell these Army creeps I was sick. I knew it, I'm gonna die, ain't I?"

"Now, wait a minute, calm down," said Michael hugging the sobbing soldier.

"No, you're not going to die, not just yet. There's a ninety-nine percent chance this is a benign growth which can be removed completely by surgery. It's called a meningioma. This will mean a medical discharge for you and you're out of the Army," said Michael, as reassuringly as he could.

"Oh, no, he's not," came a voice from behind them. "Nobody gets out unless I say so," said Colonel Anderson who had angrily barged into the room.

"What do you mean by hanging up the phone when speaking to a superior officer? I'll have you court marshaled for this, Rizzuto."

"What I mean, Colonel, is that this man has a meningioma."

The Colonel's facial expression told Michael that Anderson had long since stopped functioning as a physician and that Michael would have to explain it to him in layman's terms.

"He has a benign brain tumor that is pressing on his optic nerve and causing those headaches which no one had paid any attention to for several months."

"What?" said the Colonel.

"That's right, Colonel. It was missed for all those months because of the way you run this medical facility. There's no real basic equipment; the staff is overburdened with trivia and bureaucracy, such as *congressional inquiries*.

Instead of screening the patient's with good nurse triage they are quickly shuffled through like so many cattle. Go ahead, call your court-martial together, Colonel. I'll be very happy to answer all their questions regarding this man's undetected brain tumor; the easy access to illicit drugs that exists in this stockade and many other revealing little tidbits," said Michael, deliberately trying to control his seething anger.

Several long moments of silence followed as the Colonel and the Sergeant Major began to sweat.

"Ah . . . well, never mind the court martial, now. We'd better make arrangements to transfer this man to the Neurosurgery Unit at Walter Reed General Hospital, right away," stammered the Colonel.

"Yes, sir, Colonel," snapped Sergeant Schultz with a crisp salute. "Right away, sir."

"Oh, and bring his *entire* medical record and all other papers pertinent to this case to me. No need to bother yourself with the bureaucratic quagmire, Rizzuto. I'm used to it, I'll handle everything from here," said Colonel Anderson as he left hastily and with a quick, casual salute.

Sergeant Schultz who was gathering the papers and other medical records said, "That was a nice pick-up and a brilliant diagnosis, Dr. Rizzuto. We're going to have to keep your around here for awhile."

"Thanks, Sergeant Schultz but any fourth year medical student, given adequate time and equipment, could have done the same," said Michael.

"But you won't be getting any of the *official credit*, though."

"What do you mean *official credit*?" asked Michael.

"Well, you see, that's why the Colonel wanted the entire medical record and all papers. He'll write up this case and its disposition, sign his name to it and take all the credit for saving Paterson's life. You'll be lucky if you get a casual mention in the file."

"No matter, I'll tell you what my wise, old dad used to say about that, he said, 'you can take the credit, I only deal in cash," said Michael smiling. "As long as Paterson gets the surgery he needs," he added.

"What about those guys at Walter Reed? Do they know what they're doing?" asked Michael.

"Oh, yes sir, no need to worry there. They really know their business. All the top brass go there for their brain surgery. They operated on the Vice President's niece a few years ago," said Schultz.

"Good. I'll call the 'head-crackers' out there today to fill them in on the details," said Michael.

"That might not be such a good idea, sir."

"Why not? It's only common professional courtesy among physicians. You don't have to worry, I won't take away from the Colonel's thunder. He'll get all the credit. He needs it, I don't."

"Whatever you say, sir. Anyway, you've already made your reputation around here. Before nightfall everybody on and off Post will know about this and your true role in it. Whenever there's a real medical-problem case you can bet you'll get a call," said Schultz.

Michael blushed.

"I'm sure there are plenty of other good doctors on this Post," said Michael.

"Oh, sure but you're the new kid on the block. You'll be the star for a long time to come."

"Let's not blow this all out of proportion, Schultz. Let's just finish up here, I've got to get over to the hospital. I'm already three hours late."

"No need to worry about that, sir. I'm sure the word has reached the hospital already. Everybody will be covering for you, now," said Schultz trying to reassure Michael.

CHAPTER EIGHT

Bleeding Out

"PARRISH, YOU ARE a loser. Here I keep you supplied with clean needles, good drugs and you still screw up anyway," said Sergeant LaRocco.

"But that wasn't charity. Remember you made quite a few bucks off me and my buddies," said Parrish.

"That's besides the point. I tried to make you a good soldier. You said you wanted to go to 'Nam and kill gooks."

"Yeah, that's right. I gotta get some of them for getting my brother Virgil."

"Well, you'll never get there now. Look at these charges: operating a stolen military vehicle under the influence of alcohol and heroin; hitting an MP and then stealing his vehicle to try to escape. You're hopeless."

"I couldn't help it. All this Mickey-Mouse, Army-chicken-shit stuff was just driving me nuts."

"If you could just cool it for a few weeks you'd have been shipped *In-Country* soon and you'd be out of all that and get your chance to kill some 'Cong."

"Can't you help me beat this rap? Sarge."

"I don't know. These charges are some pretty heavy stuff."

"Just think of all the bread you'll loose if I go to Leavenworth. They'll probably investigate into how and where I got my stuff, and all my buddies, too."

LaRocco immediately had visions of his planned retirement and the small gambling establishment he dreamed of owning and running in Las Vegas. Parrish could see the wheels turning in LaRocco's head and could almost read his thoughts.

"A thousand bucks a week buys an awful lot of roulette wheels and slot machines," said Parrish, trying to set the hook.

"Maybe there is something I can do," said LaRocco smiling. "Maybe I can pull some strings with the Colonel and get you into the rehab program at Camp Bullock instead."

"Hell, that's just another stockade except it's outdoors," said Parrish.

"No it ain't," said LaRocco. "It's only a twelve week program and if you pass you go to 'Nam. But if you don't, you get to go to Leavenworth."

"Yeah, well I guess I'll at least have some chance that way of getting to kill some V.C.," said Parrish.

"Right, but you've gotta keep your nose clean. And you gotta get me some more customers while you're on the inside."

"Okay, I can manage that. I'll bet there are hundreds of pot-heads in that compound," Parrish agreed.

"One more thing, though. The price will be double for each fix but with free syringes," said the Sergeant

"Oh, you lousy blood sucker."

"Now I gotta be practical, Bobby Joe. The risk and the penalties are at least doubled for me to get that stuff into the camp. It's only right that the price has got to be higher," he said.

"Okay, okay but now I want a piece of the action," said Parrish.

"What? Why you little dirt-ball I ought to let you rot in jail," said the Sergeant as he wrapped both hands around Parrish's throat.

"Now, now Sarge, don't you want a nice fat retirement fund?" said Parrish, gasping for breath.

LaRocco let go of his grip.

"At double the price you won't even notice my ten percent," said Parrish.

LaRocco grabbed him by the throat again and squeezed even tighter.

"All right, all right. Seven percent then." said Parrish.

He tightened his grip more until Parrish's face turned purple. Then the Sergeant let go and threw him to the floor.

"You'll take five percent and like it or you'll go to the boot hill cemetery."

"Yeah, yeah five percent is good. I'll take it," said Parrish struggling for air. "Besides, I need the bread to pay for my stuff. And if I don't get mine you don't get your stash," he added.

LaRocco agreed reluctantly. "Okay. But if I catch you skimming anything off the top you're one dead pot-head. Now I'll go talk to the Colonel to see if I can get you into Bullock. And you'd better keep your ass out of trouble. No fights, no battling the guards, no nothin'. You got it?"

"Right on, right on. I got it."

Sergeant LaRocco found Colonel Anderson in his usual place and situation in the lounge area of his office. There was the usual coffee cup filled with bourbon, golf balls scattered over the artificial green surface with a few balls in the cup, the copy of 'Stars and Stripes' lying on the floor, all the standard props the Sergeant was used to seeing.

"Good morning, Colonel," said the Sergeant giving the official, crisp salute.

"At ease, Rocky. Sit down, have some coffee. . . or whatever. It's all there in the usual place."

"Thank you, Sir," said LaRocco. He gently touched the outside of the two sterling silver coffee pots to determine which one really contained the hot coffee. He took the lid off the cold pot, brought out the bottle of whiskey and poured it half-and-half with coffee into the cup .

"I need a special favor, Colonel," he said.

"And what might that be?"

"There's a pot-head in the stockade who's up for court martial. I'd like to give him a try at rehabilitation at Camp Bullock. His name's Parrish, B. J."

"Do you have his file with you?"

"Yes, Sir. It's right here," he said handing the manila folder to him.

"H'm, it seems to me I've heard that man's name somewhere before," said the Colonel.

"Could be Colonel. He's a real loser, been in and out of the stockade all the time. Recently he wrecked a stolen military vehicle and assaulted an MP non-com."

"Oh, yes, I remember him now. I don't think I can help you with this one, Rocky. He's a real bad apple. They're sure to throw the book at him."

"I think you should reconsider this case Colonel. Sure, he's the worst of the lot but just think how good you and the General will look if the Rehab Camp is successful with the worst druggie in the Army. You'll be legends in your own times."

"True, that would be a real feather in our caps but the risk is too high. It's clear from his record that he is not rehab material," he said.

"There is one other factor to consider, Sir. He can boost are retirement funds even more. He's the one that has been making those anonymous gifts you and me have been getting in the mail lately."

The Colonel nervously cleared his throat.

"Now, Sergeant, I've told you before I don't know anything about that and I don't want to know where they come from. Besides, I donate mine to the building fund for a retirement home for wounded veterans back in my home town," said the Colonel clearing his throat again.

LaRocco smiled, sipped his coffee and leaned back on the hind legs of his chair while the Colonel mulled over the situation.

"Well, perhaps you're right, Sergeant. It's the Army way to give every man the benefit of the doubt and every chance to make good. I'll speak to the General. Consider it done."

"Thank you, Sir. I brought a copy of the transfer order with me in case I was able to win the Colonel over. It's on the bottom of the stack. If you would be so kind as to sign it *now* I'll get the wheels rolling," said the Sergeant in a tone that sounded more like a command than a request.

The Colonel signed the papers and walked toward the phone on his desk.

"Corporal, get me General Forsight on the line," he covered the mouth piece of the phone with his palm. "Close the door on your way out, Sergeant. And have the corporal make a copy of that order for me."

"Yes, Sir," said LaRocco. He closed the door and left the office walking past the corporal's desk without stopping.

"Did the Colonel need me for anything, Sergeant? I want to run over to the PX for a minute," said the corporal to LaRocco.

"No, corporal, he didn't need anything at all. You run along. I think he'll be on the phone with the General for quite a while."

"Thanks, Sergeant," said the corporal and left. The transfer order was never copied and LaRocco was confident that the regular bourbon consumption of the day would erase any memory the Colonel might have of its very existence.

*   *   *

For the next several weeks the O'Maras and the Rizzutos tried to adjust to a new lifestyle in a remote Army Post outside the small town of Junction City, Kansas. Actually, the U.S. Army Post was larger in population and geographical area than the town was. Therefore, their lives were more or less centered around the activities on the Post. Junction City was devoid of any family type activities. There wasn't even a movie theater other than a drive-in which only showed adult-type, x-rated films.

The main street of the town, and the few side streets were lined with the usual complement of whore houses, bars, pawn shops and tattoo parlors. But it did have three banks which were staffed by many vice-presidents who were from the ranks of retired Army officers and non-comms.

"Well, Joe, how are things going at Camp Bullock Rehab?" asked Michael.

"Rehab? What rehab? There's no rehab going on there. The inmates . . . I mean rehabees, still get all the illicit drugs they want. There's very little counseling, if any," said Joe.

"You mean to tell me there are no group therapy sessions, individual psychotherapy meetings, no withdrawal programs?" said Michael.

"No, not really. Oh, yeah the Post 'shrink' sees the really psychotic ones but he's overworked and understaffed and can't possibly do all that's really needed. They do show some films to the men on the evils of drug abuse but they all sleep through them. The whole thing is a farce," said Joe.

"I'll bet you're exaggerating again. It can't be that bad. You just can't see the Army doing anything right, can you?" said Michael.

"Well, you're welcomed to come down anytime and see for yourself. I'll tell you what, let's switch duties for a week. You take Bullock and I'll take the stockade. And you can draw your own conclusions. What do you say? Is it a deal?" asked Joe.

"Okay, it's a deal. But not until next week. I have some things at the hospital which need my personal follow-up," said Michael.

"Good, next Monday then, we'll switch for the week," agreed Joe.

"So what's happening at the hospital, Michael? Seen any good cases, lately?"

"No, it's been more of the usual colds, nervous diarrhea, and faked backaches. You know nothing special. Certainly nothing to go into the hospital for treatment."

"Then why are they in the hospital if they're not that sick?"

"I asked Colonel Anderson that same question. He hemmed and hawed but it came down to keeping the hospital as full as possible to look good on the record. What a waste," said Michael.

The next morning after sick call Michael was called to see a young black man in the emergency room.

"What's up, Phil," Michael said to Phil Carter the medical officer on duty. "Not more of the usual 'I'm-to-sick-to-be-in-the-Army' nonsense."

"Good grief, Mike, you're beginning to sound more like Joe everyday," said Carter.

"You know, Phil. You're right. Sorry, I guess it kind of grows on you. Fill me in on the case," said Michael.

"This kid's a nineteen-year-old black male complaining of intermittent abdominal pain up on the left side of the belly. Strange thing is that the pain increases with exercise but it also increases when he's lying flat. It's better only when he sits up with his knees buckled up against his abdomen and leaning forward. What do you make of that?"

"That is an unusual pain pattern," said Michael. "It doesn't sound like a gallbladder or stomach problem. It fits more with trouble in the pancreas or spleen."

"Bingo," said Carter. "You got it. The kid's got a huge spleen, I mean, **huge**. It must be ten to twelve times bigger than normal size."

"Wow, that's one gigantic spleen. Are you sure?"

"I may only be a family practitioner but even a first year medical student couldn't miss this one. It is truly humongous."

"Then it's got to be a blood disorder of some kind. Nothing else causes a spleen that so enlarged, at least not in his age group and not in this part of the world," said Michael.

"Let's go check it out," said Michael as they walked toward the examining cubicle where one Private Larry Baker lay on a gurney.

"Private Baker, this is Captain Rizzuto," said Phil.

Baker started to stand up to salute Michael but stopped and grabbed his left side, leaned over and then eased himself back on to the gurney in obvious pain. "Sorry, Sir," he said grimacing.

"It's all right, forget the formalities, Private. Here, let me help you," said Michael while he and Carter helped Baker back on to the stretcher bed.

"I'm Dr. Michael Rizzuto," said Michael reaching out and shaking Baker's hand. "I guess you really do have some kind of pain there. Can you lie flat for just a second so I can examine your abdomen?"

Private Baker hesitated to assume what he knew to be a position that was painful for him but he tried. Michael put his arm on Baker's shoulder.

"Now, I know that position makes it hurt more but I'll only keep you there for a second. I'm sorry but I have to feel your spleen. I promise I'll be gentle as possible." Still Baker was reluctant.

"Okay, I'll tell you what. As soon as you feel you can't tolerate the pain any longer you raise your right hand and I'll back off and you can sit up right away. Deal?" said Michael.

Baker nodded his head and slowly eased himself down into the supine position with Michael's help. The pain commenced immediately. Michael lightly, but firmly, placed his hand behind Baker's back and slowed his descent on to the mattress.

"There you go. Now try bending your knees up, that might help a bit," said Michael.

"Yeah, that does help," Baker smiled and continued his slow descent to the stretcher bed.

"That did help, Captain, Sir. It still hurts but not as much. I can handle it now," he said.

"Good, that's great . . . what's your first name?" asked Michael.

"Larry, Sir.

"Okay, Larry. Now, you hold it right there for a second. I'm going to lightly place my fingers on your belly but I'll start way down here in your left groin. You put your left hand on top of my examining hand so you can see how lightly I'll touch you. Then I'll slowly walk my fingers up you abdominal wall toward your left shoulder. If I begin to hurt you, I want you to shoot up that right hand of yours right away to give me a signal to stop. Okay? Here we go."

Michael started his examination and proceeded just as he had said he would. After progressing only two or three inches out of the groin Baker's right hand shot straight up. Michael removed his hand immediately. The frown on Michael's face frightened Baker who then broke out in a cold sweat. He bolted to the sitting position despite the pain it produced.

"What is it, Doc? It's something real bad, ain't it? I got cancer or leukemia or something, don't I? I'm gonna die, ain't I?"

"Easy, easy Baker," said Michael, trying to sooth his fears.

"No, I don't think you have cancer. Leukemia would be a possibility but nothing else fits with that diagnosis. No, I don't think you have leukemia either. I don't know what you have, yet. But I'm going to find out what you do have and treat it, if we can," said Michael.

"Here's his blood count, Mike," said Phil Carter. "And believe it or not, it's normal. Red blood cell count, white blood cell count, platelet count—everything normal. How do you figure that?"

"What about his blood count on his induction physical? Do we have that?" asked Michael.

"Yep, and it's normal, too. And we have other previous blood counts from his high school physical and college football physical. They're both normal, also."

"This *is* a puzzle," said Michael.

"It's still something bad, ain't it? Doc," said Baker more calmly.

"I don't know, Baker. We just don't know. But you're going into the hospital, right now, for some tests until we do know. But I'll tell you what we do know at this point. You have a massively enlarged spleen, some ten to twelve times bigger than normal," said Michael.

"Spleen? What's that? In simple language now, Doc. I had eighteen months of college but that was on a football scholarship and you know how much college stuff you learn playing football, zilch."

Michael nodded his head in disgusted affirmation.

"Well, Larry, putting it simply, the spleen is a small organ about the size of your fist which is tucked up under your ribs here on the left side," said Michael pointing out the normal location of the spleen under his own left, front ribs. "It has lots of jobs to do but it mostly destroys old blood cells and then helps make new ones from the old materials." Michael said this while mimicking the destruction and construction of particles with concise, hand gestures the way any self-respecting Italian-American would do.

"But what makes the spleen get big, no huge, like mine?" said Baker.

"If we were in the tropics you might have some weird parasite like Kala-azar. You haven't ever been to the tropics, have you? You know like South Africa, South America, places like that?" asked Michael.

"No, I ain't never even been out of the U. S., never even got out of South Carolina, 'til now," said Baker.

"Anyway," continued Michael, "if you were in your fifties you could have some chronic leukemia but your normal blood counts rule that out, too. What we have left are some rare, hereditary blood disorders. You haven't ever been told you had any blood diseases, like anemia or anything like that have you?"

"No, Sir, never," he answered.

"What happened to your football career? Was that ended because of an athletic injury?"

"No, it was ruined by this left side of mine. Every time I got hit it hurt real bad for a long time. But then it started hurting me all the time even when I didn't get hit. So they washed me out of the program."

"I see. Then what about Sickle Cell anemia? You know what that is don't you?" said Michael.

"Yeah, I know about that. It's the black man's blood disease but I ain't never had it."

"What about the members of your family? You know like your mother, father, brothers, sisters, cousins or your children?"

"No, none of them had it, neither. I don't know about my father, that bastard ran away when we was all little. Wait a minute, I had a stepbrother that had 'Sickle Cell', but he died when he was about ten years old, I think."

"Is that it? I got Sickle Cell and I'm gonna die like Ned? But he was always getting sick. He was always in the hospital getting blood transfusions, and he was always at the emergency room getting shots for real bad pain, and such. I ain't never been sick a day in my life, 'til now," said Baker.

"No, you don't have Sickle Cell Anemia. At least not the usual variety because you're not anemic," said Michael.

"Anemic? What's that?" said Baker.

"Anemic means your red blood cell count is much below the normal value," said Phil Carter.

"And mine ain't low?"

"No, Larry it isn't. And that's one of the confusing factors. Get him a bed on my ward will you, Phil? I'll write some orders for some special blood tests and x-rays. And make sure he doesn't walk anywhere. Take him up on a gurney or in a wheelchair. I don't want that spleen to experience even the slightest jar. It's really tense and under high pressure. It could rupture with the slightest trauma. I don't want anyone else examining it without my supervision," said Michael, immediately heading for the medical library to bone up on Sickle Cell Disorders.

The next morning Michael was presenting Baker's case to the other staff doctors who had unofficially organized themselves for teaching rounds once a week to keep themselves sharp. They originally invited Colonel Anderson to attend but he never did, until today.

"Well, Doctors, what kind of cases do we have for today?" asked the Colonel.

They were all startled by the Colonel's attendance until Joe O'Mara looked out the hospital window. It was pouring rain and there was a tornado-warning for the entire day. Then they all immediately realized that the Colonel's daily golf outing had been rained out.

"I was just presenting a baffling case, Colonel, but I can fill you in on what you've missed so far," said Michael. He then proceeded to give the Colonel all the clinical details as he had learned them since Baker's hospital admission. The Colonel was as puzzled as everyone else.

"Therefore, until we get some results of the special tests ordered from the University of Kansas Medical School we don't have any answers," said Michael in conclusion.

"Can I get out of here now, Doc?" said Baker.

"No, Baker, it's too unsafe, just now," said Michael.

The Colonel pulled Michael aside and whispered, "are you sure he's just not faking it? You know you've got to watch *these people*, they have a lazy streak a mile wide," he said.

"Who do you mean by *these people* ?"

"The Negroes, of course. You know what I mean," said Anderson.

"No, I'm afraid I don't know what you mean, Sir. Besides, lazy or not you can't fake a massively enlarged spleen, Colonel. As I've said it's ten to twelve times normal size," said Michael unable to believe the Colonel's ignorance.

"I suppose you can't fake that but I just don't trust *them,* all the same. There's a lot of malingerers among his kind," said the Colonel.

"Colonel, that's the dumbest, goddamned thing I've ever heard," said Joe O'Mara.

Michael blushed with embarrassment and the Colonel flushed with anger.

"Come on, Joe, back off," said Michael.

"Well, it *is* only the Negroes that get this Sickle Cell Anemia, isn't it?" said the Colonel, trying to shift the emphasis to the clinical topic.

"Not exactly, Colonel. The vast majority of these cases are young, black people but many non-black Mediterranians also have Sickle Cell Disease or one of its variants. It's occasionally seen in Arabs, Greeks and Italians," said Michael.

"Really, I wasn't aware of that," said the Colonel.

"Well, all we can do for him now is keep him away from any trauma to that spleen and await the blood test results from U. of K.

"Nurse, no physical activity for this man. Oh, and since he's a medical curiosity everybody's going to want to examine his spleen which could be dangerous. No more than once a day is that spleen to be palpated and put up a sign reminding everyone that it's to be done *very gently*," said Michael.

*   *   *

Three days later a special delivery, registered letter arrived at Michael's private quarters from the U. of K. He wasn't taking any chances with the reports getting lost at the hospital, which happened frequently. Michael came home when his wife called him about the reports. He opened them hurriedly but read them very carefully.

"I knew it, I knew it," he said, feeling exonerated .

"What is it, honey? Good news or bad?" said his wife.

"I guess it's a little bit of both. I'll explain later. I have to check the Army medical corps Regs to get this kid a medical discharge," said Michael.

He hurried to his office and found the Regulations for medical discharge. First he looked in the index under Sickle Cell Disorders—-nothing was listed. Then he thumbed through the various disease categories.

"Gastrointestinal tract, Heart, oh, here it is, Hematology. It's has to be under this section," he said to no one in particular.

The entire section consisted of only one small, manual sized page with only six Hematological disorders listed.

"I can't believe this. Only six clinical Blood Disorders? That's crazy." He leafed to the front to find the latest revision date.

'Last revised in 1949. This is incredible. No revisions since before the Korean War. There must be a later edition,' he thought.

The medical library had no more recent revisions, either and the librarian knew of none.

"I'll check with Colonel Anderson. He must have a more current edition," he said.

Arriving at Colonel Anderson's office, he noted the wall-clock said, 2:18 PM but only the corporal was in the outer office. And the Colonel's private office was empty.

"Where's Colonel Anderson, Corporal?" asked Michael.

"The sun is shining, there's no chance of rain, it's a warm 68 degrees, now where do you think the Colonel would be, Sir? The same place he spends every nice day beginning at noon," said the corporal.

"The golf course?" said Michael.

"Right, with 'Eversharp'. Give the good Doctor a cigar."

Michael ordered a Jeep up from the motor pool, refused a driver and drove himself to the officer's club golf course still clutching the regulation book in his hand. The officer running the officer's club would not let him drive the Jeep on the course so he rented an electric golf cart and drove around until he found the Colonel on the ninth tee. The Colonel was just about to tee off and was addressing the ball.

"Hey, Colonel, Colonel Anderson, wait a minute. I must speak with you on an urgent matter," said Michael skidding the cart to a gravel bouncing stop just behind the tee. The Colonel swung and whiffed the ball.

"Goddamn it, Captain Rizzuto, you messed up my tee shot. What in hell's name could be important enough to interrupt a tee shot?" said the Colonel, infuriated.

"A man's life, Colonel, that's what," said Michael.

"Oh," said the Colonel. "Why? did some drunken, hillbilly soldier get all shot up in a tavern brawl again?" he said.

"No, Sir. This is an innocent young man who never should have been inducted into the Army in the first place. I can't believe they missed that huge spleen on his pre-induction physical exam," said Michael.

"Oh, really?" said Anderson, not showing much shame.

"The way they shuffle those guys through they could have missed a two-headed chimpanzee," said Michael. "Anyway, it's Private Baker. You remember the man from the ER with the massive spleen? The test results are back from U. of K. Here let me drive you back to your office. We've got to check the most recent regulations," he added.

"Are you crazy? I'm in the middle of a golf round, here. I've got a three under par riding on this hole. Can't it wait until I'm finished?" said the Colonel.

"I don't think so, Sir. The Regs I have read will not allow for this man to get a medical discharge."

"Well, all right, if you insist," said the Colonel, reluctant to leave his game.

Michael explained the dilemma to the Colonel on the drive back to the hospital.

"You see, Colonel, the Regs don't have Sickle Cell Disorders listed at all," said Michael.

"Here, let me see the manual. No, you're right but they do have chronic anemia listed. Why won't that work?" he said.

"No, it won't, because he's not anemic, his red blood cell count is normal. He has compensated for his disease by making more red blood cells," explained Michael.

"Well, then he doesn't have Sickle Cell Anemia. So he stays in the Army," said the Colonel.

"But here's the results from U. of K. They show that he has a variant called Sickle Cell-Hemoglobin 'C' disease. These patients don't get anemic but they have massive spleens which easily rupture and poses a threat to their lives. If they're stationed in a remote area where surgery cannot be done immediately, they all die."

"Remote, you mean like in Vietnam?" said the Colonel. "Yes, I can see you point. By the way what's Sickle Cell-Hemoglobin C disease mean?"

Michael started to give a scientific explanation but after a few minutes he could see the Colonel was so out of touch with Medicine that it was just like explaining to a layman. He backed up to the beginning and started all over again.

"Well, to put it simply, as you know people, with Sickle Cell Disease have only one kind of hemoglobin in their red blood cells— the Sickle, or 'S' hemoglobin. They get very anemic, have many severe pain episodes, multiple hospitalizations and blood transfusions but they seldom live past the age of thirty-five years."

"And this man, Baker, has had none of those things?" asked the Colonel.

"No, Sir, he has not. Now, Private Baker has two kinds of abnormal hemoglobin in his red blood cells the 'S' type and the 'C' type. They rarely become anemic, don't have severe pain episodes or don't need blood transfusions but they have tremendously enlarged spleens, like Baker does."

The Jeep pulled up in front of the hospital and the Colonel hurried into the front door of the building with Michael close behind. They examined the regulations carefully without finding any new revelations.

"But, Colonel, you can't keep this man in the Army without endangering his life whether he's in combat or not," said Michael.

"I'm sorry, Captain but Army regulations are the law around here. No anemia, he stays in."

"But Colonel those damned Regs are at least twenty-five years behind the times. They just don't apply in modern medicine."

The Colonel shook his head vigorously, went into his office swinging the door shut in Michael's face. Michael caught the door with his foot, kicked it hard against the wall and then slammed it shut once he was inside.

"Now look, *Doctor* Anderson, you've got to do something to get this kid a medical discharge or he'll die out in the Kansas hills somewhere and his life will be on your head," said Michael leaning across the Colonel's desk, his voice straining to hold back the screams, with his face fire-red. The Colonel cringed, leaning back in his chair, but persisted in his decision.

"I'm sorry, *Doctor* Rizzuto, but I can't do that. You let too many of *these people* get out of the Army and before you know it every . . . Negro will be trying the same thing. He stays in," he said.

Michael relaxed his white-knuckled grip on the edges of the desk.

"All right, Colonel. If you won't do it. I'll do it myself," said Michael.

"You're perfectly free to try, *Captain*. But, without my signature you'll never get a waiver of the Regulations."

Michael stood frozen, silent for several seconds, still leaning on the desk. You could almost here the wheels cranking in his head and feel the brain waves emanating from it.

He thought, 'Okay, then, if I can't get them to change the Regs, I'll just have to use the Regs as they are. I'm just going to have to make Private Baker anemic."

"What are you thinking, Captain? Don't do anything foolish or in violation of the Regs. You just might find yourself attending sick call in the jungles of Vietnam, if you do."

"To borrow a phrase from Joe O'Mara, stuff it, Colonel," said Michael in a rare display of disrespect and disregard for authority. "Stuff it," he said again stomping out of the room.

*   *   *

It was 2 a.m. in the Rizzuto apartment. "What are you doing up so late, honey?" said Michael's wife. "It's past two in the morning."

"I couldn't sleep, so I am reading up on Sickle Cell Disorders."

"Where did you get all those books and journals?"

"I borrowed them from the hospital library," said Michael.

"But, how? The library is locked at this hour," she asked.

"Yeah, but the officer of the day—-the ER Doc—-has the key. I offered to take his next night call in the ER if he would unlock it for me. He agreed," said Michael.

"Oh, I see. So just another night alone for me with the kids and the TV set," she said.

"I'm sorry, honey. That's the last time, I promise. But this could mean this kid's life."

"Yes, but isn't it always that," she said in frustration, then, she regretted having said it. "I'm sorry, I understand, honey," she said kissing his forehead but she knew in her heart that it would not be the last time for Michael.

The following morning, on hospital rounds, Michael carefully examined Baker's spleen which was growing larger and more tense by the day. Michael's facial expression revealed his deepening concern and Baker picked up on it immediately.

"What's the matter, Doc? It's getting worse, ain't it?" he asked.

"I'm not sure, Baker. I'm just not sure," Michael lied and Baker knew it. "Report to my office around noon after I finish rounds today. We need to talk in private. And don't walk over, use the wheelchair. That's an order, soldier," said Michael, smiling.

At noon Michael found Baker sitting outside his office securely fixed in his wheelchair.

"Been waiting long, Baker?"

"Yes, Sir, I've been waiting here since you told me to meet you an hour ago," he said, not trying to hide his impatience.

"Oh, I see. Come on in and close and lock the door behind you," said Michael.

Michael picked up the phone and called the switchboard operator," This is Dr. Rizzuto, I'm not to be disturbed, except for medical emergencies, until I call you back."

"Yes, Doctor, I understand," said the operator.

"Am I gonna die, Doc?" asked Baker.

"Not if I can help it, Baker. Here's the situation in a nutshell. You have a special kind of Sickle Cell Disorder. But these stupid Army Regs don't list your condition for medical discharge. They only list Chronic Anemia, which you don't have. But I do think you should get a medical discharge but Colonel Anderson won't recommend a waiver."

"So what can I do, Doc? This here spleen hurts more and more every day," he said.

"What we have to do is bring your red blood count down—make you anemic. But it has to be done slowly and carefully without hurting you . . . too much," said Michael.

"Can you do that, Doc? Is it possible?"

"Yes, it is. But there are some risks involved, for you."

"Risks? What kind of risks?" said Baker.

"Look Baker, there are only two ways to do it. The first is to put you on a shellfish-only diet and wait six to nine months for you to become anemic. Well, we just can't wait that long. The second way . . ." Michael hesitated.

"Yeah, what's the second way?"

The second method is to remove some of your blood, slowly, carefully from a vein—-say a half to a full pint—every week. It should take five to six weeks to get your blood count down from the normal of four million to about two million. Then you'll be anemic and be eligible for a medical discharge."

"That don't sound too bad. I've donated blood at the blood bank before for my cousin who's got Sickle Cell. It was easy. I didn't flinch," said Baker.

"That's good that you've had the experience. It does help a bit. But, this is a little different and a lot riskier." said Michael.

"How's come riskier, Doc?"

"First, there's the risk of making your spleen grow larger and even rupture if I remove too much blood, too fast."

"Oh, oh, that don't sound too good," said Baker.

"But I think I can cover that risk. We'll do the blood removal here in the hospital, but after hours, and in a place very close to the operating room. I've talked to my surgeon friends and they've agreed to be available for emergency surgery if your spleen does rupture. I've assembled all the operating room equipment and it's standing by in the operating room. But it is well hidden. So, if it happens we'll have your spleen out within minutes and you'll be okay," said Michael.

"So, if it happens what are you going to tell the Colonel and the General?"

"Don't worry about that, I've already done the paperwork to cover that if we have to operate. All I have to do is insert the date."

"Man, you've really been working on this, Doc, ain't you? Why? How come you're so interested in me? You don't hardly know me . . . and a black man yet."

"Why? because it's my duty and it's the right thing to do. The life of every person I take care of is my responsibility. If I can save that life or lessen the pain of death I must do it regardless of rules, regulations, race or even laws. There is no other choice. It must be done."

Baker sat opened mouthed and awed.

"Sorry, Baker, I didn't mean to get up on my preachy soapbox."

"It's okay, Doc, I don't mind. I just ain't use to getting equal treatment," said Baker.

Michael paled, nodded his head in recognition of the centuries of wrongs suffered by Baker's race.

"Okay, if my spleen pops you ain't gonna let me die by operating. What else?"

"The second part of the blood removal deal is a bit . . . well, gross and painful," said Michael.

"Hot damn, something tells me this is the bad news part. Right?"

"Yeah, more or less. You life will not be endangered by it but there will be more, and unusual type of pain."

"What's that mean?"

"You know that every doctor, nurse, corpsman, officer and non-com knows how to check for needle tracks on the arms and legs of all the guys on this Post. Even Colonel Anderson knows how," said Michael.

"So what? I ain't no druggie," answered Baker.

"But they won't know that, or believe it, if they see the tracks from the blood removal. They're sure to report it. There's only one way I know of to avoid being found out."

"Oh, yeah, and what's that, Doc?"

"The dorsal vein of the penis," said Michael.

"Say what?" said Baker.

Michael produced a colored, anatomical drawing of the penis with its blood circulation system and explained it to Baker.

"You see, here" said Michael pointing with a pencil, "on the underside of the penis is a large vein we can use to get the blood out. It's good characteristics are that the vein is large and easy to get a needle into. And secondly, the needle tracks will not be visible unless someone flips it over," said Michael, trying to be as cool, scientific, and matter-of-fact as possible.

"Now, wait a minute, Doc. Ain't that kind of dangerous, messing with a man's private parts like that?"

"No, not really. There's no danger to your life by the procedure. Even if the needle slipped and went too deep you can't die from it. You see, the penis is not a vital organ."

"Speak for yourself, Doc. It's real vital to me," said Baker.

Michael laughed. "No, I don't mean it that way. Of course, sex and the sex organs are important. I meant that injury to, or even removal of, certain organs will not kill a person. You know, organs like your appendix, gall bladder, or even the spleen. You can live a normal life without them."

"Oh, I see, I dig you, now. But that's a very tender part. It's gotta hurt a lot, don't it?"

"Yes, Baker, it will and that's the tough part. We can't put you to sleep with an anesthetic or even numb it with novocaine. You'll have to bite the bullet, so to speak," said Michael.

"I don't know, Doc. I'm scared, real scared," said Baker.

"Yes, Baker, so am I. If I'm caught doing this it could mean jail for me and the end of my medical career."

"Yeah, them's big stakes, ain't they?"

"Yes, for me, the biggest."

"Well, if you're willing to gamble that much on my getting out I guess I can take a little pain."

"All right, that's settled then. We'll start tonight. Meet me here at about 11 pm. The lights in my office will be out but I'll be inside waiting for you. Don't knock, just let yourself in."

"Whatever you say, Doc."

"Don't go yet. I want to get some blood from you now to document your blood count before we start removing the pint of blood. Then we'll get another blood test every week after each withdrawal until your blood count is down."

Michael drew Baker's blood from a finger puncture instead of a vein to avoid even what could be considered a legitimate needle track.

Later that night Baker wheeled himself as quietly as possible to Michael's office making sure that he was not seen by anyone. He opened the unlocked door, noiselessly, and there was only a soft thump when he closed it. Michael had put tape over the latch to try to muffle the hapless 'click'.

"Baker, over here," Michael whispered from a darkened corner of the room. He had all the apparatus ready and waiting. He helped Baker up onto the table after assisting him in removing his trousers and underwear.

"Here's two morphine tablets. Take them. They should help to relieve some of the pain and sedate you a bit," he said.

"Can't you give me no shot of morphine or something?" asked a frightened Private Baker.

"No, I can't. Remember what I said about visible, extraneous needle marks?"

"Yeah, right. Okay," Baker said, relenting.

"Are you ready for the first round?" asked Michael.

"I guess so, Doc, as ready as I'll ever be."

Michael rolled up a small hand towel and handed it to Baker. "Here, put this in your mouth and bite down on it, real hard. It'll help muffle any sounds you might make."

"Why? I ain't gonna yell, Doc. I ain't no baby."

"I know you're not, Baker. It's just a precaution in case you forget."

Baker settled back on the table gripping its edges tightly with both hands. His legs, feet and torso were extended out straight and were rigged.

Michael swabbed the dorsal surface of the penis with alcohol and inserted the needle as quickly, but as gently, as possible into the vein. Baker let out with a muffled but dangerously loud groan.

"Hold it, Baker, hold it in. I know it hurts, buddy, but we can't risk any noise. Bite the towel, bite it as hard as you can. Harder, harder," said Michael hoping to distract Baker's attention from the pain.

After a few minutes Baker relaxed all his muscles but his pajama top and the bed sheets were drenched with sweat. The blood began to flow from the vein and through the tubing in a strong, steady stream into the vacuumized bottle sitting on the floor under the table. Michael moved up to Baker's head, put his hand on his shoulder and began wiping the perspiration from the young soldier's face and neck.

"Hang on, fella. Only a few more minutes and we'll be done. The bottle is about half full now. Try to relax," Michael whispered.

Baker tried to speak but in muffled, strained tones.

"Don't try to talk now, Larry. Try to think of something pleasant. Let's see. How about home? Think of home, your house, your room, your girl." Michael felt him relax and his eyes brightened. "What about your girl, Larry? Do you have a girlfriend?"

Baker nodded his head and tried to smile in spite of the towel in his mouth.

"Good, good. Then think of your girl, . Imagine you and she are dancing. You're real close with both of your arms wrapped around her waist. The music is real slow and romantic. You are both swaying gently to the music, your eyes are closed."

Baker stopped sweating, all his muscles relaxed and he let loose of his grip on the table. He opened his eyes, removed the towel from his mouth and began humming softly. Michael didn't stop him.

After thirty minutes the one pint bottle was filled with blood and Michael ran an equal amount of saline solution in through the same needle in Baker's vein so that he would not black out from the fluid loss.

"All right, Larry, we're done for tonight," he said as he helped Baker back into his wheelchair after he had dressed. "How do you feel?" said Michael.

"Okay, I'm okay. A little dizzy, maybe, but okay."

"Great. The dizziness will pass in a few minutes. Just sit here for a little while. I want you to drink a couple of quarts of liquids tomorrow and the next day. If you begin to feel weak tomorrow you call me immediately then ask for help to get back in bed right away."

"Sure, Doc. Man that was quite an experience, a real trip," said Baker.

"Was it very bad? Was the pain too much for you? Can you do it again for another four or five times? It's still up to you, Larry. We can quit anytime you say so."

"No, no it's okay, now. Since I went through the first one I ain't so scared no more. Let's keep doing them 'til we're done. I can handle it."

"Good. You've got a lot of guts, Larry. I'll give you that. How does that spleen feel? Is the pain any different?—better or worse, I mean."

"No, it's about the same."

"Yes, I thought so. It's too soon to have any real change just yet," said Michael.

"So, we're all set for next week, then. But we'll do it on a different day and time just to avoid any obvious pattern which might arouse suspicion. Let's see, today's Tuesday. Next week we'll do it on Wednesday at about 10:30 pm. Is that okay, Baker?"

"Yeah, sure, Doc, that's fine."

Michael wheeled Baker back to the ward, helped him into bed and said good night. Baker's red blood cell count that first day was four million which is exactly in the normal range of 4 to 5 million.

A week later Michael checked Baker on rounds with all the other doctors present, including Colonel Anderson. The Colonel attended rounds almost every week now since his conversation with Michael about Baker's medical discharge. He kept very close watch on Michael and Joe. Michael was examining Baker's spleen while Joe checked his hospital chart.

"Hey, I think your spleen is a bit smaller, Baker. Maybe an inch or inch and a half," said Michael breathing a subdued sigh of relief and winking at Baker.

"Yeah, and his red blood count is down a little," said Joe.

"Let me see that chart," said Colonel Anderson.

"It's right here, Sir," said Joe as he pointed out the lab sheet, well aware that Anderson had not checked a patient's chart in months, maybe years. "There it is, 3.8 million," he added.

"And how do you account for that, Captain Rizzuto?" said the Colonel.

"I don't know, Sir. I can't explain it. Maybe it's a lab error. I'll run the test again myself," said Michael.

"That won't be necessary, Captain. I'll take the lab director's word for it since he is a career Army man. It's probably just a temporary change. Are you drinking a lot of fluids? Baker," asked the Colonel.

"Yes, Sir, I am. I've just been feeling real thirsty lately. I don't know why, I just do," said Baker casting a quick glance at Michael.

Joe picked up on it instantly.

"Well, that explains it then. Just check it every week to make sure it doesn't continue to drop. How's the pain in your spleen? Baker," said the Colonel.

"Oh, it still hurts real bad when I move, Sir," said Baker assuming a facial expression of discomfort. Michael nodded his head, ever so slightly, to Baker when the Colonel was still looking at Baker.

And so it went week after week. Michael and Baker continued their clandestine blood letting sessions every week for five more weeks. Michael made sure he checked Baker's blood count the following morning after each pint of blood was withdrawn. After the first week 3.9 million, then 3.1, 2.8, 2.2 Baker's blood count continued it's slow, steady descent. Michael brought all the medical records, lab reports and the Army regulations to the Colonel's office bright and early after redoing the red blood cell count which verified the last reading of 2.2 million.

"Chronic anemia, Sir," said Michael placing all the papers on the Colonel's desk while he was still finishing a putt on his green carpet.

"What? What the hell are you talking about, Captain? Who has chronic anemia?"

"Private Baker, Sir. His last red blood count was 2.2 million and that meets the requirements of the U.S. Army regulations. Baker deserves a medical discharge," said Michael.

"What? Let me see those records. H'm-m-m, well, it's only been six weeks that it's been low, that's not quite chronic enough. We'll wait another month to see if it stays down," said the Colonel.

"But, Colonel, the value of 2.8 and even the 3.1 before that were clearly anemic values."

"No ifs, ands, or buts about it. I said we'll wait another four weeks and that's what you'll do. And that is an order, Captain. Do I make myself clear?"

"Yes, Sir," said Michael.

Michael knew, however, that if he didn't continue the weekly blood lettings the red blood count would slowly rise back to normal. He went to break the news to Baker.

"No sweat, Doc, I can do it now without the pain-killer even. Anything to get out of this 'pit' and to see the Colonel squirm," said Baker.

"All right, then, we'll continue but I think we can get by with just one half-pint at a time, now. We'll try it that way and see how it goes."

"Right on, Doc, right on," said Baker smiling.

For the next four weeks they continued their weekly rendezvous with the removal of the half-pint of blood. Baker's red blood cell count remained essentially stable between 2 and 2.3 million. Michael walked triumphantly to the Colonel's office one month later, as ordered, with all the blood counts.

"Good morning, Colonel. The one month waiting period has passed and Baker is still anemic. I've filled out all the necessary forms for his medical discharge. All they need now is your signature, Sir."

"I don't know, Captain Rizzuto. I think we can wait another thirty to sixty days just to be sure. After all his spleen is smaller and I think he might even be faking the pain now," said the Colonel.

Michael felt a slow boil starting in his gut but he controlled his anger and said calmly but firmly, "I think not, Colonel. If these papers aren't signed and put through it will be my duty to advise Baker to initiate a congressional inquiry."

"Don't push me on this, Captain," said Colonel Anderson, his hands trembling.

"I am sorry, Sir, but this is a clear cut case which meets the Regulations and I am determined to see this through whatever the consequences for me might be. Besides, this man's life is unequivocally in danger even if he stays *Out-of-Country*," said Michael.

"All right, Captain, you win this one but don't let it go to your head. I guarantee you that you won't find the next round so easy," said the Colonel with an outpouring of anxious perspiration, as he realized that he had encountered a formidable adversary in Michael Rizzuto.

Michael left the Colonel's office in search of Baker to give him the good news, while he whistled gleefully his favorite patriotic song, 'God Bless America'. He found Baker, took him to his office to give him a final private conference and some medical counseling.

"We win, Baker, we win. These are your medical discharge papers, signed by the Colonel and ready to go. You're out."

"Ya-hoo," cheered Baker jumping out of his wheelchair and hugging Michael who loosened up and hugged him back. A trace of tears flooded the eyes of both men.

"Now, you know, of course, your blood disease has not been cured. You still need careful medical care. I've called a great Hematologist I know at University of Chicago Medical Center near your home town. He's agreed to provide your medical care, free of charge, because now that your diagnosis has been established you'll find it impossible to get medical insurance coverage."

"Oh, yeah? I didn't know that," said Baker.

"Yes, I'm afraid that's a fact. The system stinks. They'll insure you if you're healthy but the sick ones who need the help most fall through the cracks. Anyway, you'll be getting the best care available anywhere. And my friend tells me he's doing research on Sickle cell disorders and he hopes to have some effective treatment for your condition soon."

Ten days later Michael and Joe O'Mara drove Baker to the bus station in Juniper City to catch his bus home.

"Thanks for everything, Doc. You're a real brother. I'm gonna try to make something of my life now that you've saved it. I owe you that much."

"That's great, Baker. What are you thinking of doing?" said Michael.

"First I'm going back to get my high school diploma. Then I thought I'd try for something in the medical field. You know like, lab tech, physical therapy, or something like that," said Baker.

"Good man, Baker. If you make up your mind to do it, you'll do it," said Joe.

Baker shook hands with Joe and gave Michael a long, sincere hug. As the bus pulled away Michael yelled to Baker, "hey, write to me once in awhile, if you get the time."

"Okay, Doc. And if you're ever in Chicago look me up," Baker yelled back.

"Yeah, I'll do that. What's your address?"

"I live in city housing project called Cabrini Green," shouted Baker from the window as the bus speed away from the depot.

"Well, you came out ahead on this one," said Joe. "Now let's see what you can do with the so-called 'Drug Rehabilitation Unit' at Camp Bullock. Believe me that place is one huge, freeking mess."

"Oh, I forgot about that place, for the moment. Now, don't go expecting miracles from me on this one. I'm not J.C. you know. And I can't go sticking my neck out for every cause and crusade there is. I have a wife, a family and a career to think about, don't forget," answered Michael.

Joe nodded his head several times, smiled gently and said, "now you know as well as I that you're always going to find some goddamned crusade or other to fight for the rest of your professional life. You're not fooling anybody."

Michael shook his head, shrugged his shoulders and remained quiet all the way back to the Post thinking, "Joe's right I guess. What the hell am I going to do to break that bad habit? I can't seem to help myself to resist the urge. One of these days I'm really going to get hurt, I just know it."

CHAPTER NINE

Camp Bullock

"KATHY, I'M HOME," called Michael up the stairs to the second floor of their quarters.

"I'll be right down, Michael. I'm putting the kids down for a nap before dinner," she answered.

Michael was at the liquor cabinet preparing himself a martini, a double.

"Do you want a drink, Honey. I'm making martinis, very dry, of course," he said.

"You are? Since when? You hardly ever have hard liquor before dinner. Maybe a beer once in awhile. When did you start this habit?"

"As of now. After the week I've just had I need to unwind somehow. And I'm bushed. Besides, there's very little else to do out here in the middle of buffalo grass, anyway."

"But I don't think alcohol is the solution to that dilemma," she said.

"Yes, you're right and I know it. I'll have only one," he said, stretched out on the sofa and turned on the TV to one of the three snowy channels available.

"Say, I have an idea. Let's have a party here tomorrow night. I have the entire weekend free, I'm not on call and I have no patients in the hospital. What do you say, Honey?"

"Oh, I don't know, Michael. It's kind of short notice, isn't it? Our friends might have other plans," she said.

"What other plans? There stuck here in the buffalo grass, too. All we have is each other. I don't think they'll be going into Juniper City unless they're going to a get a tattoo or the clap," he said.

"Michael! Don't talk that way." she said scolding him for his atypical crudeness.

"It was only meant as a joke, Honey. Come on, what do you say?" he said as he sneaked up behind her, tickled her ribs and kissed her on the back of her neck.

"Oh, you stinker. Okay, a party then. Who shall we invite?" she said.

"Well, let's see. The O'Maras, of course, Phil Carter and his wife. Then there's the three new surgeons and their wives. Say, what about inviting someone not in the medical field, not a doctor I mean. You know, like that couple across the court, the supply officer who just got back from Vietnam. Captain. . . what's his name?" he said.

"Maitland, Bob and Pamela Maitland," she said.

"Yeah, that's them. Have you met them yet?" he said.

"No, I haven't. But you know they are regular-army people."

"So what? They can't be all that bad. Let's invite them and find out."

"If you say so, Michael."

"I know, I'll go over right now and introduce myself. If they're not doing anything right now we'll have them over for a drink, just to get acquainted," he said.

Michael rushed across the court, cocktail glass still in his hand. Kathy watched from the front window as Michael talked to the Maitlands on their front porch. Michael was speaking and pointing to his apartment window. The Maitlands smiled and waved over to Kathy. Kathy smiled and waved back. Michael came back alone after several minutes of conversation.

"They seem like real nice people but they can't come over right now. They have some prior dinner engagement with Colonel Anderson and his wife. But they said they'd come to the party tomorrow night. I told them to come around eight-ish. Was that okay, Honey?"

"Yes, certainly, that'll be fine, Michael."

"Then tonight, my darling," he said pretending to stroke an imaginary, highly waxed set of handlebar mustaches, "we can have a party of our own once the kids are asleep," he giggled fiendishly.

"Oh, you lecherous, old doctor you. My you really are getting frisky," she said putting her arms around his neck and kissing him on the mouth. Michael reached out for her.

"No, no, not now. I have supper in the oven. Let me finish. You go up and take a cold shower. Wake the kids after you're done."

"Oh, curses, foiled again," he said as he bounded up the stairs.

*   *   *

The following Saturday night their small apartment was crowded with twelve other physicians, their wives and the new neighbors, the Maitlands. Michael was even more jovial than the night before. He had had two double martinis before the guests had even begun to arrive. Kathy was very concerned because three drinks in the last twenty-four hours was more than Michael had consumed, all totaled, in the previous six months.

The women had congregated in the living room and were talking fashions, clubs, the kids, and other activities on the Post.

The men, as usual, were out on the patio talking shop, medicine that is. Captain Bob Maitland, the only non-physician in the group, was feeling awkward and out of place.

"Oh, I'm sorry, Bob. We Docs can be real bores when we forget and talk medicine all the time. Excuse us, please," said Joe.

"Yes, it's force of habit, Bob," said Michael.

"Tell me, Bob, how many years do you have in the Army now?" asked Michael politely changing the subject of discussion.

"Twelve, I have twelve years in and eight to go before retirement. Unless I decide to go for thirty," said Bob.

"Why? Bob," asked Michael revealing a faint but perceptible glow from the alcohol. "Why would you, or anyone for that matter, stay in for any extra years?"

"Well, after thirty years of service you retire with two-thirds of your yearly salary, instead of half, as a life-time pension. You have that plus anything you can earn at any other career you care to pursue, free medical care at any military medical facility, PX (Post Exchange) shopping privileges, and so on. It can add up to a mighty tidy sum," answered Maitland.

"Yeah, sounds pretty inviting at that," said Joe.

"How old are you now, Bob?" asked one of the surgeons.

"Thirty-two, I'm thirty-two. I came up from the ranks, went to OCS—officer's candidate school—and got my commission. I was only nineteen years old when I enlisted."

"Were you in the Korean War, then?" asked another.

"No, I just missed that by a few months. Too bad, too," he said.

"Why do you say 'too bad', Bob?" asked Joe.

"Aren't you afraid of getting killed or wounded in one of these 'police actions' or 'non-wars', like this one? Those are real bullets and bombs they're using in 'Nam, aren't they?" said Michael.

"Sure, there's a risk but that's one which every *real* soldier is willing take and he accepts it as his duty," said Maitland.

"You're a mighty brave man, Bob. Even one day 'In-Country' would scare the pants off of me," said Michael visible swaying on his feet, his speech very slurred now.

"The quicker I get out of this man's Army, the better I'll like it," said Joe realizing too late that he had offended the career army man.

Phil Carter quickly realized this when he saw Maitland's face flush and he tried to shift gears.

"Say, did you hear that we are all being promoted to Majors come the first of the month," he said smiling meekly.

'Uh oh,' thought Joe O'Mara. 'Wrong topic to switch to. Maitland won't like this.'

"Oh really? Why is that?" asked Maitland.

"Well, it seems Fifth Army and the Pentagon have decided that all medical specialists with three or more years of postgraduate training or five years of medical practice should move up one grade," explained another physician.

"Big deal! The pay raise for a Major's rank is forty bucks a month and the caps and uniforms cost you about $250.00, who needs it?" said another.

Michael had seated himself on a patio chair and was just beginning to doze off when Maitland spoke up with just a hint of anger in his voice.

"I guess I'll just have to hope that those Paris peace talks don't get anywhere. If this war lasts long enough I can make Major, too. Maybe even Lieutenant Colonel before I reach retirement."

Michael's eyes opened widely, his shoulders straightened, and he sat up in his chair.

"Better yet," continued Maitland, "if I can go back for a third tour of duty 'In-Country' I'll make Major for sure since promotions come a lot faster during combat duty," he said almost baiting the non-career doctors.

"I say again, what about the chances of getting killed? Isn't three times kind of tempting fate?" asked Joe, now clearly annoyed, also.

"No, not really. Medical supply officers, like myself, are far away from the action and near the field hospitals where the Docs are stationed. And you all know how much extra protection the precious doctors get," said Maitland making sure he spoke loud enough for all to hear.

The women in the other room had picked up on the conversation on the patio and had stopped talking to listen as they strolled outside. They all could smell trouble coming.

Pamela Maitland started toward her husband with plans to lure him away but Michael was now standing very close to him.

"What about all the guys that are getting killed? What about all the women and children that are getting their guts blown open? What about them, huh?," said Michael.

"That's their problem, not mine. Those *Chinks* started this war and it's up to us to finish it. If I happen to get the benefit of an accelerated promotion, so be it," said Maitland.

Michael began to reach for Maitland, who outweighed him by about twenty-five pounds and was at least five inches taller than he. But Kathy thrust herself between them and Pamela took her husband by the arm.

"Come on, Bob, I think it's time for us to go home. This party is over for us, anyway," she said to her irate husband.

"Yes, I think you'd better go home," said Michael. "Any Regular-Army ass-hole who wants to see a war last longer so that he can get promoted is not welcomed here."

"And any undisciplined, disrespectful and arrogant goddamned quack doctors who think they're too good for the Army have got a big surprise coming their way. It's us regular Army guys that make this military tick not some freeking, deferment grabbing draftees," shouted Bob Maitland.

Michael lunged at Maitland but Joe O'Mara and the others separated them and escorted the Maitlands to the door. Sam Clayburn, a gentlemanly, soft spoken internist, accompanied the Maitlands across the court to their apartment and said, "I want to apologize for Michael and the others. I don't think he meant what he said. He's had a little too much to drink tonight and he's been under a bit too much pressure lately," he said.

"The hell, he didn't mean it," scowled Bob Maitland. "Well, he can stuff it, anyway. We don't care what he thinks. And we don't need him, or you or any other draftees. We'll win this war with or without you."

"As you wish, Captain Maitland," said Sam Clayburn. "But I think, if you'll look around you and look at history you'll find that the draftees outnumber the career people by about fifty to one. I do think you need us."

"Go sit on a picket fence and rotate, Saw Bones," growled Maitland.

"Good night Mrs. Maitland, Captain Maitland," said Clayburn.

*   *   *

Kathy was holding Michael's head under the cold water tap to sober him up as she was chastising him for his crude behavior. "Michael, what on earth has come over you? I've never seen you behave this way before."

Michael mumbled something unintelligible and continued to soak his throbbing head.

"I never thought I'd say this to you but I was actually ashamed of you tonight. Your behavior was despicable, certainly not becoming of an educated, Christian physician," she said.

Michael was sitting on the toilet-seat drying his head with a towel.

"I couldn't help myself, Honey. Those regular Army weirdoes just piss me off so much," he said.

"And that's another thing. Your language has just become disgusting, too. And this excessive drinking must stop, also. I don't care how much stress you're under. It must stop, immediately," she said.

"Yeah, Honey. Yeah, you're right," he mumbled and fell face down on the bed, unconscious.

Kathy removed his shoes and clothes, tossed his legs under the covers and left him to sleep it off.

*   *   *

Michael slept soundly through the night and well past noon next day, except for three intermittent spells of vomiting. Sunday morning usually found him awake by 9:00 am reviewing medical journals after reading the newspapers. He staggered down the stairs and into the kitchen where Kathy was preparing their usual Sunday breakfast of wheat cakes and country sausage.

"Good morning, glory. Do you want some breakfast? It's almost ready," she said.

"Oh, no thanks. I'm too sick to eat. My head is throbbing, my stomach is churning like a cement mixer and my tongue has that dark brown taste. I just need aspirin, bicarb and lots of fluids. Maybe later though, Honey" he said.

After taking the scientifically correct, but ineffective, remedy for his first hangover since his college days, Michael slept again while his family went to church.

"We're going to church, now, Michael. You get some more rest. I'm going to leave the kids at Sunday school for a couple of hours after church. And then, we have some serious things to discuss, you and I," she said.

"Oh, no," he moaned and rolled over on the sofa to go back to sleep.

Two hours later Kathy returned.

"Michael, Michael," she said softly while gently shaking his shoulder. It's me, Honey. How do you feel?"

Michael sat up, rubbed his eyes and clucked his thick tongue against his dry palate.

"A little better," he said. "I need some ice cold tomato juice. Then I think I'll try some of those wheat cakes and sausage," he stammered.

"I'll make you a fresh batch, and some strong, black coffee," she said.

He quickly drained a very large glass of tomato juice, swallowed two aspirin and went to wash his face. Half way through his breakfast Kathy sat down opposite him and began to speak calmly.

"Now Michael, we have to discuss our situation and what to do about it," she said.

"How do you mean?" he said still looking down at his food.

"I mean," she said emphatically," how are you going to tolerate two more years of Army life without becoming a drunken lout?" she said and smiled, when he looked up from his food. Then he began to recall the events of the night before.

"I guess I was pretty bad last night, wasn't I?"

"Bad! You were gross and obnoxious, to put it mildly," she said.

"It was the alcohol talking, not me. I'll go over and apologize to Bob what's-his-name and his wife. It won't happen again, I promise," he said.

"It was not just the Bob-Maitland-thing, and last night. It's this whole regular-career-Army thing, you have. I know you hate it and when you're unhappy, I'm unhappy and the entire family suffers," she said.

"I know, I know. I'll try to make the best of it for the rest of the two years," he said.

"That's not good enough, Michael. Things could be worse you know. At least you're practicing medicine and not getting grenades thrown at you. You've got to manage, somehow, to follow their rules, as crazy as they are. I'll have a nervous breakdown worrying that they'll send you to Vietnam every time you buck their system," she said and began to cry softly.

Michael slid his chair over next to hers and put his arm around her.

"I know, Honey, I know. Please don't cry." he said, kissing her on the cheek. She stopped sobbing and wiped the tears from her eyes and Michael's eyes. Michael stood up with a cup of coffee in his hand and stared out the kitchen window, that far off, wondering stare.

"I'm going to try to be a better soldier from now on and follow all their dumb rules and Regs. But there's one line I must draw. I cannot, and will not, stand by when those rules threaten a patient's life or health. I'm a doctor first—after a husband and father—and with that there can be no compromise. I must not betray myself in that regard. I wouldn't be able to live with myself, Vietnam or no Vietnam."

"Of course not, Michael. There are no other options in that respect. The welfare of your patients is your first obligation. I wouldn't expect you to abandon that principle, Michael. I wouldn't live with you either if you did," she said. They hugged and went up to the bedroom.

*   *   *

The following Monday morning Joe O'Mara parked his car in front of Michael's quarters and then knocked on the front door. Michael got up from the breakfast table and let him in. It was 6:15 am.

"Hi, Joe. What are you doing here?" Did you forget that we switched duty for a week? Remember? I'm taking Camp Bullock and you're covering my sick-call and hospital chores?" said Michael.

"No, I didn't forget. I just wanted to be with you on the first day so the regular Army non-Coms in charge wouldn't let you see only what they wanted you to see. I got Phil Carter to take your duty just for today," said Joe.

"Oh, I see, you don't trust them anymore than I do. Come on in and have some breakfast. It's too early to go just yet."

"Well, I kind of wanted to get you there early, too. You know, before anybody else was around," said Joe.

"I see, all right. Wait, I'll get my coat and cap," said Michael.

The car pulled away and headed down out of the hills where the officer's quarters were located. They descended down into the valley toward the hospital. As they approached the valley the predawn sun lighted the landscape in golden yellow stripes. Michael noticed a thin layer of smoke in the air which had a strong pungent odor.

"What the hell. . . I mean, heck, is that stink? It's awful," said Michael.

"Ah, hah the little wife's been on your back about your foul language, heh?" said Joe.

Michael blushed but ignored the comment.

"No, really Joe. What is that smell?" said Michael again.

"Well, do you remember that memo we all got last week from the new commanding General?" said Joe.

"Yes, I remember. He arrives on the Post today doesn't he?"

"That's right. Do you recall the order about no one else writing, typing or printing in red, don't you?" said Joe.

"Oh, yes, so that any order written in red we would immediately recognize as one from the General."

"Correct. Well, he also ordered the burning of all red pens, pencils, typewriter ribbons, stamp pads and even red crayons. That's what that smell is in the air. The odor of burning plastic," said Joe.

"What? You have got to be kidding. This guy must be a real nut. What's he trying to prove?" said Michael.

"He's letting everybody know who the new boss is. Taking the initiative of command, I think they call it," said Joe.

"Such a waste of money. Taxpayers money, our money," said Michael.

"Besides which, he knows he'll only be here for six or seven months then he goes to 'Nam to command a combat unit. And he wants his second gold star before he goes. At least that's what I hear through the grapevine," said Joe.

"You mean to tell me this man is going to lead troops into battle, make choices and decisions which could mean their lives? I can't believe Fifth Army Headquarters is doing this," said Michael.

"That's what I hear from the regular army non-Coms. And you know how reliable their info is," said Joe.

They were approaching the hospital now which stood like a tombstone on a slight rise at the bottom of the valley. It is shaped like the United Nations building in Manhattan except that its broad side which faces the main road was made of solid concrete instead of glass. The sun was just completing its ascent over the horizon and was casting a yellow-white glow on the concrete face of the building.

Michael glanced at the hospital which was the tallest structure on the Post at ten stories high.

"Hey, what is that on the face of the hospital wall?" said Michael.

"Where?" said Joe with a smirk on his face. As they came closer Michael could began to discern the markings on its face.

"Judas priest! Someone's painted some huge red letters on the concrete face. Get closer, will you, so I can read it," said Michael.

"Well, I'll be damned. Will you get a look at that," said Joe.

There blazoned on the face of the hospital, in large *red*, block letters was a well known quote of the times. Michael read it aloud," I'D RATHER BE DEAD THAN RED."

They both were laughing so hard Joe had to pull his vehicle off on to the shoulder of the road.

"Good God. The new General's going to have a fit when he sees that," said Michael.

"Well, he'll be seeing it very soon. His motorcade and military escort should be coming down this main road any minute," said Joe.

And come it did. The entourage of vehicles with the General's staff car in the lead, with the military band just behind it playing 'When the Caissons Go Rolling Along', suddenly stopped dead, still on the road. The General jumped out of his car and shouted, "What is the meaning of this? I'll hang the people responsible for this." The band stopped playing and the convoy sped away toward the hospital.

Joe and Michael sat in their vehicle roaring with laughter for several more minutes.

"Who the hell did such a wacky thing? It's a great gag on the General but I'd hate to be them if they get caught," said Michael.

"Beats me," said Joe. "But I loved it."

Michael looked at Joe's hands gripping the steering wheel and noticed traces of red paint under his fingernails.

"Why, you idiot, they'll castrate you and then send you to Vietnam if they find out," said Michael.

"I don't know what you are talking about Captain Rizzuto. I had nothing to do with this," said Joe smiling.

"Oh, is that so. We'd better go right to the lab at Bullock and find some carbon tetra-chloride or acetone to clean those fingernails of yours," said Michael.

Joe looked at his hands, then he looked at Michael. Again they both roared into five straight minutes of side-splitting, tear producing laughter. When they had sufficiently recovered they drove on to the Rehab Center, Camp Bullock.

"So, here we are," said Joe. "The famous Camp Bull shit."

"What's this, a new eponym?" said Michael.

"Yep, because that's exactly what goes on here. There's no rehab, no detox—just plain old army bull shit," said Joe.

Their jovial mood had quickly changed to anger, frustration and disgust. The compound resembled a Nazi concentration camp including, electrified barbed wire fencing, armed guards in towers and standing at the gates the works. The only thing missing was the ovens and torture chambers but the powerful search lights were there also.

They arrived at Camp Bullock just in time for 7:00 am reveille. The so called, 'rehabees', were standing at attention, and in formation for roll call. Joe drove close to the lines of troops, and as slowly as possible, knowing that Michael's sharp clinical eye would pick up what he hoped he would see. Michael's glance oscillated from face to face as they drove past. His glance stopped occasionally for an intense look at some of the men.

"Hey, wait, Joe. Stop here a minute." Michael jumped out of the vehicle, walked over to the lines and stood before three of the men in succession and examined their eyes.

The sergeant running the roll call charged over angrily until he noted the gold oak-leave clusters on Michael and Joe's shoulders.

"Is there something wrong, Major, Sir?" he asked.

"I'll say there is," said Joe.

"Yes, Sergeant several of these men are under the influence of opiates," said Michael.

"Excuse me, Sir?" he said. Then he noticed the Medical Corps insignia on their collars and thought to himself, 'Oh, oh, some of those smart-ass-draftee docs.'

"They're stoned on drugs, Sergeant," said Joe.

"No, no that can't be, Sirs. There must be some mistake. You see this is a drug rehab unit. We don't allow illicit drugs inside this compound," said the Sergeant.

"What's your name, Sergeant?" asked Michael.

"Staff Sergeant Douglas, Sir."

"Sergeant Douglas, after roll call you bring these three men directly to me at the lab. We'll run some blood and urine tests and then we'll see if they are on drugs or not," said Michael.

"But, Sir . . .?"

"Never mind the buts, Sergeant, that's a direct order. Just do it," said Joe.

Michael and Joe drove on to the Rehab Headquarters where the classes and the morning sick call was always held. Joe showed Michael through the building with its very few conference rooms, offices and a single large meeting room.

"Say, Joe, I didn't see an office for the camp psychiatrist," said Michael.

"No, you didn't because there isn't any office for him and we don't have a regularly assigned head-shrinker out here. We have a couple of good, well trained psychologists but none of them have any addiction counseling experience."

"Why not? We have four very well trained psychiatrists at the hospital. I'm sure they would be willing to give some time to these addicts," said Michael.

"Oh, I'm sure they would, too. In fact, they did volunteer to give some of their time. But Colonel Anderson said it wasn't necessary," said Joe.

"Why aren't they needed? What possible reason could he have for reaching that conclusion?" said Michael.

"Beats me. Except, I did note that the psych guys' commander is Regular Army but the shrinks are draftees, like us."

"Oh, I get it. There's not likely to be anyone making waves amongst the career guys," said Michael.

"Right on. And all the non-Coms in Camp Bullock are career Army people, too," said Joe.

"Hm-m, all wrapped up nice and neat in an air-tight package," said Michael.

They proceeded on to the lab to await the three men from the roll call who they had told Sergeant Douglas to send in for testing. After a twenty minute impatient wait there was a knock at the door but Sergeant Douglas alone entered the room.

"What's going on? Sergeant Where are those three men I told you to bring over for testing?" asked Michael.

"It's the Colonel's orders, Sir. He said he didn't believe that any blood tests for illicit drugs were necessary. He examined the three men in question himself and saw no evidence of drug effects, Sirs," answered the Sergeant

Michael looked at Joe in disbelief. Joe just shook his head, threw up his hands and said, "Well, what else could we expect from him."

"Sergeant I want the names and serial numbers of those three men and I want them before the day is out," said Michael struggling to contain his anger and frustration because of his promise to his wife.

"I'm afraid I can't do that, Major," he said.

"And why not? for God's sake," shouted Michael.

"There won't be enough time to do any testing anyway, Sir. Those men are flying out this afternoon, along with thirty-two other rehab graduates. They've completed the rehab program and they're being flown to their new Post assignments. . . in Vietnam."

"Why that is insane. Those men are in no condition for combat duty. They'll crack under that kind of pressure," said Joe.

"If that's all, Majors, I'd like to be excused. I have other duties to attend to," said the Sergeant. But he didn't wait to be excused, he saluted quickly, did an about-face and hurried out of the lab.

Michael started after him but Joe grabbed his arm. "Forge it, Mike, he's only the messenger boy. Okay, and he's a snitch, too, but the Colonel is the leader of this entire fiasco."

They spent the rest of the day witnessing the so called 'rehab programs' of the unit.

"Come on, let's get a cup of coffee while the inmates have their breakfast. The meetings and teaching sessions won't begin for a while yet," said Joe.

"I'm glad to hear that they do have some educational classes, at least," said Michael.

"I wouldn't jump to any conclusions just yet, Mike."

"What do you mean, Joe?"

"Just wait and see for yourself."

At twenty minutes after the hour they quietly slipped into one of the darkened classrooms where about forty men were viewing a film.

"Be quiet," Joe whispered, "we'll slip unnoticed into a back row. First take your gold leaves off your shirt."

"Why?" Michael whispered.

"So they don't gleam in the dark if the projector light strikes them and gives us away as officers," said Joe.

"I don't get it," said Michael.

"You will. Trust me, Mike and just do it."

A few heads in the classroom turned around, when the slightly opened door briefly let in some of the light, as they entered. The instructor, however, who was sitting at his desk on the podium, with his feet crossed on the desk, didn't stir. He was sound asleep with his hands folded across his lap. Most of the men in the room slept, also.

Michael shifted his attention to the screen and gasped.

"Hey, what the hell is going one here? They're showing one of those old John Wayne, World War II movies. I don't understand this," whispered Michael.

"It's called brain washing, Mike. And you thought only the Commies used that technique," said Joe.

Several of the men were smoking, what Michael first thought were ordinary cigarettes, but then he whiffed the air and detected a faintly familiar odor.

"Is that marijuana I smell?" he said.

"Well, it ain't Camels or Virginia Slims," said Joe.

Michael left his seat, abruptly, and turned off the projector while Joe switched on the lights. The Corporal on the podium jumped out of his chair.

"Hey, what the hell's going on? Who turned on those lights?" he shouted and walked rapidly toward Michael standing at the projector.

"Who the hell are you and who told you to turn off the goddamned proj . . .?"

His tirade halted when he saw Michael and Joe putting their gold Major's leaves back on their shirts.

"Begging your pardon, Sirs. I didn't know who you were," he said as he saluted smartly. For the first time in his six months in the Army Michael didn't return the salute. He looked at the Corporal's name tag.

"So, Corporal Hanover, tell me, what do you call this drug rehab educational film you're showing these men?" said Michael.

The Corporal didn't answer but he did glance at the blackboard where he had printed a subtitle in large block letters that read, 'GETTING HIGH ON COMBAT, NOT DRUGS.'

"I see. Is that your idea of a joke, Corporal?" said Michael.

"And, are you able to recognize the smell of Marijuana smoke, Corporal?" asked Joe.

"Yes, Sir, I think I can," said the Corporal.

"Then what is it I smell in this room? right here and now?" said Michael.

All the men had extinguished their smoking materials by this time.

"Tobacco, Sir, just plain, ordinary cigarette tobacco, Sir."

"You're a freeking liar, Hanover," said Joe grabbing the Corporal by his shirt front.

"Easy Joe," said Michael. "Remember, he's only a messenger, too."

Michael turned to face the classroom. "I want all you men to stand up and empty your pockets of everything you have in them and place the contents on this desk on the podium. Corporal, you take that empty waste basket and pick up every single cigarette butt from the floor and place them in the basket."

The Corporal hesitated.

"Do it now, goddamn it," said Joe.

The Corporal followed orders, albeit, reluctantly.

"Now, go get some real educational film on the dangers of drugs and instruct these men like you're suppose to," said Michael as he carried the basket of evidence out of the room.

"Where can we find a safe place to hide this stuff? Joe."

"There's a file cabinet with a lock on it in my office. It should be safe in there," said Joe.

They went into the office, poured all the evidence in a large manila envelope and locked it in the file cabinet. Michael put the only two known keys to the cabinet on a shoe string and hung them around his neck.

"What else can you show me that proves that this rehab unit is a farce," asked Michael.

"I know just the place to start, the Johns," said Joe.

"The Johns? You mean the bathrooms? Why there?"

"You'll see in a minute, just follow me."

"Okay, you've been here awhile, so I guess you know what you're doing," he said.

"First we'll get out of these uniforms. Then we'll get some green scrub suits on," said Joe.

"What for?" said Michael.

"So we don't stick out like sore thumbs, white bandages and all, walking around this place," said Joe.

Joe deliberately used the back paths and sidewalks to avoid high visibility. They arrived at the first latrine building. There was no one standing watch outside, as was usually the case. They stepped into the foyer and Joe stopped Michael and whispered, "let's take off our shoes."

But this time Michael did not question Joe's motives. He removed them and followed him inside. They entered the commode area, as quietly as possible. There was only one booth being used, at the time. Joe tiptoed up to the occupied one and went into the empty booth on the right and motioned to Michael to go into the one on the left. Michael did as Joe instructed.

Joe stood up on the toilet seat, peered over the edge and Michael did likewise. There, sitting on the toiled seat, fully clothed, was Bobby Joe Parrish with a syringe in his hand, tourniquet on his arm and injecting the giddy-fluid into a vein. The two doctors stepped down from the stools and stood outside the booth. Joe knocked on the door of the booth.

"All right, soldier come out of there and don't bother to flush anything. Just keep the syringe in your hand and step out as you are," said Michael.

After no more than a split second of hesitation Joe ran back into the next booth, reached over the divider and grabbed B. J.'s hand just before he tried to drop his paraphernalia into the bowl.

"Ouch, you're breaking my wrist. Who the hell are you guys, anyway? Didn't you talk to Sergeant LaRocco when you were assigned here?" said Parrish.

Michael memorized the Sergeant's name instantly.

"I'm Major. . . I mean Doctor O'Mara and this is Doctor Rizzuto. Now step outside the booth and don't try to ditch anything or I will break your wrist," said Joe.

Parrish hesitated for a moment. Joe reached over the divider, unlatched the door and opened it with his free hand. B. J. stepped out, slowly, tourniquet still on his arm and with a slow trickle of blood coming out of the venipuncture and running down his forearm.

"Now, step out here nice and easy like, soldier. We're not out to harm you," said Michael as he reached for a clean paper towel, removed the tourniquet from Parrish's arm and applied pressure to the bleeding needle puncture. He also looked at B.J.'s name tag and memorized his name.

"Here, you hold this towel and press firmly," said Michael with the demeanor befitting a physician.

"Yeah, we're not after you, Parrish. We're only after evidence so we can straighten out this Unit," said Joe.

"Yes, that's right. You're only a victim of this whole drug-addiction-scene. You need therapy, not punishment. We're out after the people who sell this junk to you. They're the ones that deserve the punishment," said Michael.

Michael took the syringe, needle and tourniquet from B. J. and said, "Now, do you have any other stuff on you?" B. J. hesitated again. Then he reluctantly removed three bags of white powder from inside his sock.

"Is that all of it? Do you have anything else?" asked Joe.

Parrish lowered his head and eyes, shook his head no.

"Now, don't force us to search you, man. I know all the tricks and the hiding places. I worked in a hospital in Spanish Harlem for two years, Believe it, I know where to look and I'm not easily embarrassed," said Michael.

B. J. removed a small pocket flashlight from his other sock and opened it. Two, very thin, marijuana cigarettes slipped out from where the batteries should have been.

"Now, are we finished or not?" asked Michael.

Parrish couldn't figure out why but he trusted the two doctors. He really felt they were not out to harm him. Ordinarily, he trusted no one in authority.

"Yes, Sir, we're finished. That's all of it. I'm clean, now, I swear it," he said.

"It's okay, Parrish, we believe you," said Michael as he took out a white envelope he had put in his pocket earlier for this purpose. He put all the evidence inside, labeled it with name, date, time and location, and sealed it.

"Let's see that arm," said Joe.

"It's okay, it has stopped bleeding. Get to the aid station and have them put a clean bandage on that puncture. Then report back to your unit," said Michael.

Parrish moved slowly, in some disbelief that they were letting him go. Michael patted him on the shoulder and said, "Go on, soldier, it's okay."

"Thanks, Doc," he said, and left the latrine.

Michael and Joe spent the rest of the day gathering as much tangible evidence as they could find. Joe placed the several envelopes of drug paraphernalia in the file cabinet, and locked it.

"Here, you keep one key with you, Joe. I'll keep the other. First thing in the morning I'm going to confront Colonel Anderson with this stuff and demand an investigation, and some changes for this so called 'Rehab unit'," said Michael.

*   *   *

The following morning Joe and Michael arrived at 6:12 am at the office to pick up the evidence. Joe unlocked the office door with its only key.

"Ouch, damn it," said Joe and put his handkerchief over a small puncture wound on his index finger on the hand that had inserted the key in the lock. There was a small, fresh drop of blood on the handkerchief.

"What happened?" asked Michael.

"Ah, there must have been a small metal splinter on the lock. It punctured my finger," he said.

"Here, let me look at it," said Michael.

"Nah, it's okay. See, it's stopped bleeding already. Forget it."

They entered the office, unlocked the file cabinet, and removed the large manila envelope inside which they had previously placed the other three small, white envelopes of evidence. A small drop of Joe's blood stained one of the white envelopes.

"Here, let me at least clean that puncture and put on a Band-Aide. Look, you stained one of the envelopes," said Michael.

"Yeah, okay," Joe yielded reluctantly. "Adds a nice effect to it, though, don't you think?"

"What are you talking about?" said Michael.

"You know, like a Scotland Yard investigation. Needles, syringes and an authentic drop of the victim's blood," said Joe.

"Yes, it adds real drama. Maybe we'll get the movie contract," said Michael.

Then they drove to the hospital and went straight to Colonel Anderson's office. Their arrival couldn't have been more timely. Colonel Anderson was just leaving his office with his golf bag slung over his shoulder.

"Good morning, Colonel," said Joe.

"Forget it, Docs, I'm due to tee off in ten minutes and I don't intend to be late for any reason."

"I think you'd better reconsider that decision, Colonel. This matter could mean the end of your career, a dishonorable discharge, and maybe even a prison term," said Michael.

The Colonel stopped abruptly, dropped his golf bag with a thud and turned his pale, perspiring face toward them.

"What the hell are you talking about?"

"I think we'd better go into your office for some privacy," said Joe.

The Colonel agreed and they went in and locked the door behind them. At that moment the Colonel's secretary's voice came over the intercom, "Is there anything wrong, Colonel? Can I do anything for you?"

"Just call and cancel my tee time, Corporal. Oh, and hold all my calls. I don't want to be disturbed unless it's a dire emergency," said the Colonel.

"Do you mean like the General or your wife?"

"That will be all, Corporal," he said and slammed down the off-button.

"Now, Majors, what is this all about? And be brief, I'd still like to get in nine holes."

"It's about Camp Bull shit, Colonel," said Joe smiling.

The Colonel ignored the jab.

"Do you mean the Drug Rehab Unit? What about it?" asked the Colonel

"That's the whole point, Colonel. There is no drug rehab going on in that place. As a matter of fact, those guys have access to all the illicit drugs they want," said Michael.

"You're out of your mind. We don't allow. . ."

Michael interrupted, "we have proof, Colonel. Tangible evidence including needles, syringes, bags of drug, smoked down pot cigarette butts and more."

The Colonel's hands began to tremble, the perspiration again sparkled on his brow and upper lip.

"Proof? What proof?"

"Here, try this for starters," said Joe who then tossed the envelopes onto the desk in front of the Colonel.

The Colonel picked up one of the envelopes with trembling fingers and fumbled with a letter opener to break the seal on a small white envelope. Peering inside it at the contents he stopped and smiled. Then he poured the contents out on the desk top. What came out was a collection of old pencils, pens and small nails.

Michael and Joe stared at them with shock and disbelief.

"Is this supposed to be your incriminating evidence, gentlemen?" said the Colonel laughing.

"What the blazes is going on here?" said Michael.

Then Michael grabbed the other envelopes, ripped them open and poured out their contents, also. The white envelopes contained the same bogus materials as the others. But out of the larger manila envelope fell some packs of ordinary cigarettes-Camels, Lucky Strikes, Parliaments and Marlboros. There also were several crushed out butts of the same ordinary brands.

"Well, well, well, my good Dr. Watson and Mr. Sherlock Holmes it seems your so called evidence can be found in any officers club or drug store.

Michael and Joe fell onto a large sofa next to the door and shook their heads in embarrassment and dismay. They were so stunned they were unable to speak for the moment.

"Now, if you'll excuse me, I'll get on with my golf plans. Good day, gentlemen."

When the Colonel unlocked the door his Corporal-secretary came barging into the room and before he noticed Michael and Joe sitting behind the opened door he blurted out, "Colonel they've hijacked the plane."

"Plane? What plane? And who hijacked it?" asked the Colonel.

"You know, the first plane load of Camp Bullock rehabees going to California. They hijacked it late yesterday and forced the pilot to land at a small airport outside of Anaheim," the Corporal said.

"That's enough, Corporal, hold your tongue," the Colonel shouted.

Joe and Michael jumped up off the sofa as if they had been resurrected from the dead.

"So," said Joe, "some freeking drug rehab program. The very first graduates hijack an Army transport plane on its way to Vietnam via California," said Joe laughing for joy.

"What's happened to them, Corporal?" asked Michael.

"Don't answer that Corporal. These doctors have no authority to hear anymore about this," said the Colonel with gigantic perspiration stains mapping the outer limits of the armpits of his shirt.

"If I were in your shoes, Colonel, I'd let him finish. Or would you rather wait for the investigation we'll demand from Fifth Army and then get it all from the newspapers?" said Joe feeling certain the threat, and the bluff, would have the desired effect.

The Colonel's eyes oscillated from left to right, he rubbed his sweaty palms on his pants, and slumped into his desk chair.

"You may go on, Corporal, and close that door again," said the Colonel.

The corporal continued and spared none of the lurid facts and even embellished them as he went on.

"Well, it seems they tied up one of the guards, took his 45 caliber sidearm. Then they forced the pilots to land, as I said, at a small airport outside of Anaheim, California. Then they pushed the plane into some woods and covered it up with leaves and branches.

"Did they all scatter and head for home, or what?" asked Joe.

"No, Sir, they didn't. Get this! They commandeered a couple of trucks, went to town to buy some civilian clothes, and then they spent the rest of the day at . . . Disneyland," said the Corporal.

Michael, Joe and the Corporal burst into uproarious laughter while the Colonel cringed and slouched down as low as possible into his chair.

"That'll be all Corporal," mumbled the Colonel. "If you breath a word of this to another living soul, I'll have your head. Understood?"

"Yes, Sir," said the Corporal unable to completely restrain a chuckle as he left the office.

Joe closed the office door very smartly and smugly and locked it again. Then he arrogantly reached across the Colonel's desk, switched on the intercom and said, "no calls or interruptions, Corporal. The Colonel has some very important matters to discuss with us. You got that?"

"Yes, Sir, Major," the Corporal answered.

"So, Colonel, let's discuss our plans for revamping the drug rehab program," said Joe.

The Colonel tried to muster up some courage but answered still cringing, "Why should I change anything? You have no tangible proof. You can't hurt me."

"That's true, Colonel, we have no real hard evidence but I have this good friend in Los Angeles. He's a reporter for the L.A. Times and he owes me a big favor. You see, I saved his life when I was an intern," said Joe concocting the story as he went along.

Michael picked up his cue from Joe, and added, "How do you think he would react if we told him our story?"

"Ah, yes, I can see the headlines, now. 'Army Drug Rehabees Hijack Military Plane, Visit Disneyland'. A bit too many words for a headline but I think you get the idea, don't you Colonel?" added Joe.

"All right, all right. What do you want me to change? But keep it reasonable. Don't push me too far," he said unsuccessfully feigning toughness.

Joe looked at Michael," You have the floor Dr. R."

"For starters, we want a psychiatrist put in charge of the entire program and we want one of the many 'Head shrinkers' on the Post to treat patients every day of the week, excluding Sundays, six days a week. And we don't want one of your career Army 'flunkies' running the show, we want a draftee in charge." said Michael.

"I don't think they have the time or the desire," countered the Colonel.

"Wrong Colonel. We've already talked to them about it. They have plenty of time and they'll work extra hours if they have to," said Michael.

"And, as far as desire is concerned, they said they were sick and tired of screening recruits who claim to be *'gay'* just to get out of the Army; they are bored and overburdened with seeing career Army alcoholic and neurotic wives who all think their husbands are cheating on them and who demand sleeping pills and tranquilizers," added Joe.

"Second," said Michael, "we want a fully equipped drug screening lab out there to spot check the men on a regular, periodic basis. Third, we need a 'Detox' Unit of about thirty beds with the necessary nurses and corpsmen to bring these kids down slowly so nobody dies in the withdrawal process," he added.

"Very well, I'll start the planning process immediately," said the Colonel.

"No need for that, Colonel, we've already have the entire plan written out. Here, you can sign the orders now and we'll start things rolling tomorrow," said Joe as he placed the papers down in front of the Colonel and placed a pen in his hand.

"Oh, and one more thing, you will co-sign all the records of the plan and the patient records, too, to make them appear as official as possible," said Michael.

The Colonel smiled coolly when he realized that the program could be a feather in his cap and then he quickly frowned when he realized that he could also be blamed for any misfires.

Michael read his thoughts precisely.

"No, Colonel, we're not doing this to give you the credit, although I'm sure you'll take it all, anyway. We're doing this so there will be no questions as to the validity of the orders. Unless, of course, the General has any problems with them," said Michael.

"In that case, we'd naturally refer him to you if he does question the orders. After all, you are the commander of the entire Medical Unit here on the Post," added Joe.

With all the papers signed and sealed, in triplicate, Joe packed them up while Michael used the Colonel's phone. He dialed the non-Com in charge at Camp Bullock.

"Sergeant Major, this is Major Rizzuto. Remember those instructions I left on your desk yesterday? you can begin to implement them now," he said. Michael paused and listened for a moment. "Yes, we have the orders right here, signed by Colonel Anderson. You'll get a copy of them, forthwith. Proceed as directed," said Michael curtly and hung up the phone.

"Thank you, Sir, it's been nice doing business with you," said Michael.

"Catch you later, Sammy," said Joe.

They left the office marching smartly in single file whistling, 'I'm a Yankee Doodle Dandy'.

CHAPTER TEN

Coming Down Easy

THE SUDDEN CESSATION of the flow of illicit drugs into Camp Bullock did indeed cause many acute withdrawal syndromes. However, because of the preparedness of the staff and the provision of emergency facilities to manage the problem there were no deaths and no major medical complications or residual injuries. The need for psychiatric counseling did skyrocket, as expected, but mechanisms were already in place to answer the need. Unfortunately not all the withdrawing addicts were able to stay clean.

"Come on, Sarge, I need some junk bad, man. I'll go out of my tree if I don't get something real soon," said Parrish showing visible signs of crashing.

"That's tough, Parrish. But right now things are tighter than a crab's ass and that's water tight. I ain't stickin' my neck out for the likes of you, anyway," said LaRocco.

"Then I'll have to blow the whistle on you, you son-of-a-bitch. I'll tell them you were selling dope to me and anybody who had the bread and was willing to pay your blown up prices," said Parrish, his hands trembling as he was clearly about to go into withdrawal.

LaRocco slammed Parrish against the wall of the building and twisted his arm behind his back.

"Go ahead, you little scum bag, you ain't got no proof of that, anyway. Who's going to believe a hop-head like you? It's your word against mine," he said as he released Parrish's arm and shoved him in the direction of the dispensary.

"Now get yourself over to that Detox Unit before they carry you out of her in a body bag not that anybody'd shed any tears over the likes of you."

BJ struggled up from the ground and staggered away. "I'll get even with you for this, LaRocco. Count on it," he said.

"Go on punk, beat it before I put you in that body bag myself right here and now."

Parrish didn't go to the Detox Unit but instead he sought out one of his former secondary providers off the Post in Juniper City. He knocked on the door of the run down house trailer.

"Cal, Cal," he called and knocked louder.

"Who is it? Who's there?" came the slurred words from behind the locked door.

"It's me, Cal, Bobby Joe, let me in. I need a fix and I need it bad. I'll pay you any price you want, anything, please."

The door opened just a crack and a pair of blood shot, beady eyes with pin-point pupils peered out.

"Oh, it's you, BJ Come on in quick before somebody sees you. The heat is really on, hereabouts, lately," said Cal.

"You got any junk?" BJ pleaded.

"No, I ain't. I nearly got busted last week and I had to flush it all," he said.

"Here, I got five hundred bucks. It's yours, all of it, for whatever you can get me," said BJ

"The way the MP's and the Feds have been cracking down I wouldn't do it for five thousand," he said.

"Oh, sweet Jesus," cried BJ "I need something or I'm gonna die."

"Quiet down will ya? You'll get us all busted. Okay, all I got is some homemade red wine. I made it myself," he said.

"Wine! What good is that? That ain't gonna help me none."

"Well, I heard that if you mainline it after you filtered it through a cloth it'll give you a nice buzz and you can bring yourself down with it, nice and easy like," said Cal.

"I'll try it. I'll try anything. I'm going crazy this way," said BJ

"Here, here's a whole gallon. I'll let you have for, say . . . a hundred bucks," he said.

"A hundred bucks! You're out of your skull, man. I could get it for a lot less in town in a bar," said BJ

"Not in the dry state of Kansas you can't."

"Yeah, yeah, okay. I'll take a gallon but I need it in small pint bottles so I can sneak it into the compound."

Cal produced eight, one-pint bottles which he had already filled with the red-brown, cloudy liquid. BJ held one of them up to the little light available in the dingy trailer. He saw a grey-brown sediment rise from the bottom when he shook the bottle.

"Looks might cruddy to me," he said. "I'll just give you twenty-five bucks for the lot," he said.

"Oh, that don't mean nothing. That's just some of the crushed grapes. It gives the brew more zip, don't you know?" said Cal.

"I ain't stupid, you know. I ain't gonna inject that crap into me, no way," said BJ

"Of course not. I know'd you weren't dumb. You just pour it through a rag or your handkerchief and the crud will all come out on the rag. Fifty bucks a gallon and that's my rock bottom offer," said Cal.

"All right, all right, it's a deal. But this better work. 'Cause if it don't give me no buzz I'll be back for my money," said BJ

"Sure, sure, anytime, I'll be here. All my stuff's guaranteed to work. If it don't, you get your money back," Cal said and was amazed that so many of his dissatisfied customers never figured out why he did business out of a mobile home. Within twenty-four hours he'd sell the rest of his tainted brew when the other pot-heads at Ft. O'Malley heard the news, and he knew it. Then he'd be on his way out of town in the small hours of the morning and heading to the next military instillation.

BJ walked back to the Post after dark, just sipping the wine to start with. He found a remote, unguarded part of the Post without any fencing and simply walked back to Camp Bullock.

"I ain't getting much kick drinking this stuff. I'm gonna have to shoot it up."

He sought the corner near some high, dense rhododendron bushes and prepared the paraphernalia for mainlining. In the darkness and in his drunken, impaired mental state he forgot what Cal had told him about filtering the wine. He injected one teaspoonful, and waited.

"Nothing," he said. "I don't get nothing. I'll try some more."

He injected an additional two teaspoonsful and then a third, fourth and fifth. Then his eyes began to glaze over, his visions blurred, and he started seeing weird psychedelic colors and shapes.

"Now, that's more like it," he said. "Yeah, man that'll do for starters." He got up from the ground and staggered in the direction of Camp Bullock. As he sauntered down a steep hill toward the main gate he noted the MPs standing guard.

"Oh, shit, I forgot about the twenty-four hour guards that Dr. Mike put on the gates. I'll just have to find another way in," he muttered.

He walked around the perimeter of the electrified, barbed wire fence trying to find an opening in it, or a tree branch that protruded over it.

"A tree?" he said, "there ain't no goddamned trees in Kansas. Buffalo grass, sage brush, and rhodo. . . rhodo something is all they got out here. Well, I guess I'll just have to dig my way under that fence."

But finding a soft enough spot in the hard, dry, tan Kansas clay was no easy task. Abandoning the idea of finding any soft ground he began digging anyway, using his bare hands. Besides, he was so stoned from the IV wine he was literally feeling no pain in his hands or anywhere else, anyway. After an hour of digging the wine began to loose it's anesthetic effect. The slashes and cuts on his hands, and the ripped off fingernails began to sting.

"I need another shot of that juice if I'm gonna get under that fence." He injected four more teaspoons and then threw in a fifth just for good measure.

"Yahoo," he cheered. Then he realized he was being too loud but he repeated in a whisper, "Yahoo, I'm flying again."

Two more hours digging had produced a shallow dip in the ground so that he might be able to slip into and under the fence, if he was lucky. Lying on his back he slithered into the trench and under the double row fence never touching a single strand of wire. Then he scrapped more clay and rocks together, filled the hole, and marked the spot for possible future use.

"There you are now, Honey. Now we're all set for the next time I need you," he said.

He checked around for any signs or clues he might have left. He found none except for the small fragments of skin, some fingernails and drops of blood that stained the soil. He kicked some fresh soil over these, and left the site.

"Now, let's see where I'm at. I picked just the right spot next to home."

He had unknowingly come up behind his favorite latrine-building and was just a couple of hundred yards from his barracks.

"Think I'll have me a nightcap before I turn in so it'll help me sleep." He slipped quietly into the latrine and then into his favorite end-booth, close to the door. He injected more of the wine into another vein and then drank the remaining pint of wine.

"Wow, I'm getting might hot. But this last swallow ought to cool me off," he said draining the bottle. "That should do it," he said as he struggled to stand up by pushing his hands against the walls of the booth which left two bloody but perfect hand prints on the surfaces.

After getting half-way to the upright position he stopped, abruptly, threw back his head and rolled back his eyes. Then, suddenly, his head was thrown back violently against the concrete wall and he fell to the floor. Lying between the stool and the wall his entire body shook convulsively, his arms and legs stretched out and alternately contracted and then relaxed rapidly in a typical grand-mal epileptic seizure.

With each violent tonic-clonic jerk his head intermittently struck the stool or the concrete wall with a crack. Finally after about three minutes the seizures stopped and he lay unconscious, barely breathing. A second attack had started when an MP entered the latrine for the every-hour, around-the-clock check of the latrines which was another of Dr. Rizzuto's ideas.

The MP looked inside the door, too quickly, then he started to leave until he heard the cracking sound of BJ's head striking the stool.

"What the hell," said the MP as he now went completely inside the building to investigate. He saw BJ's legs sticking out from under the door of the booth as they were jerking rhythmically.

"Holy shit, this guy's having a full-blown seizure," he said. He reached the inside latch by inserting his long arm under the door and unlatched it while BJ's feet kicked his arm. He grabbed BJ's legs and slid him out into the open area of the floor away from the objects against which his head was striking. Parrish continued to jerk violently. The MP took out his pocket-flashlight, wrapped his handkerchief around it and quickly inserted it between BJ's front teeth. Then he quickly rolled BJ on his side so that he couldn't choke or aspirate his own saliva and waited until the seizures stopped.

The MP did not try to hold the BJ's arms and legs motionless which he had learned from the doctors could cause fractures. The entire process was done exactly as Drs. Rizzuto and O'Mara had instructed when they ordered all Camp Bullock personnel, MPs, officers, non-Coms, and even the cooks, to take a course in first aid and emergency medical procedures.

The M.P. waited for the last seizure to stop, knowing when it did he would have only three to five minutes to get help before the next seizure started. Finally BJ did stop jerking and then the MP bolted out the latrine door. It took him slightly over four minutes to return with two corpsmen and a stretcher. Just as they placed Parrish on the stretcher another seizure started. The MP ran alongside the stretcher still holding BJ on his side as he had before.

"Here, let's put him right on the back of my jeep and get him right to the hospital," said the MP

"I think it would be better to take him to the dispensary first," said one of the corpsmen.

"Why? Wouldn't he be better off at the hospital as soon as possible?" asked the other corpsmen.

"If he survives that long you mean. The dispensary is closer, and besides, we could use the ambulance, give him some oxygen, and then call ahead to the hospital to get everything ready for him," said the other.

"Good point. And we could check his body temperature and other vital signs. You know, he feels awfully hot to me. I can feel the heat coming off him without even touching him," said his colleague.

They arrived at the dispensary very short order.

"Here, you put the oxygen mask on him," the corpsman instructed the M.P. "I'll check his vital signs."

"And I'll call the hospital and tell them we're bringing him in," said the other corpsman.

By this time it was 1:30 am. The corpsman called the hospital emergency room while the others worked on BJ. All the pertinent information was given to the ER Tech while they placed BJ in the ambulance.

"Hey, Mickey, they won't believe it but tell them this guy's temp just blew out the top of the thermometer, that means his temp is over 108 degrees. Ask them what we can do to start bringing it down."

"Okay, hold the line," said the ER Tech. "I'll call Dr. O'Mara, he's on call," he added.

Joe O'Mara had just fallen asleep after six steady hours of seeing the usual number of minor bumps, bruises, aches and pains, and colds—not a major illness in the bunch. His nerves, and his patience, and his tolerance were stretched to their limits. The ER Tech knocked on O'Mara's bedroom door, very gently.

"Excuse me, Doc, but we got a real sick one coming in from the boonies."

"Oh, yeah, I'll bet. It's probably just another recruit trying to get out of marching or training, or something," said O'Mara.

"Not this time, Doc. It's some guy from Camp Bullock with a body temp of over 108 degrees."

"What? You mean a hundred *point* eight, don't you?" asked Joe.

"No, Sir, I mean one-zero-eight *point* zero. They want to know what they can do to bring it down while they bring him in?"

"One hundred and eight? For Christ's sake that's almost incompatible with life. Tell them to put ice packs on his head, in his armpits, down in his groin and over his heart. If they have one, they can put a catheter in his urinary bladder and irrigate it with ice water. But tell them to do it while they drive him on in here, and make it fast."

"Okay, Major, I'll tell them."

"Ask them what his primary disease problem is," added Joe.

"Yes, Sir." said the Tech and gave the other instructions, and asked more questions while Joe got into a clean scrub suit.

"Well, what did they say about his primary illness?" he asked.

"They said he OD'd on something," said the Tech.

"On *something*? What the hell do you mean, 'on something'? Get a precise answer, *something* is not good enough. You should know that."

"Yes, sir, I do know that but they couldn't find any drugs on him or at the scene except for some smelly empty wine bottles. They don't have a clue."

"Oh, yeah, sure. A recruit from Camp Bullock OD's by main-lining some wine. That'll look real convincing on his medical record while he's in the hospital."

"I'm sorry but that's what they said, Doc."

The ambulance finally screeched to a halt in front of the ER entrance. The MP and the two corpsmen quickly carried the stretcher to a gurney, placed BJ on it and wheeled him inside. Joe ran up to the gurney and said, "What's his temp now?"

"We don't know, sir the first reading blew out the top of the thermometer and we've been winging it every since," said one of the corpsmen.

"Good grief, this guy's in deep trouble. I'd better call the internist on call. . . this case is beyond the abilities of a radiologist," said Joe.

Joe took the ice-pack off the Parrish's head, and examined his eyes and his pupils.

"There's no sign of heroin or other opiates. Hey, don't I know this kid from somewhere? What's his name?" said Joe.

The MP looked at his ID tag and said, Parrish, B J, Sir."

"Yeah, that's the kid we caught shooting-up in the latrine. I'd better call Mike Rizzuto no matter what internist is on call. Mike knows this case already."

"Well, he's the internist on call, anyway," said the ER Tech.

"Hello, Mike, are you awake? This is Joe. Sorry to wake you up but I got a humdinger down here at the ER."

"Really? What's his problem," said Michael.

"Damned if I know. All I know is that he has a temp of 108, rectally, he's had several grand mal seizures and he mainlined something but we don't know what, yet," said O'Mara.

"A hundred and eight? Okay, I'll be right down. Get a hold of all the ice you can get your hands on and fill up the bath tub in your quarters with it. Then stick the guy's body into the tub completely naked," said Michael.

"Sure, Mike, whatever you say. But get down here fast, will you?"

It took Michael about ten minutes to get dressed and to drive to the hospital ER. He rushed into the Officer-of-the-day's quarters and found Joe and the corpsmen pouring ice cubes into the tub containing BJ's naked body.

"What's his temp, now?" asked Michael.

"It's down to 106.4 but he's still having seizures," said Joe.

"That's a better temp but it's not low enough yet. Just keep putting in more ice and drawing off the water as it melts. And get me a syringe full of Dilantin so I can give if into his vein to try to stop the seizures," Michael said to a corpsman.

The other corpsman came in with two more buckets of ice cubes.

"Good man," said Michael, "but keep it coming."

"I can't, Doc," he said.

"What do you mean, you can't?" said Joe.

"I mean that's all the ice there is in the entire building. Half the ice machines in this hospital don't work, anyway," said the corpsman.

"Then we've got a real problem. If we don't get his temp down below 105 soon it will literally fry his brain," said Michael.

Joe thought for a minute and then snapped his fingers, "I got it, Mike," he said.

"What? You've got what?" said Michael.

"Never mind, Mike. You stay with him and we'll get you that ice," said Joe.

"You two corpsmen come with me," Joe said.

They went out to the hospital parking lot and got into Joe's station wagon.

"Why don't we just take the ambulance or a jeep? Doc," asked a corpsman.

"No, they're too easy to identify with all those markings. Besides, I have two large camping coolers in the back for when I go fishing."

The two corpsmen looked at each other baffled but they followed his instructions.

"Where are we going to get all this ice. Sir?"

"Just wait and see. I don't want either of you involved in the premeditation of this crime," Joe laughed.

After a five minute drive they pulled up behind the officer's club. Joe had turned off the headlights about a mile away from the club and had taken a deserted back road in.

"The officer's club?" said one of the corpsmen.

"Of course, where else can we be certain there's always enough ice? What with happy hour every night they always have a good supply on hand," said Joe.

"But it's closed now, Sir. And I'm sure it's locked up tighter than a drum."

Joe smiled, reached under the front seat and produced a tire iron and a small crowbar.

"Unless they keep that ice in a bank vault I guarantee you we'll get it," said Joe. The two corpsmen stared at each other and hesitated.

"Hey, if you guys don't want to come along I'll understand. This is strictly a volunteer mission, men. I just love that military talk," said Joe smiling.

The humor having subdued their reluctance the two corpsmen jumped out of the car and joined Joe. In a short time they had pried off the locks and had loaded twenty bags of ice cubes into the station wagon and were speeding on their way back to the hospital.

*   *   *

After another three hours in the ice bath, and after using up all the bags of ice, BJ's temperature finally began dropping and his seizures had completely stopped .

"What reading do you get now? asked Michael.

"I get . . . 103.8," said Joe.

"Great. Now let's get him up to the ward and into a bed close to the nurses' station so he can be watched closely," said Michael.

"If this goddamned nineteenth century hospital had an intensive care unit and half-way modern equipment we could put him in that unit where he belongs," said Joe.

"Well we don't, yet. But I'm working on that one, Joe. I think we'll have one in the next month or two. In fact, I guarantee it," said Michael.

"Oh, got the colonel by the balls again, have you?" asked Joe laughing.

The two corpsmen and the MP also laughed.

"I suppose you could express it that way," said Michael.

They got BJ into the bed, inserted all the appropriate tubes and IV's. Joe and Mike stayed with him through the night and relieved each other periodically for the next thirty-six hours until he was out of immediate danger. They visited BJ every hour on the hour while a nurse attended him constantly around the clock until his fever finally broke and stayed below 101.

"How's he doing, nurse?" asked Michael.

"His temp is staying down and he's had no further seizures but he's still unconscious and unresponsive to all stimuli—verbal, tactile or otherwise, doctor," she answered.

"Yes, I expect he'll be in a coma for quite some time yet," he said.

"How long do you think, Mike?" said Joe.

"Another seven to ten days. Maybe even as long as two to three weeks. It's hard telling. We'll have to feed him through a stomach tube. We can never get enough calories in through a vein for that long," said Michael.

"What about the tests? Did they give you any answers about what he OD'd on?"

"Yes, they sure did, indirectly. Sure, we found a high blood alcohol but it wasn't high enough to cause this coma and sky-high fever. But we did found this other stuff in his blood and urine and it did match the composition of that sludge we found in the bottom of those wine bottles."

"You mean this kid actually did mainline that wine? How are you sure he just didn't drink it and flood his entire system with the sludge also?"

"Because we found the same elements in some syringes and needles he left in the latrine," said Michael.

"That's incredible. How strung out can you get?" asked Joe.

"Oh, it's not unusual when the supply of hard stuff is cut off like we just did at Camp Bullock. When I was a resident in a Spanish-Harlem hospital I saw junkies who had injected airplane glue, marijuana tea, Darvon. You name it, they've tried it," said Michael.

"How did those junkies make out? I mean did they survive?"

"They all died. Every one of them I'd taken care of died from injecting that kind of crap into themselves," said Michael.

"So BJ's got the cards stacked against him, doesn't he?" said Joe.

"Yes, I'm afraid he does. He is young, however, but it's still going to be a long, slow road to recovery," said Michael.

But nine days and nights later, under the diligent care of Joe, Michael and the nurses, BJ regained consciousness. And after another three weeks he was actually sitting up in bed taking light nourishment.

Colonel Anderson, after he'd heard the entire story, accompanied the other doctors on rounds just to check on BJ's progress and also to be sure Parrish had not blown the whistle yet on the Colonel and Sergeant LaRocco.

"How's Parrish doing?" the colonel asked Michael.

"He's coming along fine, Colonel. We started his physical therapy and speech therapy programs yesterday. He's making progress," he said.

"What has he said so far? Ah . . . I mean has he said anything coherent, yet?" asked the colonel.

"No, not yet. He just utters unintelligible sounds right now and an occasional syllable but no complete words or phrases yet. It'll come in time," said Michael puzzled by the colonel's interest.

"Good, good. He had just gotten his orders for Vietnam just before this happened, you know?" said the colonel.

Michael was stunned. He turned and looked at Joe. Joe just shook his head in disbelief as Colonel Anderson walked away casually.

"Did he say what I thought he just said?" said Michael.

"Yeah, you heard right," said Joe.

"He can't be serious. Even if this kid recovers all his mental and physical faculties there's no way he could survive In-Country. As a matter of fact I think he should get a medical discharge based on psychiatric grounds," said Michael.

"I'm sure you're right but it seems like they've got their minds set on his going to Vietnam," said Joe.

After three more months of intensive, daily therapy, under Michael's meticulous supervision, BJ did have a complete mental and physical recovery but his psyche was still sick. And his addiction potential was still there and it always would be especially during times of extreme emotional stress.

Nevertheless, Michael personally, and privately, prepared Parrish's medical discharge papers. He also prepared himself for another confrontation with Colonel Anderson and the Army bureaucracy. But BJ had no residual *physical* damage from his overdose incident. All his tests and x-rays were normal, as was his physical examination. Even his psychological tests were normal but borderline. Addiction potential, like suicide potential, was a difficult thing to quantitate or document. Michael knew that, and he knew that Colonel Anderson knew it, and was counting on it.

Nevertheless, he knocked on Colonel Anderson's office door, which was now so familiar to him like a kind of rampart-symbol. Michael heard the same squirrelly voice, trying to sound tough, as it bid him to enter.

"Oh, it's you. What is it this time Rizzuto? I'm very busy," said the Colonel.

Michael silently placed Parrish's discharge papers in front of the colonel.

"And what is this? Medical discharge papers for . . . Parrish. Are you crazy? I'm not signing these. He has no discernible residual medical injuries, physical or mental, that I can see. Take them away."

"But, Colonel, you know as well as I that this kid is unstable and not cured of his addiction potential. Sure, he's been off everything for months but that doesn't mean he's cured," said Michael.

"It does to the Army, and to me. And that's good enough for Fifth Army Headquarters," he said.

"Come on, Colonel, it's just like dried out alcoholics. They may be dry but they know the potential is still there. The AA, and even the alcoholics, admit that openly," he said trying to subdue his anger.

"Documentation, Major Rizzuto, you need documentation of a persistent addiction potential, and you don't have that. So he goes to Vietnam. And this time no amount of coercion from you will make me alter my decision."

Michael had no ammunition other than his medical intuition and judgment which he knew was wasted on Colonel Anderson.

"If he goes to Vietnam, he'll die. If he doesn't get killed in combat he'll get sick again from shooting-up some adulterated substance. His central nervous system . . . his brain, can't stand another traumatic challenge like the last one, and you know it," Michael was shouting now, "and his death will be on your head, Colonel."

The colonel sat back calmly, clasped his hands behind his head, tilted his chair back, and smiled. "You're dismissed, Major Rizzuto. And another word on this matter and you'll find your ass in some Vietnam rice paddy right next to Parrish's."

Michael knew he had met his Waterloo but couldn't accept it.

"But, Colonel . .," he started to say but the Colonel interjected.

"And close the door softly behind yourself on the way out. Oh, and take these papers with you." He tossed the file at Michael who caught it, turned and left the office.

*   *   *

Two weeks later, after a quick refresher basic training course on guerrilla warfare, BJ Parrish was on his way to southeast Asia and to almost certain death.

CHAPTER ELEVEN

Not Fit For Man Nor Beast

"ALMOST ONE FULL year in this Army and ten months at Ft. O'Malley and they're still handing us the same old crap," said Joe as he and Michael drove down to the hospital to make rounds.

"What do you mean, Joe? What is it this time?" asked Michael.

"Would you believe I got word yesterday that they expect all the Docs to accompany the veterinarian once a week to check out an old Army hay-burner, a nag," he said.

"What? You mean a horse? I didn't know the Army still had any horses," said Michael.

"Oh, yeah. His name is Scout. It seems he was the last horse commissioned by the U. S. Cavalry. I hear he's real old now and barely breathing," said Joe.

"Why don't they do the humane thing and end the old guy's misery?" asked Michael.

"Oh, they couldn't do that. You see, he's suppose to be buried with special honors so he's got to die of 'natural causes' or 'in combat'."

"You're kidding," said Michael.

"Nope, I have seen the plans for the ceremony. A big parade is planned, with brass bands, grandstands, speeches, the works. Even the President of the United States will be invited to attend," said Joe.

"I don't believe it. You're making this all up as you go along, aren't you?" said Michael.

"No, I'm not. Have you ever known me to make up stories?" said Joe laughing.

Michael looked at him and rolled his eyes.

"Well, disregard that last question. But, you'll see for yourself. You should find your own notice for making the sick visits, along with your weeks of assignment, on your desk, any day now."

"Yeah, I probably will find it, but that doesn't mean the big-funeral-ceremony part is true."

"Fine. I'll bring you the original itinerary for the whole show tonight," he said.

"Go on. How can you manage to do that? You're not a magician, you know," said Michael.

Now it was Joe's turn to roll his eyes.

"Ah, disregard that last remark," said Michael and they both laughed.

"Let's just forget about that Army nonsense for now and concentrate on our medical duties." said Michael. "I can only stand just so much of that 'Mickey Mouse', Army stuff at one time."

"Sure, Mike, whatever you say," said Joe but he was feeling deep concern for Michael's spirits, of late. "Hey, Mike, are you okay?" he added.

"Sure, I'm fine, fine. I just need some time off and away from this place," answered Michael.

"What's happening at the hospital? Have you had any interesting cases lately?" asked Joe.

Michael's face and eyes brightened with the change to his favorite topic of discussion.

"No, not really. Just more of the same minor illnesses, congressionals, and that I-need-to-get-out-of-the-Army stuff."

"I hear there's a new load of casualties coming in today from 'Nam. There might be some challenging cases in that bunch for us," said Joe trying to raise Michael's spirits.

"Yeah, maybe so. But you know, it just doesn't seem right for us to look for challenges stemming from the battle injuries of a senseless war, like this one," said Michael.

"Yeah, I know what you mean. I have mixed feelings about that, too. But we're only human, Mike, even if we are doctors. We've spent years in learning to practice medicine, so naturally, we like to do it. Besides, we can't carry all the burdens of the world on our backs. Well, maybe you can, but I know I can't," he said.

Michael didn't answer. He was reluctant to admit to anybody that his burden-carrying-back might be growing weaker.

After their usual third cup of coffee in the doctor's lounge, they went to the admitting-office to look over the list of new patients arriving from Vietnam. Michael ran his index finger down the long list of patients' names, ignoring the rank and serial numbers, but he did read the diagnoses after each and every one of the names.

"Anything special or critical on the list, Mike?" said Joe.

"No, just the usual cases of malaria, hepatitis, undiagnosed fevers, two pneumonias, you know, the routine stuff," he said.

Then Michael turned and began to walk away from the desk when his eye caught a familiar name on the list of psychiatric admissions.

"Highsmith, C. D. I might know this one. There couldn't be two people with that same name," he mumbled.

"What? Who did you say? Mike," said Joe.

"You remember Highsmith don't you? Joe."

"Highsmith, sure. Old C. D. Highsmith the lawyer turned corpsman from Ft. Sam Houston. What's he here for?" asked Joe.

Michael ran his finger over to the diagnosis column, it read, 'Post-Traumatic Stress Syndrome'. Michael repeated the diagnosis aloud.

"What the hell does that mean?" said Joe.

"It's today's equivalent of the old terms 'shell shock' or 'battle fatigue'," said Michael feeling his usual disgust for the military pseudonyms.

"What? Not Highsmith. I always thought he was as solid as the Rock of Gibraltar. It must have been something real heavy to make him crack," said Joe.

"They say a few months In-Country with the VC has made the most stalwart of men crumble. But you're right, he's the last one I would have guessed would mentally disintegrate," said Michael.

"Come one, let's go ask his shrink if it's okay for us to talk to him," said Michael.

"Why ask anybody?" said Joe.

"Because it's only the courteous thing to do with a colleague. Besides, we might be able to give him insight into C.D.'s case and maybe we can help. And the Psychiatrist might want to see C.D.'s reaction when he sees old, familiar faces. Who's got his case?" asked Michael.

"Let's see. Sidney Greenspan. I know Sid, he's a good 'head shrinker', too. He'll be no problem for us," said Joe.

"I hope he can help C.D. who is a good man. After corpsman school at Ft. Sam, he told me he was thinking of going to medical school. Did you know that? Joe."

"No, I didn't. I'll bet you had something to do with that," said Joe.

"No, I didn't force him or even suggest it to him," replied Michael.

"That's not what I meant. You turned on his juices, man. He saw the *chief* in action and was inspired," he said.

Michael blushed but didn't reply.

They paged Dr. Sidney Greenspan who was in a group therapy session at the moment.

"This is Dr. Greenspan speaking."

"Hi Sid, it's Joe O'Mara. How're you doing, buddy?"

"Fine, Joe, I'm fine. What can I do for you?"

Joe related the facts to him about knowing C.D. Highsmith at Ft. Sam Houston and before he was sent to Vietnam.

"Oh, yes, that could be very helpful. Wait for me to join you. I'd like to be there also to see how he reacts to familiar faces," said Dr. Greenspan.

Joe turned from the phone and looked at Michael standing nearby. Of course, he only heard Joe's side of the conversation. Joe said to him with a smile, "you smart-ass."

"What? What are you talking about? Joe."

"Never mind, never mind, I'm just thinking out loud."

Joe turned his attention back to the phone.

"What's his problem, Sid? Is he in real bad shape?"

"Prepare yourselves for a real shock. You may not even recognize him in his current state. He's catatonic, Joe," said Sid.

"Oh, I see," said Joe, with a soft gray shadow coming across his face.

"He just sits in one position all day and night. He won't eat or sleep. It must have been some major emotional trauma he experienced."

"Yeah, yeah, I understand, Sid."

"What did he say?" asked Michael.

Joe decided not to share the gory details with Michael.

"Like I said, no problem. He'll meet us outside the Psych ward in ten minutes or so. He said he wants to observe C.D.'s reaction when he sees us, just like you said, smart-ass," said Joe trying to end on a humorous note, and left it at that. Knowing the way Michael gets too attached to patients he tried to think of some way to soften the blow and break it to Michael gently. But he knew, as did most physicians, that there is no easy way to reveal bad news to someone.

They sat outside the locked Psych ward waiting for Sid Greenspan.

"You know, Mike, this Sid Greenspan is a real cracker jack psychotherapist. I've seen him work miracles on some real tough cases when he was only a resident at Bellevue Hospital in New York," said Joe.

"Yes, you already told me that, Joe. I'm confident he'll be able to help CD. Did he say how bad off he was?" asked Michael.

Joe didn't answer.

Michael nudged Joe with his elbow. "Huh, what did he say? Joe

"Joe, didn't you hear me? I asked you a . . ."

Sid Greenspan turned the corner and greeted them, and Joe sighed with relief.

"Hi, Joe. This must be Dr. Michael Rizzuto. I'm glad to meet you Mike. I've heard some good things about your clinical acumen. Makes a guy feel good way out here in the Kansas boonies to know there's a sharp Internist around in case you or your family gets really sick."

"Thanks," said Michael.

"We all know that few groups get more heart attacks then we doctors do, and that half of us die on the spot, and the other half only has a chance with someone like you around," said Sid.

Michael was beginning to feel quite uneasy with all the flattery. He changed the subject abruptly.

"Can we talk to Highsmith now? Do you think he can handle it?" he said.

"Didn't you tell him, Joe?"

Joe didn't answer but turned and looked away.

"Oh, I see, you didn't tell him," said Sid.

"Tell me what?" said Michael.

"Highsmith hasn't spoken a word to anyone for six weeks, ever since whatever caused his problem happened. He's catatonic. I doubt he'd even recognize you and if he does he'll show no response, no change in facial expression, not even any eye movement. He just sits there and stares off into space," said Sid.

Michael tried, albeit unsuccessfully, not to look taken aback but inside, he was.

"What was this traumatic event, do you know?" asked Joe.

"No, not yet. We haven't questioned any witnesses yet but there's one on his way over here to talk to me. I'm to meet with him in an hour. You're welcomed to sit in if you want."

"Yes, thanks, we'll do that," said Michael trying to appear detached and clinical.

Sid Greenspan unlocked the Psych ward door and they walked into the day room. Michael and Joe looked around the room at the men lounging, playing cards, watching TV or reading. Michael's glance stopped at a man sitting, legs crossed Indian-style, in front of the large bay window. It was C.D.Highsmith. Despite all the horrifying things Michael had seen as a physician it was still difficult for him when it was someone he knew and liked.

"Try not to startle him. He gets hysterical and combative, sometimes. Come around from the side and let his peripheral vision pick you up first before you confront him head on," warned Dr. Greenspan.

Michael and Joe moved slowly around Highsmith's left side, moving their arms as well as their legs slowly until they were almost facing him. Highsmith didn't move or turn his head or even his eyes.

"Hi, C. D. It's me Dr. Rizzuto from Ft. Sam and Dr. O'Mara, too. You remember him don't you? the clown of Ft. Sam Houston," whispered Michael grinning.

C.D. still sat frozen, back straight as a rod, bare chested, one hand resting on each knee, head and eyes straight ahead. No sign of recognition, no response.

"You must remember Field Service School at Ft. Sam. Don't you recall that we gave you your corpsman training before they sent you to Vietnam?" said Joe.

Sid Greenspan noted a minor muscle reaction from C.D. Highsmith.

"Careful now," he said. "I think you brushed by a sensitive nerve fiber there. Change the subject away from . . . you know where," he said cautioning them.

Highsmith's facial expression changed, his lip muscles began to quiver slightly, and his eyes blinked rapidly.

"Remember we talked about you maybe going to Med School because you were such a good corpsman?" said Michael.

The lip tremor stopped and all his muscles again went rigid, and Highsmith lapsed back into the catatonic state.

"I don't think that is going to do it, Michael. We'll just have to take the risk of shocking him and approach the only topic which illicited any response," said Sid Greenspan.

"Isn't that dangerous, Sidney?" asked Joe.

"Yes, it is somewhat chancy but we'll have to take the gamble to try to take this kid out of his catatonic state or he may be lost to the conscious world forever," said Dr. Greenspan.

"I'll start out cautiously. You men back me up and add a familiar name, place, situation or person here and there. Are you ready?" asked Sid as all three men sat on the floor, in the same Indian-style, in front of Highsmith.

"I'm Dr. Greenspan, C. D. I'm one of the Post shrinks you know, a Psychiatrist. Anyway, I'm due to go In-Country in a few weeks and I think I can benefit from the experiences of someone who's been there, like you. What can you tell me about the place you know where I talking about, *Vietnam*?"

C. D. began to twitch, his eyes began blinking rapidly again and the perspiration poured off him like a shower.

Dr. Greenspan panicked and tried to back off.

"Okay, okay," he said quickly, "let's forget that for now. Tell me what you remember about Ft. Sam," he added.

But it was too late, the stimulus had been applied and Dr. Greenspan didn't know how to remove it, in Highsmith's case.

C. D. began a slow, rhythmic swaying of his body while still in the sitting position. First he swayed slowly from left to right, then from front to back. A low-pitched moaning began emitting from his throat. At first the sound was very soft, then it gradually increased in volume as the rate of his swaying increased. His teeth were tightly clenched and they began to grind audibly as he was practically forcing the sounds out between the spaces in his white, closely aligned teeth. The sweat was now running off in torrents.

"Corpsman, nurse, somebody, get me a sedative injection for this man, quickly," yelled Dr. Greenspan.

Michael and Joe tried to hold C. D. back by physically subduing his swaying, but without success.

"My God, he's as strong as an ox," said Joe.

Sidney Greenspan looked around desperately for the nurse with the syringe full of sedative but there wasn't anyone there, yet.

"Don't let him hurt himself," said Dr. Greenspan.

"Tell them about Sylvia, C. D.," said a loud, unfamiliar voice coming from behind them at the main entrance to the ward. Everyone turned around toward the door. Highsmith began to slow down his swaying and moaning.

"Tell them about your girl, Sylvia, C. D.," the voice repeated more loudly. An infantry Corporal walked, as quickly as he could, toward C.D., although the man was considerably slowed by the crutches he carried and the plaster cast on his leg.

Highsmith's swaying continued but slowed even more and the volume of his moaning diminished also.

"Who are you, Corporal?" asked Michael.

"Corporal Isaac Wyers, Sir. I was in C. D.'s outfit with him in 'Nam. I also witnessed the whole incident that caused this problem with him," said the Corporal.

"Go on, Wyers, he seems to recognize your voice," said Dr. Greenspan.

The Corporal hobbled around in front of Highsmith while Michael and Joe hung on to his shoulders. The two doctors flailed back and forth, then to the left and to the right, like two rag dolls nailed to a fence in a tornado.

"It's me, C.D. It's Isaac Wyers from 'C' company. What was it you said was Sylvia's favorite song? Remember you told me once outside of Da Nang but I forgot it?" continued Wyers.

Highsmith's movements and moaning continued to slow quite measurably.

"Was it 'Earth Angel' or 'Unchained Melody' by the Righteous Brothers? I always get those two mixed up," said Wyers.

He set his crutches down, and sat on the floor, with the help of Joe and Michael, who had since let go of C. D. Highsmith, who's swaying and moaning had almost come to a halt, now. The perspiration had slowed to a trickle from the tip of his nose and the ends of his bare, tightly flexed elbows.

"It's okay, C. D. It's okay if you can't tell me the name of the song. I have the name written down somewhere," said Wyers, trying to be gentle and consoling as he slid himself closer to him. "I do remember that she went to Howard University under grad with you. Then she went on to get her Teaching degree while you went to Law School," he added.

Highsmith stopped his swaying completely, now, but he was still moaning ever so softly, almost inaudibly.

"'at a way, C D, keep it cool, man. Just think about Sylvia, and home, and getting out of this freeking war and this stinking Army."

Wyers' hands were now resting on CD's knees as he continued his soothing words.

"That's it, that's it," he continued until Highsmith had stopped moaning and twitching, at long last.

Just then the nurse arrived with the syringe full of sedative.

"I don't think we'll need that now, thank you, Nurse," said Dr. Greenspan.

"Why don't you just lay down on your mat now, C.D. and get some shut-eye," said Wyers.

Joe O'Mara pulled a blanket off one of the nearby beds and folded it lengthwise next to Highsmith. He rolled over on to it and collapsed in total exhaustion.

"He'll be okay, now. I think he'll sleep for three or four hours. Just don't let anybody disturb him or try to put him in bed or anything," warned Wyers.

"Funny, that's just the way he was when I found him in that yoga-like position next to the jeep with all those dead bodies lying around," added Wyers.

"Let's get some coffee while you tell us the rest of the story," said Sid Greenspan.

Michael and Joe helped Wyers up from the floor and onto his crutches. They walked down the middle aisle between all the ward beds, and passed all the other patients who had been sitting on or had stood at their bedsides mesmerized by the entire scene. Now some of them cried softly, some rolled over into the fetal position onto their beds to sleep while others stood still frozen at their bedsides.

The four men walked slowly to Dr. Greenspan's office. They all stopped along the way to hug, stroke and console several of the more distraught patients. The distance of about twenty five feet seemed more like twenty five light-years.

"I want all the nurses and corpsmen out here among these people until I get back. Don't leave any of them alone, especially Highsmith," said Dr. Greenspan.

"Yes, Sir," answered the Head nurse.

The three Doctors and the Corporal finally reached the office, went inside and closed the door.

*   *   *

"I seen it all happen from a hill overlooking this clearing near the Mekong Delta. I took some shrapnel from a mortar shell in this here leg, and the VC left me for dead. My platoon had scattered after the ambush and we got separated."

"How did you manage to walk with that leg all torn up?" asked Michael.

"At first I crawled on my belly for a mile or two until the VC were gone, then I used my M-16 as a crutch to walk the rest of the time. It was slow and painful at first but I managed. Anyway, I finally got to this hill and I saw this big clearing. It must have been two miles down the side of this steep hillside to the clearing below.

There was a lot of rice paddies in the valley. The one closest to the bottom of the hill had three Vietnamese villagers working in it. I was resting up, drinking some water from my canteen and eating some C-rations to get my strength back before starting the climb down. I knew it was going to be tough and dangerous. It was real steep, man. I was scared, with this bad leg and all.

Next thing I know I see this APC you know an Armored Personnel Carrier with a Red Cross on it driving into the clearing. It was moving real slow like it was checking out the three workers in the rice paddy. There was three of them in the field, like I said. Two were guys and one was a girl. They couldn't have been more than thirteen or fourteen years old. But age don't mean nothing with the Vietcong. You learn that real quick In-Country."

"Was Highsmith alone in the APC?" asked Sid Greenspan.

"No, there was three wounded guys. Two walking wounded sitting in the back tending to this other guy on a stretcher. He was hurt real bad. I could see the blood all over him, even from where I was. The other guys were sitting up and seemed okay. One had his arm in a sling and the other guy had a bandage around his head. And C.D., he was driving, and then they stopped near the three Vietnamese.

"And then what happened?" said Dr. Greenspan.

Anyways, C D, and the guy with the bandage on his head got out to check out the three kids farming. It looked like they talked to them for a bit to try to get a feeling for whether they were VC or not. They seemed satisfied and turned to walk back to the APC. And that's where they made their big mistake."

"What do you mean? 'big mistake'," asked Joe. "They had checked them out, hadn't they?"

"Yeah, but still you don't never turn your back on no possible VC, no matter what. You keep your eyes on them and you back away, real slow like. If they so much as twitch or even bend over to work again before you get a safe distance you blow them away. Those guys must've been pretty green, the GIs, I mean."

"You could kill a lot of innocent people that way, Corporal," said Michael.

"You stop thinking about that, Doc after you see a half-dozen of your buddies with their guts blown out by old ladies and school kids."

Michael nodded.

"What happened next?" asked Sid.

"Like I was saying, they turned and walked back to the APC. The wounded guy was climbing back in and C.D. was going around to the driver's side, that's probably what saved him. Then three VC bent over, put their hands into the water and came up with some grenades. They pulled the pins and threw them into the APC. They blew all those three guys twenty feet into the air. C.D. was thrown about ten feet away by the blast. Must have only stunned him, though.

The three VC started to try to run through the knee-deep water. It slowed them down quite a bit. Then C. D. seemed to just go bananas.

He started yelling for them to stop. They didn't. Then he picked up one of the automatic weapons of the GI's and started blasting those VC in the back. He just kept on firing and yelling long after the three of them had went down. Next he jumped into the paddy and kept shooting the dead bodies until the clip was empty. Must've put fifty rounds into them altogether."

"What did you do next?" asked Sid.

"I didn't know what to do, to tell you the truth. If I yelled to him or fired a shot in the air to get his attention I was afraid the VC would get me, too. I decided that it wouldn't do no good, anyhow. C.D. was just kneeling down in the water in a state of shock. He wasn't moving a muscle or nothing.

So I started down the steep hill, using my weapon as a crutch again, as fast as I could go. It took me near three hours to get down to the edge of the clearing, and all the time I couldn't see what C. D. was doing or if they got him, too. I fell down that hillside five or six times, I did. My leg was paining me something terrible. But, finally, I made it to the clearing's edge, about three or four hundred yards from the APC."

"Was Highsmith anywhere in sight?" asked Michael.

"Yeah, I couldn't believe some of the VC didn't get him, too. But, there he was sitting on the ground in front of these six sticks poking out of the ground. At first I thought they were small trees or bushes. When I got closer I could see that's not what they were. And C.D., he was just sitting there a rockin' and a moanin'."

"What were those sticks, then?" asked Joe.

"I'm coming to that, Sir. They was grave markers."

"Grave markers?" said Joe.

"Yep, that's what they were. C.D. had dug them six shallow graves for his buddies and the three VC. Dug them with his bare hands. I could tell because his hands were all cut and bleeding with the dirt still sticking to them. And you could see his hand prints all over the mounds of dirt where he patted them down."

"That sounds unbelievable. Are you sure about that, Corporal?" asked Michael. He immediately regretted asking when he realized he had offended Wyers by questioning his veracity. He dropped the subject.

"The adrenaline of hysteria and acute Psychosis can give some people amazing strength, determination, and freedom from physical pain," said Dr. Greenspan.

"Yes, of course, I remember that now," said Michael.

"Wait, you haven't heard the half of it yet. Those markers weren't just any old sticks, no Sir. C D, he made crosses from the rifle bayonets for his three buddies, figuring they was Christians, and hung their dog tags on them. Tied the cross pieces together with their shoelaces, he did. I guess he calculated that the VC was heathens, or Buddhists, or at least not Christians. Their grave markers was just some branches from the bushes."

"Well, at least he still had his cognitive powers in tact," said Dr. Greenspan.

"Yeah, whatever," continued Corporal Wyers. "But the most amazing part was what he put on the VC markers. One had one of these wooden carved figurines on a leather string. You know, it looked like one of the crazy letters of their alphabet. The second marker was a Swiss Army knife with a GI's rank and name on it. The third one was a photograph that was laminated in plastic. In this picture was a GI with his arm around a young oriental gal that was pregnant. The face of the GI was scratched off, though. I guess he left her and she was pissed off at him."

"Was there a baby or its body anywhere around?" asked Michael.

"No, Sir, there weren't none. But that one grave had a big bulge in the middle of it. You know, like the belly of a pregnant lady."

"You don't know if the woman was still pregnant, do you Corporal?" asked Joe.

"Yes, Sir, I found out soon enough that she was. I dug that one up, at least until I could see the belly. I just had to know. It was all tore up by the bullets, the belly, I mean. Most sickening sight I ever laid eyes on and I'd seen some pretty gory ones in 'Nam. It made me throw up. Then I covered it up again. It must have been that sight that blew C.D.'s mind."

"What was C. D. doing all this time?" asked Sid.

"He was still just sitting, and a rockin', and a moanin'."

"Did he say anything or move, or do anything?"

"No, Sir, not until I started walking him out of there. Then he just held on to my hand like a little child and followed right behind me until we came on some of our guys, about an hour later."

"Thanks, Corporal. Would you mind telling that story again to my secretary so we can get it into the written record? Highsmith deserves a commendation, and so do you for that matter, for getting him back to safety," said Sid Greenspan.

"Not at all, Sir. But, I don't need no medals, I just need my medical discharge and a ticket home. And C.D.? It ain't going to do him no good, no how."

"No, it won't but it might make his family feel better. I think I'll write them a letter," said Michael.

"What are the chances C.D. will come out of this catatonic state, Sidney?" asked Joe.

"Theoretically, with today's modern drugs and some psychotherapy, I'd say his chances are fifty-fifty. But it'll take a long time and a lot of therapy sessions. We'll start both of those first thing in the morning," Sidney answered.

Michael, will you do his physical examination, x-rays and all the necessary blood tests to check him out for any hidden medical illnesses?" asked Dr. Greenspan.

"Certainly, Sidney, I'll start today and have it all done in a couple of days. The report will be on your desk before the end of the week."

* * *

Two weeks later Michael found the memo and the schedule on his desk for examining the horse, Scout, with the Vet.

"Do you believe this garbage?" said Michael.

"Don't say I didn't tell you so," said Joe. "When are you scheduled to examine the nag?" he asked.

"Tomorrow morning at 7:00 am," he answered.

"Would you mind if I joined you?"

"I thought you had your own schedule to check him, too?" said Michael.

"I did, but I traded with one of the other Docs. I'm just a radiologist, don't forget. What do I know about examining hearts and such?"

"Sure, you can come along if you like. I'll pick you up at your place tomorrow morning at about 6:45," said Michael.

"Oh, no, no, Major Dr. Rizzuto. Haven't you learned anything about military ways in your many months in the Army?" said Joe.

"What are you talking about, now?" said Michael.

"The 'Scout' is too special for ordinary procedures. We meet the Vet at his office and a staff car, with a jeep escort, picks us up and takes us to his stable from there. Good God, man, don't you know anything?"

"That's crazy. What for?" said Michael.

"The way I understand it, it's to make sure that the only Vet on the Post is not killed by enemy fire. Because then 'Scout' might die of neglect and that would be a terrible blow to Army morale."

"Come one, get serious. What's the real reason?" asked Michael.

"Well, I've been told that some of the Veterinarians objected to a once a week visit. They thought that they were over doing it a bit. Can you believe those guys? The Army *never* over does anything," said Joe.

"Yeah, right, frugality is their motto," said Michael.

"Anyway, some of the MDs and Vets didn't make the weekly visits but said they did on the records. That's also the reason the MPs accompany the two of them. They actually court-martialed one of the Vets, I heard," said Joe.

"Why? so the MDs and the Vets could fink on each other if one doesn't show?" asked Michael.

"Now you're getting to understand the Army way. But that didn't always work, either. Sometimes both agreed not to go and waste their time, and also not to fink on each other. And that's the reason that the MP escort is always composed of two career military types," added Joe.

"Unbelievable," said Michael.

"Oh, I don't know, it sounds reasonable enough to me," said Joe, and they both laughed.

The following morning Michael and Joe drove to the Vet's office. The MP jeep was parked at the curb waiting for the Vet and the M.D. to show. But with Joe along, the five passengers made the vehicle too crowded, so the Vet suggested that he, Michael and Joe follow in his car.

One of the MPs, a Captain Brighton, asked, "might I inquire why you need two MDs on rounds today, Sirs?"

"Well, you see, Major Rizzuto here doesn't know very much about medical care and all, so I came along to help him out," said Joe smiling.

The Vet chuckled because he knew of Michael's reputation as an astute clinician. The M.P.s got in their jeep, and the three physicians followed in the Vet's car to the stable.

"By the way, my name's, Captain Steve Casper, D.M.V. You can call me Steve except when the brass is around," said the Vet.

"Hi, I'm Joe O'Mara and this is Mike Rizzuto."

"Yeah, I know, I've heard about both of you."

"Now, Steve, you mustn't believe everything you hear. Unless, of course, they're nasty rumors," said Joe.

"Are you the only Vet on the Post, Steve?" asked Michael.

"No, there are four of us, all together."

"Four Vets? Why so many? I mean what do you do all day long besides take care of Scout?" asked Michael.

"Ostensibly, we're also supposed to care for the small herd of buffalo they keep here on the Post. But the real reason is to take care off all the pets the officers, the retirees and their wives have," said Steve.

"Isn't that against regulations? I mean, to provide Vet care to their animals?" said Michael.

"Yes, it is but we don't mind. It's what we do for a living anyway. I'd go out of my mind with boredom if I didn't do it. Plus the fact that we might go to 'Nam if we refused to do it."

"Vietnam? What possible use could a Vet be In-Counrty?" asked Joe.

"I have no idea but I'm sure the Army could cook up something. Anyway, I'm not risking it. I'll clean Scout's stall if they ask me to."

Michael and Joe nodded in affirmation. They finally turned off the main blacktop road on to a concrete paved, two lane side road. They approached a red brick building placed in the middle of a large Kansas meadow. The well groomed, one story building was ringed by a dozen tall shade trees. On the south side of the stable was a corral area rimmed with steel posts and railings similar to those used for highway guardrail work. Another exact duplicate corral area was attached to the north side of the building for use during the hot summer days. The entire area containing the building, the trees and the corrals, was surrounded by another steel ring of fencing.

"Would you look at this set up. You'd think that they had Man-O'War, or Citation or some other million dollar race horse housed here," said Michael.

"Yep," said Steve. "Nothing's too good for the Scout. Wait until you see the inside. Did you notice there weren't any windows in the building?" he added.

"Yes, now that you mention it. How come?" asked Michael.

"The whole place is climate controlled. It has the same temperature, humidity and barometric pressure day and night, all year round," said Steve.

"This place must've set the taxpayers back a pretty penny or two," said Joe.

"Half a million is what I heard," said Steve.

They stopped at the main entrance gate to the facility where two MPs stood guard. They checked the orders of the men in the escort jeep, and then they waved them all on through the gate.

The five men then passed through the only door into the building after another M.P. checked their IDs. The next stop was an ID check at a desk similar to the kind found in the best hotels. It included a luxuriously carpeted waiting room with leather chairs, a coffee-maker, magazines and coat racks. The only thing missing was the TV set and a gift shop. Again the five men were checked, but this time by a nurse at the desk.

"Is that gal at the desk an RN, or what?" asked Joe.

"No, she's a veterinarian's assistant," said Steve. "She is First Lieutenant Cloweter doing her shift now."

"You mean there's more than one shift?" asked Michael.

"That's right. Three shifts a day with twenty-four hours coverage, three hundred and sixty-five days a year," answered Steve.

Michael immediately thought, 'and there's a shortage of RNs at the hospital so bad that some weekend days and nights there's only a corpsman to staff the wards.'

The stall area was large enough to stable at least five horses. The floor was covered by clean, fresh smelling, snow white wood shavings not the usual, less costly straw. The shavings layer was at least ten inches deep and if felt like walking through fresh fallen, powdered snow on the ski slopes of Utah.

"Just like walking on a cloud," said Joe.

"This place is immaculate. There's no droppings, no yellow urine stains, no foul odor, nothing. How do they do that?" asked Michael.

"The stall area is cleaned every four hours and the wood shavings are completely replaced every twenty-four hours," said the M.P. on duty.

Michael glanced at but did not closely examine several dozen wooden crates stacked against the wall behind them as they came into the area.

At the far corner of the stall stood 'Scout', a tired, sway backed, gentle, old black gelding who was too weak even to eat the bucket of oats placed before him. A Corporal dressed in a white lab coat was helping the old boy by hand feeding him the oats a few kernels at a time. A large alpaca-lined sling was strapped under the horse's belly, its ends were anchored to some ceiling beams by leather strips. The pitiful animal could not even stand on his own.

"This is downright inhumane treatment, Steve," said Michael.

"This poor old guy should have been put out of his misery long ago," said Joe.

"Not so loud you guys. This place is loaded with the General's spies," said Steve.

"I don't give a damn about the General's spies or the General, either. You've got to do something about this suffering animal. It's no more than you would do in your private practice," said Michael.

"Easy, old boy, easy there," said Joe placing one hand gently on the horse's neck and stroking his long nose with the other. "How you doing, fella, heh? Are they keeping you here against your will? I'll bet you're just yearning to be with your old buddies in that great box canyon in the sky, aren't you? Yeah, that's my good old fella."

The horse turned instinctively in response to Joe's gentle voice and soothing manner. His large brown eyes spontaneously returned the affection Joe offered.

"Hey, you've got a real good way with animals, Joe. That's the most spark I've seen out of him in more than a year. You've missed your calling, Doc," said Steve.

"Sometimes, I feel the same way. Unconditional love, that's what this old guy is giving me. It's something most humans have a hard time practicing," said Joe.

Steve examined Scout's hooves, teeth, eyes and ears while Michael distracted himself from the repulsive scene by examining the animal's heart and lungs.

"I think this horse is in severe congestive heart failure. Did you know that? Steve," Michael asked.

"Yes, I know. He's already on digitalis, diuretics and a low salt diet," said Steve.

"Exactly, but that's what is prolonging his agony. It's proper treatment for humans but it's like whipping a crippled ox to make him move. You just can't make it work anymore by pushing it. It's just not right," said Michael.

"I know, I know," said Steve clearly uncomfortable with the confrontation. "But what can I do? It's the General's orders. Scout must die of natural causes or in combat or he'll be dishonored. I've got no choice."

"Who'll be dishonored? The General or Scout?" asked Michael pressing the point.

Steve didn't answer but went about his business of checking out the horse. Joe just stood silently next to Scout giving all the affection and understanding he could muster. He was very somber but his mind was churning.

"Who gives him his medication?" whispered Joe to Steve.

"I prepare it ever day and the Vet assistant or the corpsman gives it to him by injection. He's too weak to swallow even the smallest pills, now," said Steve.

"Oh, Jesus God, man. You call yourself a Vet, a guardian of the quality and quantity of life of the animal world. You're a hypocrite," said Joe loosing his temper.

"Easy, Joe, settle down. It's not Steve's fault. All the fault lies with the commander of this Post and his stupid pride," said Michael.

"I'm sorry, Steve. I didn't mean what I just said. I just lost my head for a minute. I take it all back," said Joe shaking Steve's hand and patting him on the back. "I just got this hard-to-control temper when I see people and animals suffering needlessly. I know you feel the same otherwise you wouldn't do this work," he added.

Steve turned pale, his shoulders sagged and he stared down at the wood shavings.

Joe continued softly so that only Steve and Michael could hear what was being said. "It's like Michael says, it's the General's fault not yours. I know you love old Scout the way we do. And I know that if you could now I'm only saying, *if,* mind you if you could slowly decrease his medication doses, then one day the end would come quickly and painlessly. And nobody would be the wiser. It would look just like a death due to so called 'natural causes', whatever the hell that's supposed to mean."

Steve fussed and fidgeted with his instruments and medication bottles but didn't say anything or even acknowledge that he understood what Joe's was suggesting.

"Let's just say, if you cut the doses by maybe, ten percent a day, in about two weeks he'd just go to sleep, real peaceful like. That would do it, don't you think, Mike? Look, even Michael says that would work. There'd be no sedatives or poisons to trace in the blood or urine. Isn't that what you use in your private practice to put suffering animals to sleep, sedatives at such?"

"No, no it isn't. We use high doses of potassium intravenously. There's no pain or distress of any kind that way. The heart just stops beating and they go to sleep," said Steve solemnly.

"That's exactly what would happen if Scout's digitalis dose was slowly reduced, say just ten percent a day," said Michael as scientifically and as clinically as possible.

Steve just nodded his head and packed up his gear. Then the three physicians walked slowly back toward the exit, not speaking until Michael broke the silence.

"Hey, what's in all those wooden crates? There must be fifty of them," said Michael.

Joe moved closer to examine the writing on the crates. He used his pocket flashlight to read it because of the dim lighting in this rear corner of the stable.

"Horseshoe nails," he read aloud. "Would you believe they're crates of horse shoe nails," said Joe.

"Are there any other horses on this Post?" asked Michael.

"No, Scout is the only one," said Steve.

Joe looked again at the crates and read further, "two thousand nails per crate. Can you believe that? Scout would have to live another fifty years to use all of these."

"How often does the furrier change Scout's shoes, Steve?" asked Joe.

"Never, he hasn't had shoes on since I've been taking care of him and that's coming on two years now. His hooves are too brittle for them. And of course no one has ridden him in years. The strain of a work out would kill him," said Steve.

"Let's get out of here. I'm getting sick to my stomach at the sight of this kind of waste and cruelty," said Michael.

"What do you think it costs for a crate of these nails, Steve?" said Joe.

"Oh, I'd say about fifty dollars a crate," he answered.

"Let's see, a hundred thousand horseshoe nails, fifty crates at fifty bucks a crate, that's twenty-five hundred dollars. My dad busted his ass for forty-two years as a refrigeration repairman and he never earned more than five thousand dollars a year and he died without a dime in the bank. Those nails represent almost a half years salary for him. Don't those Army jerks realize people work hard for this tax money they throw around like water?" said Joe.

"That's typical Army policy for you," said Michael. "Just think how many bandages or syringes that could buy. It's no wonder people cheat on their income taxes, they know the government will only throw the money away, anyway."

Steve drove Joe and Michael back to his office to pick up their vehicle but very little was said until they arrived back at the office. Steve's car stopped at the curb, Michael got out but Joe hesitated long enough to remind him, "just ten percent reduction a day in dose, Doc. That's all it'll take. No pain, no more suffering," he said.

Steve turned and stared into Joe's eyes silently.

"So long, Joe, Michael. I don't know if we'll run into each other again except maybe at the officer's club or the PX. Keep your noses clean and stay out of Vietnam."

"Yeah, Steve, you too. Drop by the hospital sometime. We'll buy you lunch," said Michael.

Michael and Joe drove off to the hospital.

"Do you think he'll do it?" asked Michael.

"I'm not sure. He's pretty scared of going to Vietnam. But he did say he's been in the Army almost two years so he should be close to finishing his hitch. Maybe if he waits until just before he gets out he may be safe by then."

"Yeah, maybe. But if it's still a few weeks or even months away Scout will have to suffer all that much longer. I hope he doesn't wait that long," said Michael.

"Yeah, me too."

They arrived at the hospital just as five ambulances were bringing in the evacuated wounded from Vietnam. They had no sooner stepped inside the door when Michael was paged to 'report to the ER, stat.'

"Oh, oh, somebody must be in big trouble. I'll see you up on the ward, Joe," said Michael.

Michael trotted toward the Emergency Room. As he hurried into the ER he proceeded immediately to the examining cubicle with the most activity and the most white shoes showing under the curtain around it. Having guessed correctly he found several corpsmen and nurses actively giving CPR to a young infantryman.

"What've we got? Kelley," he asked the Head nurse.

"I don't know yet. We haven't had time to check his medical record, yet. They brought him in having a grand mal seizure, then everything stopped. No blood pressure, no pulse, no respirations. We got right on it," she said while filling a syringe with adrenaline.

Michael moved to the patient's head to survey the situation. The man was pale blue and lifeless. The only body movements visible were those of the corpsman compressing the patient's breast bone and the expansion of his lungs by a rubber bag attached to a tube into his mouth and windpipe. The bag was being slowly compressed by a nurse. Michael quickly examined the infantryman's eyes for any signs of brain death.

"Pupils are not dilated, yet. He's still getting oxygen to his brain. Keep going with the CPR. "You, Miss," he instructed another nurse standing by, "please start another IV in his other arm and run in some Ringer's Lactate Solution with two ampules of Sodium Bicarb."

The nurse responded immediately. Michael watched the cardiac monitor for thirty seconds nothing electronically happened, only a straight line, except for an occasional feeble, erratic blip.

"Nothing!" said Michael. "Quick, give me the syringe of adrenaline with a long cardiac needle on it," he instructed nurse Kelley.

Then he felt for the proper space between two ribs on the left side of the chest and plunged the long needle through into the heart.

He pulled back on the plunger of the syringe until he saw bright red, oxygenated blood flow into the syringe to be sure he was in the heart chamber. Once he was certain of it's proper placement he quickly injected the cardiac stimulant into the heart. After quickly withdrawing the needle he glanced at the monitor still nothing but a straight line. Everyone waited for instructions. Then Michael recalled something he had read about a way to jump start a stopped heart.

Suddenly and without warning he delivered a powerful single blow to the patient's breast bone with his tightly closed fist. Everyone was startled by this new, strange maneuver. Some thought Michael had gone berserk. Michael looked at the monitor again and the straight line was now interrupted, sporadically, by three or four consecutive and distinctly normal heart beats. But there were still long delays between the small groups of beats. He delivered another powerful, closed-fist blow to the sternum. Now the monitor showed larger and more frequent groups of normal complexes.

"How much oxygen is he getting?" he said.

"Two liters a minute, Sir," answered the nurse.

"Increase it to six liters. Open up both of those IVs to full until we get a blood pressure that's stable and above 100 over 60."

"BP is now fifty over zero," said a corpsman.

"That's better but not good enough. Keep checking it while I check his medical record for clues. Come and get me if the BP drops again or if the it goes over 100," said Michael.

Michael and the nurse searched through all the scattered equipment, bed linens and tubes to find the file. When he found it the name written on the edge of the file instantly caught his eye. PFC, Parrish, B. J.

Michael rapidly spun around back to the patient to look more closely at the face he had scarcely noticed before.

"Hey, it is him," he said to no one in particular just as Joe O'Mara walked into the area.

"Do you always talk to yourself after bringing a guy back from the brink?" joked O'Mara.

"Oh, hi Joe. Yes, I mean no. I just realized who he is."

Joe looked at the man. "Hey, it's B. J. Parrish. I thought he'd gone to 'Nam."

"He did but he came in today with the other wounded guys only he isn't wounded, at least not on the outside, as far as I can tell."

They immediately had the same thought and went back to check his arms for needle tracks.

"Yep, there they are as clear as day," said Joe.

They both could clearly see the several needle track marks above and below the current IV needles which were running in the life-sustaining fluids and medications.

"Yes, he's been at it again," said Michael.

"How's his blood pressure doing?" he asked.

"It's up to 70 over 40, Sir."

"Good, he's getting there. Check his temperature, too. It it's over 100 degrees, let me know. And run a drug and toxic-substance screen on his blood and urine."

"For what substances, Sir?"

"Everything and anything they can test for. This guy's mainlined some strange materials in his time," said Joe.

"You tried to tell that idiot, Colonel Anderson, that B. J. wasn't fit to go to 'Nam," said Joe.

"Yeah, but he wanted him off this Post for some special reason. I think I know what that was but I have no proof," said Michael.

"We'll have to forget that for now and try to find out what B. J. has been shooting up," he added.

"His blood pressure is stable at around 110 over 70, Sir. And his temperature is elevated at 104.4," said the nurse.

"Great blood pressure. Okay, transfer him up to the ICU and tell them I'll be up to check on him in a few minutes," said Michael.

"Yes, Sir," she answered.

"Here, Joe, you take half his medical record and I'll take the other half. Let's see if we can find a clue as to what B. J. was shooting up."

They began sifting through the pages, and very carefully examined even the smallest bit of information.

"Hey, he was stationed at Mylai until a few days ago," said Joe.

"You mean the same Mylai where all those civilians were supposedly massacred by some of our guys?" asked Michael.

"Yep, the very same place, and B. J.'s platoon was involved," said Joe.

"Do you suppose B. J. did any of the actual shooting?" asked Michael.

"I don't know. They don't give any details here to indicate if he did or not. No matter. Even if he was only a witness or even remotely involved this kid would crack," said Joe.

"Yes, you're right. This very kind of incident could be the flash-point that pushed him over the edge. Well, this will be enough to get him the medical-psychiatric discharge we thought he should have gotten in the first place, if he survives, and right now that's a big if," said Michael.

"You think he's in a real bad way then?"

"I'm not sure yet. It depends on whether or not he has had any severe, and permanent brain damage. The problem is, we don't have an EEG machine, or a an experienced Neurologist on this God-forsaken Post who can read one. It's like doing heart surgery with the mask over your eyes instead of your mouth and nose."

"Well, now you know what Sir William Osler had to deal with a hundred years ago," said Joe.

Michael smiled but was not appeased by the joke and very quickly became sullen again. They sifted through the record further until every scrap of paper had been examined, on both sides.

"You know, somebody should have picked up B. J.'s distress signals," said Michael.

"Why, what do you mean?" asked Joe.

"Well, look at all these sick call visits in 'Nam. Sometimes he was in twice in one day, and he was in at least ten to fifteen times a week. And they were all for potentially stress-induced symptoms," said Michael.

"Yeah, you're right. I can see that now. Look at these sick call notes; chronic headaches, insomnia, horrifying nightmares, vomiting, bed wetting, a twenty-pound weight loss. Who the hell was commanding that unit over there in 'Nam?" asked Joe.

"Oh, oh, that explains it," said Michael.

"How do you mean?" said Joe.

"Don't you remember our own beloved General who went over with the outfit from here? It was that screwball who ordered the burning of all the red pencils and pens. The one who'd rather be 'Dead than Red'."

"Of course, the same nut that kept the troops working out on the high bars in weather so cold their hands stuck to them and their skin peeled off down to the bones, when they let go. Yeah, he would ignore those signals from B. J.," said Joe.

"Let's go up to the ICU and see how B. J. is doing," said Michael who immediately headed for the stairs.

"Hey, hey," said Joe grabbing Michael's arm, "that's seven flights up, Mike. That's why they put elevators in this place."

"Oh, come on. It'll be good exercise for you. I do it all the time," said Michael.

"No thanks, you go ahead. I'll meet you up there. I'm liable to collapse before we even get to the third floor."

"But that's exactly the point. This is the way to avoid poor cardiac conditioning. If you do this everyday you won't have a heart attack," said Michael.

"Please, please, Mike, spare me the preventive medicine lecture. Besides, everybody expects radiologists to be fat and out of shape. I wouldn't want to disappoint my peers," said Joe.

*   *   *

"How's he doing, nurse?" asked Michael.

"His vital signs are stable; blood pressure 120 over 70, pulse 108, temperature down to 102 with ice packs and aspirin. Respirations are a problem, though. He has not had any spontaneous breathing without the help of the respirator," she said.

"What about the test reports regarding drugs and toxic substances?" asked Joe.

"Nothing reported back yet, Sir."

"How's his urine output?" asked Michael as he looked at the glass reservoir catching the urine draining from the tube in B.J.'s bladder.

"Hold it, there's something strange about the urine in that container," said Michael.

"In what way?" asked Joe.

"Come here, closer, look at it," said Michael.

"I don't see anything unusual," said Joe.

"Wait a minute until the surface settles."

They waited until it did settle and Michael switched containers.

"There, do you see it now? You have to move your head slightly so that the light hits the surface just right," said Michael.

Joe moved his head to several different angles. "Oh, yeah I see it now. I looks like gasoline or oil floating on the top of a pool of water," he said.

"Right, except that it doesn't have the color of gasoline or motor oil. It's another kind of oil," said Michael.

"But, how do you get oil in your urine? I mean, what kind of disease condition causes that?" asked Joe.

"Well, assuming the container was clean and had no oil in it to start with, there's only one condition I know that causes that to happen," said Michael.

"Oh, really, and what condition is that? 'Boy wonder, asked Batman'," said Joe.

"Fat embolism after a fracture of the long bones," said Michael.

"Yeah, I remember now. But that's only after massive, multiple bone fractures. Did he have any broken bones?" said Joe.

"I don't think so but we're going to find out. Why don't you take him down to the x-ray department and get some films of all his long bones, shoulders to ankles, and let's find out," said Michael.

"Right you are. What are you going to do in the meantime?"

"First, I'm going to change that urine receptacle again in case it wasn't clean, and free of oil or soap. Then I'm going to take this container to the lab and analyze it to see if we can figure out what kind of oil this is," said Michael.

Joe prepared to move B. J. in his sick bed to the x-ray Unit. Michael changed urine containers and then headed to the lab. About an hour later Michael went down to x-ray to examine the films with Joe.

"We checked all the films, twice," said Joe. "Not even a small hairline fracture, anywhere."

"I figured that," said Michael. "Anyway, hairline fractures wouldn't matter even if they were multiple. The fractures have to be massive, multiple, and in the long bones, to make oil appear in the urine," said Michael.

"What did the urine assay tell you? What was that oily substance?"

"You'd never guess in a million years," said Michael.

"What? What? So tell me already," said Joe.

"Peanut oil. It is peanut oil," said Michael.

"Now wait a minute. I thought I'd heard it all. Are you sure?"

"Here, smell it yourself," said Michael handing him a vial of the extracted oil.

"That's what it is all right. But how do you get a 'high' from peanut oil? And where would a GI in Vietnam get pure peanut oil to inject in himself?"

"One question at a time," said Michael.

"Corpsman," said Michael calling over a Spec 3 from B. J.'s outfit, "tell him about it, Specialist."

"It's quite popular, Sir, whenever things are really tight and they can't get any of the hard stuff. They get peanut butter in small containers to put on crackers that come in their C-rations," he said.

"But how do they get the oil out of it?" asked Joe.

"They use a clean, cloth sack or a handkerchief, although cheese cloth or a nylon stocking is better. They pool the small amounts of peanut butter each of them gets. Then they put it into the cloth and twist it as tight as they can until the oil filters through and they collect it in one of the empty cans."

"Okay, that answers the second question. Now, how do they get strung out on it?" asked Joe.

"They suck it up into a syringe and shoot it up," said Michael.

"And? so what?" asked Joe.

"The glob of oil goes through the heart and lungs and blocks the flow of oxygen, momentarily. The heart flutters and skips beats for a few seconds during which no blood or oxygen gets to the brain. That brief interruption in flow to the brain causes a giddiness, a kind of fainting spell. That is, if they're lucky," said Michael.

"What do you mean? 'lucky'," asked Joe.

"I mean, if they're lucky enough not to stop the heart completely and die instantly," said Michael.

"It can't be much of a high compared to heroin," said Joe.

"When these guys are desperate enough, Sir, they'll take anything they can get."

"So you think that's what happened to B J?" said Joe.

"Yes. I think his heart stopped long enough to cause extensive brain damage. How extensive, I can't tell yet. It's too early, after the immediate event, to measure the extent of brain injury."

"Do you think he'll make it, Sir?" asked the corpsman.

"I don't know, yet. It's just to early to estimate his chances," said Michael.

"What are the odds like?" asked Joe.

"I'd say, fifty-fifty," said Michael. "He's young and that's a plus for him."

"What are the negatives?" said Joe.

"The recent stress and strain of combat, his weight loss and general malnutrition, which resulted because it was ignored for so long. The chronic drug abuse has taken it's toll, too. There's always some immeasurable but significant damage to heart, liver and kidneys which slowly worsens over time, in addicts," said Michael. "Come to think of it that makes it more like 70-30 against survival, for him," he added.

CHAPTER TWELVE

Pulling the Plug

A WEEK PASSED by and B. J. had not yet regained consciousness, or showed even the smallest sign of improvement. Michael started to visit him twice a day instead of the standard once a day, seven days a week. He left instructions that he was to be notified of even the slightest change in his condition, day or night.

"Mike you can't keep up this pace. You'll end up in the hospital as a patient yourself," said Joe.

"I've got to, his life is my responsibility," said Michael.

"Now wait a minute, where the hell did you get that dumb-shit notion?" said Joe.

"I could have made the Colonel keep him out of Vietnam, if I had pushed a little harder," he said.

"Oh yeah, sure, you and Jesus Christ, maybe. You know, you really piss me off sometimes with all this super-dedication-and-guilt crap," said Joe as he slammed his hand down on the table top.

It was the first time Michael had ever seen Joe truly angry with him. He was quite taken aback and disturbed by the realization.

"Okay, okay, cool it will you. I'll only see him once a day. Does that satisfy you?"

"That'll do for starters. Now, what about transferring him to Walter Reed Army hospital or one of the other major military referral center hospitals?" asked Joe.

"I've already thought of that option. I'm afraid he wouldn't survive the traveling in his current condition," said Michael.

"So what's next, then?" asked Joe.

"I thought I'd ask Colonel Anderson to have a neurologist and a neurosurgeon fly in with an EEG machine and one of those new Echo encephalograph machines," said Michael.

"Oh, yeah, I read about those new Echos. It actually takes pictures of the brain from sound waves. It's kind of like the sonar used by the Navy to pick up submarines. And they are very sensitive. I heard they can visualize a filling in a tooth," said Joe.

"Now, all I have to do is convince the Colonel of the need," said Michael.

"What's to convince?" said Joe. "The kid's dying, isn't he? What more could he need to persuade him? Come on, I'll go with you for moral support, as if you needed it," he said.

*   *   *

"Is the Colonel busy? corporal," asked Michael.

"Oh, he might be trying to sink a twelve foot putt. Of course, that is important business but nothing life threatening, I'm sure. Go on in, I'm sure it's okay," said the corporal.

Michael knocked once on the office door and was about to knock again because there was no response when Joe abruptly opened it.

"Wait until he answers the knock, at least," said Michael.

"Nah, we might catch him napping this way and that would crumble his defenses," said Joe smiling.

"Sure enough," said Joe, after opening the door quietly.

The Colonel was stretched out, leaning back in his desk chair with his feet on top of the overturned waste basket. There was a copy of the 'Stars and Stripes' opened and draped over his face. He was snoring softly.

"Ten-hut," yelled Joe, as loud as possible, as he elbowed Michael in the ribs.

The Colonel jumped to his feet to find Michael and Joe standing at attention in front of him in a full, stiff-elbowed salute. The Colonel's face was an ashen white, and his speech was stammering.

"What the hell is the meaning of this?" he blurted out.

Sorry to startle you, Sir. We knocked but we didn't hear an answer. We were afraid you might be ill, so we came right in, Sir," said Joe.

"Oh, oh, I see. At ease, then," said the Colonel rubbing the sleepiness out of his face and eyes. He shook his head to clear away the clouds.

"Well, what is the problem? And be quick about it. I have lots of important business to attend to, here," he said clearing his throat. Joe smiled and Michael kicked Joe on the ankle. Joe's face turned serious.

"It's about Pvt. Parrish, Sir," said Michael in his best tone of faked respect.

"What about him? Is he getting any better?"

"No, Sir. His kidneys and liver are beginning to show some signs of early failure. That's the purpose of our visit," said Michael.

"Why don't you fly him out to Walter Reed or Letterman?" said the Colonel.

"I doubt he would survive the travel ordeal, Sir, and. . ." Michael hesitated.

"So then what's the idea coming to me?"

"I'd like to have a neurosurgeon, a neurologist, an EEG and one of those new Echo machines flown in here to assess his status," said Michael.

"You can't be serious, do you realize what the cost of such an operation would be? If it were the General, or some VIP that would be another matter. No, it's out of the question."

"It would not be as expensive as that fancy, climate controlled horse barn keeping that Army-nag alive," mumbled Joe.

"What's that, O'Mara?"

Michael kicked Joe's ankle again, only harder this time.

"Nothing, Sir. Just thinking out loud."

"There'd be very little cost, Colonel. They already have the equipment available and I don't think those specialists would demand any extra pay," said Michael.

"And they could hitch a ride on one of the transport planes that fly in here everyday. You know, like your buddy Colonel Watkins does when he flies in to have a weekend of golf with you," added Joe.

The Colonel frowned. This time Michael slapped Joe across the shoulder.

"Forget it, Rizzuto, O'Mara. There's no way that I would authorize such a request. You'll have to make do with what we have here," said the Colonel.

"But, Colonel . . ." said Michael, almost pleading.

"Forget it, Mike. You're not going to convince this horse's ass. Let's go," said Joe.

"O'Mara, I've had enough of your insolence. . ."

They walked out of the office, Joe slammed the door.

"Great, just great. You really appealed to his better side, didn't you? What'll we do now?" said Michael.

"Forget it. He hasn't got a better side, only a blind side and an Army side. Besides, I've got a better idea anyway," said Joe.

"Oh, really? And what's that, a magic carpet to transport B. J. in the blink of an eye?"

"You might say that," said Joe confidently, "except the magic carpet will come to us," he added.

"All right, let's have it. What kind of crazy scheme have you thought up now?"

"Maybe not so crazy. Look, I have this good friend of mine, a neurosurgeon, stationed at Walter Reed," said Joe.

"So what makes you think he'll come out here to see B. J.?"

"It so happens this guy owes me a couple of favors. It also happens he's a little crazy and he likes to buck the system, too, any system, just for the sheer joy of it," said Joe.

"You mean like you?" said Michael.

"Yeah, and like you, too. Only we're not as serious about as you are. We do it for the fun. Anyway, let's go to my office and I'll give him a call."

"What about the neurologist and the equipment? Do you think he can get those, too?"

"Sure he can. If it's against the rules and regulations he'll do it," said Joe.

"What is it that gives this guy such great powers?" asked Michael.

"He's the best goddamned neurosurgeon on the entire east coast, that's what his power is. If the President needed his head cracked Sam would be the one they'd call. He's already operated on the wife of a senator and some RVN Army General."

Joe picked up his phone and dialed the Post operator. "Hello, Gloria, yeah, this is Dr. O'Mara. I need to place a call to Walter Reed Army Hospital, please."

"I'm sorry, Dr. O'Mara but you know we have to clear all those calls through Colonel Anderson's office," she said.

"Oh, come on Gloria, this call was the Colonel's idea. He asked me to make the call for him," said Joe.

"Is it Army business?" she said.

"Of course, what else could it be?"

"Now, Major. You have been known to bend the rules a bit, you know. What particular Army matter is involved?" she asked.

"A . . . a, we're requesting some new special piece of medical equipment. It's a new device for. . . for painlessly piercing ear lobes. You know like the holes you put your earrings through.'"

"Oh, really. Are the doctors going to be allowed to do that now?" asked the operator.

"Oh, yes, yes. There's a great deal of risk of infection incurred if you let just anybody do it and this device practically eliminates the risk," he said.

"Will the machine just be available for military personnel or will the civilian, Post employees be allowed to get it done?" she asked.

"Yes, technically speaking, it is just for military personnel. But I'm sure there will be exceptions made for special, cooperative personnel. Dr. Rizzuto is right here with me. He says he'll put you right at the top of the list. You'll be the first as soon as the equipment arrives."

"Oh, how nice of him. What department did you wish to speak to at Walter Reed?" she asked.

"The neurosurgery department, Gloria. And thanks a million."

She dialed the number and waited for the connection after for a few phone-line transfers.

"Shall I call Dr. Rizzuto for an appointment?" she asked while waiting.

"Oh, no Gloria. He'll call you as soon as he receives the new device. It may take a few weeks, or months," said Joe clearing his throat.

"Oh, thank you so much, Dr. O'Mara. You're a dear."

"Don't mention it, Gloria . . . to anyone. It'll just be our little secret, for now," he said.

"Your party is on the line, Major."

"Neurosurgery department, Walter Reed hospital, Sergeant Henderson speaking," said the young female voice.

Joe covered the mouthpiece of the phone and said to Michael," it's just like Sam to have a young lady run his office. I'll bet she's a real looker, too."

"Hello, is anyone there?" she said.

"Oh, yes, sorry, this is Major Joseph O'Mara, Medical corps, Ft. O'Malley, Kansas. I'd like to speak to Lt. Colonel Sam Murphy, please."

"I'm sorry, Sir, the Colonel is in conference at the moment. He'll return your call later," she said.

"Listen, honey, you just slink your shapely body into his office, sit on Sam's lap and tell him Joe O'Mara, M. D. is on the phone. He'll take the call and he'll be damned mad if you don't tell him."

"Oh, oh, you must be a good friend of the Colonel's. I'll tell him you're on the line. . . over the intercom," she said clearly flustered.

"Hey, Joe, long time no see. How are you doing? I didn't know you were in the Army, too," said Lt. Colonel Sam Murphy.

"Yeah, I try to keep it a secret. I've been in about sixteen months. I'm stationed at a place called Ft. O'Malley, Kansas."

"Where? Is that in the U. S.?" mocked Murphy.

"Yeah, it's kind of the armpit of the universe. But, you know me, I make do and try to have fun wherever I'm at. Listen, Sam, I need a big favor."

"Sure, anything for you, Joe. You showed me some good times when we were hospital Residents, and I owe you a few favors. Name it, and it's yours."

"This Internist friend of mine has got a tough case out here and we need your expert help with it. This infantryman suffered some severe brain damage after he OD'd. We need a good neurological evaluation and we don't have the staff or the equipment," he said.

"No problem, Joe. Just have your hospital Commander sign the papers to air evac him here and I'll see him right away," said Murphy.

"There's the hitch. Mike Rizzuto, that's the Internist, doesn't think the kid would survive the trip," said Joe.

"Well, then just have him send an authorization for me to fly out and I'll be there in the next twenty-four hours."

"We've already asked him, and he refused to do it," said Joe.

"Why did he refuse? He's a doctor isn't he? Surely he can see the medical necessity of the situation," said Murphy.

"If you only apply the definition of *Doctor* very loosely, he's one. I don't think he's managed a medical case in ten or fifteen years. And, besides, he's one of those career Army, Gong-Ho types. He won't bend the Regs. You know the kind," said Joe.

"Yes, I do, Joe. But they're not all that way, Joe. We've got some really great Docs here. I'd let them take care of me or my family, anytime."

"Well, we're not so lucky out here on the frontier. Mike Rizzuto's real good but he's a draftee like me and with no power, either. What do you say, will you do it, Sam?" asked Joe.

"I'll have to see what I can do. I can probably swing it. I'll call you back in a couple of hours," said Murphy.

"Wait a minute, Sam. We need a few other things. Hold on, Mike will tell about them" he said and quickly thrust the phone into Michael's face.

"Thanks a lot, you coward," whispered Michael with the mouthpiece covered.

"Yes, hello, Lt. Colonel Murphy, this is Mike Rizzuto," then he paused to listen.

"Okay, then, Sam it is", said Michael. "Yes, he's in a complete coma, on a respirator, and his kidneys and liver are beginning to fail. He's only twenty years old," said Michael as the youth of B. J. struck him for the first time.

"I think we'll need a neurologist to come out, too," said Michael.

"What for? "asked Colonel Murphy.

"To interpret the EEG and the echo."

"I thought Joe said you didn't have that equipment, out there in Kansas."

"We don't. We, a . . . we thought, maybe, you could bring them with you since they are portable, anyway," said Michael.

Joe covered his face with his hands and cringed.

"Wait a minute, I don't know about this. That's a big risk to take. Let me talk to Joe again," said Sam Murphy.

Michael handed the phone to Joe. "He's balking at bringing the equipment. He wants to talk to you again."

"Hey, Sam what's the hang up? I know it's against the Regs but that's half the fun for guys like us," said Joe.

"Yeah, I know, Joe, but this is a little bit more risky than I thought. Even though I'm not career Army I could still get my ass in a sling if I'm caught. I don't think I can chance that," said Murphy.

Several seconds of silence ensued as Joe thought of a new approach.

"Say, Sam, how's your wife, Alice?" he said.

"What? Oh, she's doing okay. Why?"

"Do you remember that x-ray Tech we knew in residency? What was her name again? Oh yeah, I remember now it was Dawn, that was it. We used to call her 'Mary Mattress Back', recreational counselor to all the interns and residents," said Joe.

Several more seconds of silence followed but Joe could feel Sam's uneasy squirming in his chair.

"Your wife never met her, did she? You know like at any of the Christmas parties, or anything like that," Joe asked.

"No, no . . . she never did," said Murphy.

"No, of course not. How could she? I don't suppose she's ever heard any of the stories about Dawn either, has she? Nah, why would she?" Joe continued.

"Joe, Joe you bastard," said Sam Murphy. "This is blackmail, low down, dirty blackmail. I didn't think you were like that, I thought you were a friend of mine?"

"I am your friend, Sam. And, no, I wouldn't blackmail you if push came to shove. But that should tell you how important this is to me and Mike."

"Yes, I see your point, Joe, and I can see, now, how serious you guys are about this guy, Parrish. Oh, what the hell, I'll do it. What's the worst that could happen if I'm caught? Maybe a dishonorable discharge and a court-martial. I'm getting out in seven months, anyway. I'll just change my name and open a practice in Alaska or Tahiti. I hear those Eskimo babes are something else," said Sam laughing.

"Same old Sam, that's exactly what I was counting on. But listen, I do want you to be careful and if anything does happen you can lay off the whole scheme on me. I mean that. Keep Mike Rizzuto's name out of it, too," said Joe.

"Now, hold on a minute," said Michael softly as he tried to take the phone away from Joe. They wrestled for a moment and Joe got Michael in a head lock and put his hand over Michael's mouth. While holding Michael immobilized, he continued. "So when do you think you'll get here, Sam?"

"Let's see, today is Thursday. I prefer to come on a weekend to avoid suspicion. I'll be there this Saturday afternoon," said Sam.

"With the neurologist and the equipment?" asked Joe.

"Yep, the whole ball of wax," he said.

"No reservations, no misgivings, no regrets?" asked Joe.

"Nope, this is now a team effort just like the old days of residency—the same unbeatable team of O'Mara and Murphy," he said.

"Let's go get 'em, Tiger. See you Saturday," said Joe.

Joe hung up the phone and released Michael from the head lock.

"What are you trying to do, kill me or what?" said Michael.

"No, I was just trying to keep you from screwing up the deal with your righteous indignation. There's no sense in all three of us going down if we can't pull this one off. You know I don't give a shit about what people think, or about the Army," said Joe.

"Do you think I care about the Army, or this stupid war, anymore?" said Michael.

"No, no I know you don't. But you've got too much conscience for your own good. Your soul would bleed for the rest of your life if you we got court-martialed, or anything," said Joe.

Michael didn't answer and they both sat there for awhile to let the entire scheme, and it's risks, sink in.

*   *   *

The following Saturday they went directly to the Post airport to wait for Sam Murphy and his entourage to arrive. At 12:01 p.m. they drove up to the control tower in a heavy Army truck with a diesel powered hydraulic lift platform on the back.

"I see you called in another one of your IOUs," said Michael.

"You mean the truck? No, no. I just walked into the motor pool yard and took it. There was nobody around and the keys were in the ignition. So I just drove it out the gate," Joe said, stretching the truth quite a bit.

"Yeah, sure. No guard, no mechanics on duty? They just left the gate open and the keys in the vehicle by accident? Sure, Joe, tell me another one," said Michael.

"Right, I mean it. Why, I can't even remember the name of a single person who works at the motor pool. My memory for names has just suddenly become a total blank. Say, what did your say your name was?"

"Okay, okay. Just park the truck in the back and be sure your memory reminds you to take the keys out of the ignition," said Michael.

"Keys? What keys?" said Joe laughing.

They went to the front door of the main waiting room of the airport. It was locked, as it usually was on weekends.

"I guess we'll just have to wait out here in the cold, Joe. With this constant Kansas wind we could get frostbite before the plane arrives," said Michael.

Joe nervously checked his wristwatch several times. At exactly 12:15 a Spec 4 unlocked the door and said, "the coast is clear, Doc, come on in."

Michael looked at Joe. Joe looked up toward the lightly clouded sky and whistled the tune to 'God Bless America' as they went inside.

"What? What? Don't look at me like that, Mike. I had nothing to do with this. I don't even know this guy's name. Do I? Sergeant—-what's your name again?"

"Never mind, we don't want to know," said Michael.

They followed the Sergeant inside who then lead them directly to the control tower.

"Isn't the tower supposed to be off limits to everyone, even the General?" asked Michael.

Joe and the Sergeant didn't respond. They both just whistled 'God Bless America'.

Michael just shook his head and smiled.

After waiting about an hour the radio in the tower suddenly came alive at Ft. O'Malley's usually inactive airport.

"This is U. S. Army transport 7-4-6 Foxtrot requesting clearance for an emergency landing at the Ft. O'Malley airport," crackled the voice of the pilot.

"Seven-four-six Foxtrot cleared for immediate emergency landing on runway one-two-niner, left," said the tower operator.

"Emergency landing? What emergency? Is this Sam Murphy's plane or someone else's?" asked Michael puzzled and clearly agitated by the situation.

"Cool it, Mike, cool it. Sam and I worked this plan out. You know these guys have to file a flight plan with an approved destination. They're actually scheduled to land at the Abilene, Kansas airport, not Ft. O'Malley, and the records have to show that. The pilot owed Sam a favor and this is the pay off. He'll make his emergency landing, take on some extra fuel, while we unload the equipment, for the record, then he'll fly on to Abilene. That was his original destination to drop off some Presidential Papers at the Dwight D. Eisenhower Presidential Library," explained Joe.

"And what about getting Sam back to Walter Reed?" asked Michael.'

"Easy. The plane goes back to Walter Reed on Monday morning as scheduled. It has another 'emergency landing' here, picks up Sam, the neurologist and the equipment and nobody is the wiser and the record is complete and accurate," said Joe clearly proud of his scheme and it's execution.

Ten minutes later the transport touched down on runway 129L and taxied to the fuel depot. Joe drove the truck over to the apron next to the fueling area, the cargo door opened and out stepped a redheaded Irishman, 6 feet, 4 inches tall, about two hundred and sixty pounds. Michael assumed he had been a collegiate athlete, like Joe. They went over and greeted him.

"Hi, Sam," said Joe, who then fainted a soft, left jab to Sam's mid-section. "Hey, you're getting soft in your old age. You've got to get to the gym more often," he said.

"I can still take you in three rounds or less," said Sam Murphy. They sparred for a few seconds, laughing.

"This is Mike Rizzuto," said Joe.

A tall, petite, very attractive brunette also stepped off the plane. Joe and Michael glanced over at her as Sam shook Michael's hand. "Hi, Mike, glad to know you. Joe has a very high opinion of you and your ethics. How did you ever get hooked up with a bum like him?" said Sam Murphy.

"Oh, his soul's not as black as he likes to make everyone believe it is," said Michael.

"Say, Sam, who's the looker that just got off the plane? Never mind, never mind, don't answer that one. I should've known you'd have some good looking companion to keep you company for the weekend," said Joe.

"Are you kidding? Don't I wish. No, she's a straight arrow like Mike here. I've been trying to put 'the make' on her for months, now. But she's all business and she's the best neurologist in the whole damned Army. That's what you asked for wasn't it? the best," said Murphy.

"Doctor, Major Terry Mitchell meet Joe O'Mara and Michael Rizzuto. Joe's the one you've got to watch out for. Mike, he's good and pure like you," Murphy said.

"Hello, Joe, Michael. I understand you have a tough head-injury case on your hands," she said.

"Hello, Dr. Mitchell happy to make your acquaintance," said Joe shaking her hand for longer than was customary until she pulled it away. "You're right, Sam, she's just like Mike. All business, and get's right down to brass tacks, too, doesn't she?" he said.

They walked to the truck as the plane crew unloaded the equipment from it's cargo area. Joe and Sam walked ahead laughing and clowning around. Michael and Dr. Mitchell followed behind discussing the clinical details of B. J. Parrish's case.

"How about some coffee or lunch before we get started, if you haven't already done it?" asked Joe.

"I'd rather get started right away, if you don't mind. I'd like to have this case all worked out before the weekend is over," said Dr. Mitchell.

"Sure, Terry, whatever you say," said Sam Murphy.

"We'll give you some more background into the case along the way. Is that okay Dr. Mitchell?" asked Michael.

"Terry, please call me, Terry. I'm not your matronly, regimented great-aunt or your nanny. I believe in getting on with it but we are all equals, colleagues, here. Agreed guys?" said Terry Mitchell.

"Agreed," they all answered in unison.

"All right, Michael, fill us in," she said.

Michael delved deeply into Parrish's past medical history of drug and other substance abuse including the homemade wine incident. He revealed B. J.'s past criminal record and his family background as he knew it. The discussion veered off into one regarding Ft. O'Malley, Colonel Anderson, and the military attitude toward medical care, in general.

"This guy, Colonel Anderson, must be a real 'whack head'," said Sam.

"I can tell you it's not that way at Walter Reed, Letterman General or any of the other U. S. Army teaching hospitals. I've spent some time at almost all of them," said Terry.

"Of course, that's the way it should be at any teaching hospital, military or otherwise. But what about the places out in the boonies, like this? Just because we're small and remote doesn't mean we still can't, and shouldn't, deliver the best possible quality of care. After all, quality care is up to the individuals on the professional staff and not dependent on place or physical plant. I wonder how many other small military Posts have this low a quality of medical care," said Michael.

"Good point," said Sam.

"Maybe someone should do a study and look into that question," said Terry.

They all silently mulled over the suggestion for a few moments.

"Very good, then, Doctors, I think I'll look into that possibility when I get back," said Terry.

'You know, small and remote should not be synonymous with mediocre. A medical facility should be as good as its personnel want it to be, not the other way around," added Michael.

"Correct," said Sam Murphy. "And it should not be a matter of the commanding hierarchy or the delivery system limiting the quality or quantity of care" he added.

"And that's especially true here at Ft. O'Malley where most of the troops are screened and then trained for duty 'In-Country'," said Joe.

They all fell silent and digested these thoughts in the remaining ten minute drive to the hospital. The four physicians went immediately to Parrish's bedside and began their examinations. The electronic equipment was set up, and the EEG and echo-encephelogram were done, and interpreted. Three hours later all the data had been gathered and it was time to put their heads together.

"Now, I'll have that cup of coffee," said Dr. Terry Mitchell.

"Yeah, I can use it, too. This is one tough case. I doubt we could find anything in the medical literature about the effects of injecting peanut oil into the human body," said Sam Murphy.

"Let's go to my office. I have a coffee pot and some fresh donuts," said Joe.

They sat around the conference table with the x-ray films on a nearby viewbox, the EEG and Echogram were on the table, and all of Parrish's medical and service records were stacked in the middle.

Joe passed the donuts which a corpsman had brought from the hospital cafeteria. Sam took a chocolate glazed. Terry and Michael passed on the donuts and just took their coffee black and without sugar. Joe settled on a cheese-Danish.

"So, what do you think?" said Michael looking at Sam.

"It's clear that there has been extensive brain damage including the centers which control respirations, body temperature and other vital functions. Of course, he's young and may have a family background of strong powers of recuperation," said Sam Murphy.

"Do you think he can make it?" asked Joe bluntly.

"There's also the question of his will to live and he has been in coma for what, two weeks now?" added Murphy.

"Let's cut the happy-horseshit, Sam. This isn't grand rounds at University Hospital," said Joe.

Dr. Murphy paused for a moment to bring himself down to the point of conclusion.

"I think he's had it. Maybe one chance in a hundred thousand of regaining consciousness but he'll be left with major, residual neurological deficits. I mean no speech, no communication, very little mobility, if any," said Murphy.

"In other words, he'll be a vegetable," said Terry Mitchell. Her choice of terms surprised everyone.

"Since we're calling them like we see them that's essentially what Sam is saying, isn't it?" she added.

"So you agree, Terry, with Sam's assessment?" asked Michael.

"No, not entirely. I think his 1 in 100,000 prognosis is too optimistic. I don't think he has a snowball's chance in hell. Sorry to be so frank, but that's my honest opinion," she said.

Everyone was silent for some time.

"Do you think we ought pull the plug on the respirator and make him a DNR (do not resuscitate) case?" asked Joe.

"That's between Parrish's family and Michael, since he's the primary care doctor," said Sam Murphy, and Dr. Mitchell nodded her head in agreement.

"There aren't any known living relatives that we can find. We've been trying to reach someone, anyone in his family, for a week. We contacted the police and the family Doctor in his home town, in Georgia. There are no relatives there. The Doctor said there was an alcoholic stepfather but no one knows where he is or if he's even still alive," said Michael.

"So, I guess the ball's in your court, Michael. You'll have to make the decision for him. What are you going to do?" asked Dr. Mitchell, as she place her hand on his shoulder.

"I don't know yet. I'm going to think on it, for awhile," said Michael.

"Oh, oh, you're getting emotionally involved here, Michael. You know that's not wise for a physician to do. It'll only cloud your medical judgment and impair your ability to make objective decisions." said Dr. Murphy.

Joe rolled his eyes and held his breath knowing that Sam had said the wrong thing, to the wrong doctor, at the wrong time.

"Don't give me that esoteric, medical school crap, Sam. These are people we're dealing with, not new cars on an assembly line. If you don't care about them as people you can't do anything '*for them*' you can only do things '*to them*'," said Michael, trying to restrain his frustration as best he could.

Sam realized his error in his choice of words and said, "sorry Mike, I didn't mean it that way."

Michael calmed himself down and took several deep breaths followed by a deep sigh of frustration.

"No, I'm sorry, Sam. I know you didn't mean it that way, either. You were just spouting back that garbage they threw at us in Medical School about emotional detachment, I know that," he said.

The group spent the following day relaxing, talking shop, visiting with Michael and Joe, and the Rizzuto and O'Mara families—-and checking on B. J. Parrish twice a day at the ICU.

In the meantime Michael spent two sleepless nights, supported by his wife Kathy, mulling over his options.

The following morning Joe and Michael accompanied Sam and Terry to the Post airport to catch the transport which was making its second 'emergency landing' at the Ft. O'Malley.

"I want to thank you both for all your help," said Michael shaking their hands. Terry let go of his hand, hugged Michael, and said, "you've got a tough call to make, Michael, good luck."

"Yeah, thanks a ton," said Joe, who then noticed one less crate being loaded onto the plane.

"Hey, Sam I think you forgot something, there's one crate missing from your load," he added.

"Oh, yeah, that's the one containing the Echo machine. I left it at the hospital for you guys. You need it here more than I need it at Walter Reed. Anyway, we have several others and this was a portable one that wasn't getting used much," said Sam.

"You could get in big trouble for ripping off government property, including jail time," said Joe.

"Not really. I bought that one myself to use when I get back into private practice. Consider it payment for the room and board, and the coffee and donuts, and for breaking the monotony for us," said Sam.

Sam jumped quickly onto the plane and Terry Mitchell followed, immediately behind him. They waved to Michael and Joe and then shut the aircraft door.

The drive back home and to the motor pool was a quiet one for Michael and Joe. Joe pulled up in Michael's driveway. Michael opened the door to get out.

"What are you going to do, Mike? I mean, about B. J. and the respirator."

"I have no other choice. To do anything else wouldn't be fair to B. J. or his family, if there are any of them still alive. I'm going to detach the respirator tomorrow morning, on rounds."

"Don't you think you should have a lot of witnesses present so there aren't any accusations later," asked Joe.

"I don't give a damn about that, Joe. My conscience is clear. I know I'm doing the only humane thing, and if B. J. could communicate, I know he'd say the same. Besides, it's my duty to make those decisions when there's no family to guide me."

"I think you've made the only choice you could, under the circumstances. I'll see you tomorrow, Mike. Try to get some sleep, you look like hell," said Joe, and he drove away.

*   *   *

The following morning Michael detached B. J. from the respirator, himself, instead of using an intermediary nurse or corpsman, as was the usual procedure. He wanted to bear the sole responsibility for his decision. There was no fanfare, no attorneys or administrators involved. There was just lots of documentation to substantiate his decision and his individual burden for it.

B. J. remained alive, but in a vegetative state, for another sixty hours until his respirations spontaneously ceased. His death seemed peaceful and painless.

*   *   *

The phone rang at Michael's home around 3:00 a.m. and a nurse told him that B. J. had expired.

"Yes, thank you for your help, nurse. Tell the rest of the ICU staff thanks, also. Oh, and leave a message with the switchboard operator that I'll be in late tomorrow. I need some extra sleep. Good night and thanks again," he said.

*   *   *

Next morning Michael arrived at his office at the uncharacteristic hour of 11:20 a.m., still looking like hell but, prepared to jump back into the boiling cauldron. He began by opening his mail and checking the in-box for memos. A large, red-trimmed, manila envelope marked, 'Top Priority', lay on the top of the stack.

He opened it slowly, deliberately and completely. He slammed it down on his desk, and said, "I don't believe this! I'm not going. I don't care what they do to me I'm no going and that's all there is to it."

He picked up the envelope and its contents and walked hurriedly to Joe O'Mara's office saying aloud, "I'm not going to go."

He burst into Joe's office as Joe was dictating x-ray reports into a machine.

"Whoa, whoa, Michael, slow down, man. What's the problem?"

Michael was beside himself with anger and was, at first, unable to speak.

"Wait, wait. It's almost lunch time, anyway. Let's talk about it over lunch," said Joe, who knew very well what the topic of conversation would be since he had also received his own red-trimmed, envelope and had read its contents.

The hospital cafeteria was, as usual, full of Medical officers including doctors, nurses and other hospital support personnel. Colonel Anderson was sitting at a corner table with his usual covey of cronies.

"Now, eat your lunch, drink your beer, calm down, and tell me peacefully what the problem is," said Joe.

"Peacefully? Calm down? Did you see that memo about the funeral for that . . . that horse? Scout," said Michael indignantly.

"Yes, I saw it. I guess he passed on last night, or the night before. I hope it was peaceful and painless for him, like it was for B. J.," said Joe.

"Yes, I do too, but you don't see any big-ass, million-dollar, two day, memorial parade and services for B. J., do you?" said Michael, growing more uncontrollably angry by the moment. He jumped to his feet and repeated loudly, "Do you?"

"Come on, Mike, sit down. Take it easy," said Joe.

The cafeteria had suddenly fallen entirely silent. All the usual clanking of plates, tinkling of silverware and background conversation was frozen in the silence.

Michael shouted at Joe again, "DO YOU?" Then he walked directly over to Colonel Anderson's table, with all eyes in the room following him through the petrified stillness.

"Well, get this Colonel Ass-hole, I'm not going to your stupid, Army horse funeral even if it is under the pain of possible court-martial. Send me to Vietnam if you want, see if I give a shit," he added.

"Major Rizzuto, that will be enough. Go back to your table and sit down," the Colonel ordered.

"Not by a longshot, Doctor Anderson," he added sarcastically. "I don't see you arranging a big-deal funeral for a poor kid who just blew himself away with peanut oil just because he didn't want to go back 'In-Country' to kill more innocent Vietnamese women, and kids. Where's his memorial, hah? Where is it?" Michael was still shouting.

Neither the Colonel, nor anyone else in the cafeteria, moved or uttered a sound, until Joe walked over to Michael who was now leaning limply on the back of a chair, emotionally spent.

"Come on, Michael, let's go back to your quarters. You need some more rest. You'll feel better after you get a good night's sleep," said Joe.

Michael said nothing but walked, dragging his feet, with Joe's help, out through the cafeteria doors.

Colonel Anderson was still standing amid the dead silence with all eyes now focused on him. When he realized that he was now the center of attention his knees shook, his fingers grew icy cold, and beads of cool sweat appeared on his brow.

"As you were," he commanded, trying to shout but unable to do so. "As you were," he said again, and fell back into his chair.

All eyes turned back to their plates, the clinking and clanking of utensils resumed but there was no more audible chit-chat until the Colonel and his entourage started to leave the cafeteria. He stopped at the door, turned back to the room full of people, and said, "and *all of you will attend* the memorial parade and funeral for Scout, including Major Rizzuto if he's still 'Out-Of-Country' when the time comes." Then he left the large, stunned crowd in the cafeteria.

*   *   *

The memorial parade and funeral procession were scheduled to start at 10:00 in the morning. Colonel Anderson went to his office, as usual, at 8:00 am, before the ceremonies started, to handle some routine paperwork.

Joe O'Mara and three other medical officers were waiting for him outside his office. The Colonel was startled and dismayed by their appearance at this time, and so close to the start of the parade.

"What are you men doing here? What do you want? You should be forming up for the parade," said Colonel Anderson.

"That's exactly why we are here, Colonel," said Joe.

"We're not going to the parade," said another medical officer. "not any of us," he added.

"You're not, what? Very well then, as you wish, gentlemen, In that case, you will all be court-martialed, along with Major Rizzuto, and you will suffer the consequences," said the Colonel.

"That's just fine with us, Colonel. But then who's going to run your hospital, your emergency room, and your sick-call duties?" asked one of the officers.

"Oh, I think we can manage without just five medical officers. We'll have to double up on some duties but I'll work it out, I assure you," he said.

"No, no, Colonel, you don't get it. I don't mean just us four and Michael I do mean 'all' of us. We're here speaking for all the doctors, all the nurses, all the pharmacists and Vets on the Post. The whole shebang," said Joe, "the entire medical crew," he added.

"What? How dare you challenge my authority? I'll not knuckle-under to your blackmail again. . ." The Colonel tried to go on, until he realized that all four men were deadly serious in their declaration. Then some characteristic cool, sweat beads again appeared and he licked his drying lips.

"You're all bluffing, you wouldn't leave all those sick patients unattended, you couldn't," he stammered.

"Oh, yes, you are right, we're not about to let the patients suffer because of Army stupidity. There will be one emergency doctor in the hospital, and one RN on each ward at all times but for 'real' medical emergencies only. But there will be no routine, scheduled medical services in operation," added another medical officer.

"You . . . you can't do this to me. I won't stand for it. . ." stammered the Colonel.

"We'll see about that. You watch us do it, Colonel. Don't look for any of us at that parade or the funeral services because we won't be there. And you just make one move against Mike Rizzuto, or anyone of us, and we'll all walk out," said Joe.

"And all the local newspapers, the Kansas City Star, and the 'Stars and Stripes' will be notified before-hand to witness the entire ordeal, 'your' ordeal, that is, Colonel," added another.

Then the four men left the office as Colonel Anderson slumped back into his overstuffed, executive chair appearing quite pale and shaken.

*   *   *

As ten o'clock, the parade starting time, approached, Michael and his family sat at home discussing the possible consequences of his authority-defying actions.

"I know it's hard on you and the kids, honey, but if I have to go to Vietnam because of my stance on this, I probably won't be anywhere near any of the combat areas," said Michael.

But his wife wasn't at all consoled by his reassurances. She had seen enough TV news, and read enough about the carnage 'In-Country', to know that American military personnel, of all types, were being killed all over Vietnam. There really were no 'safe havens' or sanctuaries. Not even the hospitals were off limits to the Vietcong. Kathy, and the kids, were crying softly, now.

The doorbell rang, Michael went to answer it, and was glad to momentarily escape the discomfort his family was suffering. He opened the door to find Joe, Phil, and two other medical officers standing on the doorstep.

"Joe, Phil? What are you guys doing here? You're suppose to be at the parade for Scout," he said.

"We've decided we wouldn't go, either. A form of group-protest and civil disobedience, I guess you'd call it," said Joe smiling.

"Oh, no you don't. What in hell . . . I mean, blazes made you do a dumb thing like that?" said Michael.

"We did it to make you feel guilty," said Phil. "Just kidding, Mike. We did it because you are right and you don't deserve any punishment when you are right," he added.

"Besides, we're not alone in this, I mean, not just the four of us. Do you think you're the only Doc who can be a hero?" said Joe.

"What are you talking about?" said Michael.

"Never mind, never mind, just come with us. You too, Kathy, and bring the kids along, too" said another doctor.

Michael and Kathy hesitated, and then Michael started to object, "But . . ."

"Never mind, just follow orders for once, will you?" said Phil.

"Orders? What are you talking about?" asked Michael.

"I was drafted six days before you were, so I'm your senior officer, in rank. Now get moving, soldier," said Joe.

They all squeezed into Joe's station wagon and drove in the direction of the hospital.

"What is this? Where are we going?" asked Kathy.

"Trust me on this one, Kathy. Everything is going to be okay. Just trust me," said Joe.

They pulled up at the hospital's back-entrance, and then proceeded to march down the back stairs in military formation. The kids lead the way, and were enjoying the marching to the military tune, 'The Gary Owen', they were all whistling.

They stopped at the cafeteria doors, "Company, halt, one, two," shouted Joe.

They swung open the doors to find all of the medical officers standing and applauding as Michael, Kathy, and the kids were lead down the aisle formed by the men and women of the Ft. O'Malley Medical Corps. Kathy cried some more, the kids waved, and marched in jubilation, but Michael was flabbergasted.

"Oh, Michael," Kathy sobbed. Michael put his arm around her shoulder to help her walk to a kind-of-headtable, set up in the front of the room for them.

"Joe, Joe, you wonderful nut. How's this going to help anything?" asked Michael, having difficulty trying to speak above the applause.

"It'll help, believe me. We also told the Colonel we were all going to miss the parade and if he retaliated in anyway, against anyone, we'd go on strike," said Joe.

"And he bought that?" asked Michael.

"Yep, and when we showed him this declaration signed by everybody here, he almost choked on his tongue. I wish you could have been there to see it, Mike."

The hospital's chief cook, whom Michael had treated and cured of a previously undiagnosed hypoglycemia, had prepared a special lunch. Which included a large cupcake with a small birthday candle sticking in its red, white and blue icing, for each and everyone there.

Some kind of 'victory celebration' just seemed appropriate to everyone. The lunch and the lighting of the individual candles was enjoyed by all, but especially by the kids who ran around to blow out each and every one. They tried to coax Michael into making a victory speech but, to no one's surprise, he declined

Suddenly a corpsman busted through the double doors shouting, "Major Rizzuto, Major Rizzuto," and the spell of euphoria was quickly broken.

"What is it, corpsman?" said Michael.

"It's Colonel Anderson, Sir. He collapsed on the reviewing platform at the parade. They think he's had a heart attack. The ambulance is bringing him in now," said the corpsman. The wailful sound of the ambulance siren could be heard in the distance.

"So, why bother me, corpsman? There's a doctor in the emergency room, isn't there? He can handle it," said Michael.

For the first time since the day he had entered Medical School, Michael felt an ambivalence, a conflict between his sense of duty and his personal feelings for a patient. Although there had been other patients he had disliked, he never hesitated before.

"But they said the Colonel asked for you, Doctor. He said, 'I want Dr. Rizzuto to handle my case and no one else'," said the corpsman.

Michael hesitated, only momentarily, but he did falter as he looked at his wife.

"All right, I'll be right with you," he said, then he bolted out of his chair reaching for the stethoscope in his pocket. He ran up to the emergency room with Joe O'Mara not far behind.

Just as they entered the ER, Colonel Anderson went into a cardiac arrest. His head was thrown back, his eyes rolled up under his eyelids, and all four limbs contracted violently.

Michael applied cardiac compression while Joe gave mouth-to-mouth respirations. The electrode paddles of the cardiac defribillator were applied to the Colonel's chest, and after two jolts his cardiac rhythm was stabilized, as were his vital signs.

"I think he'll be okay, now. Transfer him up to the intensive care unit, I'll be there in a minute," said Michael.

"Another close one," said Joe.

"Yeah," said Michael. "That new defibrillator does it's job very well," he added completely detached, to all appearances.

*   *   *

Colonel Anderson survived his heart attack, with Michael's diligent care, but he did have severe, residual heart damage. He left the hospital after a stormy, seven week recovery period. Then the Colonel received a honorable, medical discharge just four months short of his thirty years retirement date. This early discharge, of course, negated his retirement benefit of two-thirds pay, on which he had planned and conducted his career.

The Army also tried to deny Anderson full medical disability benefits which almost equaled his lost retirement pay. However, Michael felt, on a purely clinical basis, that the Colonel was entitled to the full disability allowance, so he persisted and fought for those benefits for the Colonel, until the Army reversed it's ruling.

Colonel Anderson retired to his home near Bethesda, Maryland, and in close proximity to the National Institutes of Health hospitals.

Michael and Joe received a Christmas card from the Colonel and Mrs. Anderson every year, until the Colonel's death, four years later.

Michael and Joe finished out their Army tours of duty without going 'In-Country' or even leaving Ft. O'Malley, Kansas.

After his hitch, Michael settled into the private practice of Internal Medicine in a small, mid-western city. He continued to practice medicine as he thought best for his patients, and, thus, inevitably continued to struggle against the system and its bureaucracy.

Joe O'Mara returned to join his colleagues in the same radiology group he had been associated with prior to his conscription into the U. S. Army.

Eventually, of course, the Vietnam War came to an end but not without leaving behind many deep scars and unresolved issues for both sides.

THE END